"This must have been a bad week for you, Abbie. Your father's leaving was a real shock. Is your mother taking it hard?" Stuart asked.

"Don't talk about Mama," Abbie said, and there was a sound of tears in her voice that alarmed her. She didn't want to break down and cry before Stuart's penetrating gaze.

"Then," he went on, "there's the matter of Douglas taking your cousin Lorena out driving this afternoon. "Are you going to sit by and let her get away with it?"

"How can I help it if Douglas prefers her company?"

"Lorena is—Lorena, and she has some things you lack. But Abigail Garrett has qualities Lorena lacks. Don't forget that. You've got both the North and the South in you, Abbie. Use it. Go after Douglas yourself."

"All my life I've liked him," she told him simply.

"It's because I love him too, Abbie, that I want to see someone stop Lorena."

Another Fawcett Juniper title
by Phyllis A. Whitney:

THE FIRE AND THE GOLD

STEP TO THE MUSIC

Phyllis A. Whitney

"We join ourselves to no party that does not carry the flag and keep step to the Music of the Union."

— RUFUS CHOATE

FAWCETT JUNIPER • NEW YORK

RLI $\dfrac{\text{VL: grades } 6 + \text{up}}{\text{IL: grades } 7 + \text{up}}$

A Fawcett Juniper Book
Published by Ballantine Books

Copyright 1953 by Phyllis A. Whitney

Library of Congress Catalog Card Number: 53-8425

ISBN 0-449-70058-5

This edition published by arrangement with Thomas Y. Crowell Company

Manufactured in the United States of America

First Ballantine Books Edition: February 1986

For
my daughter Georgia,
who has helped through
all her growing-up years

With grateful acknowledgement to the Staten Island Institute of Arts and Sciences and to the Staten Island Historical Society, which made available to me their collections of books, newspapers, and historical records concerning the Civil War years on Staten Island.

With special thanks to Herbert Magruder, who first introduced me to Staten Island history, and to Miss Mabel Abbott, Miss Dorothy Smith, Dr. Henry G. Steinmeyer, and Dr. Otto Eisenschiml for their interest and help.

Contents

1

A Day of News

Spring rains had done the roads of Staten Island their usual ill turn and, despite the clear, thin sunshine of early April, there were carriage ruts and yellow puddles of water everywhere. Abbie Garrett started across the Shore Road, her hoops bouncing as she hopped from one oozy spot to the next.

She was in the middle of the road when the approach of a pair of bays forced her to snatch up her skirts and jump for the plank walk in front of Mr. Pine's store. She was just in time to escape the arc of muddy water thrown out by the carriage wheels.

For a moment she looked indignantly after the reckless driver. Then whirling to enter the store, she nearly collided with the delivery boy on his way out with a huge basket of groceries. He grinned and stepped back to let her through the door.

"Sorry, Miss Abbie. You always move so fast a fellow can't see you coming. Say—your friend Hannah Phillips is inside."

Her annoyance faded as she thought of the news she had for Hannah. She managed a smile and some confused thanks and stepped into the store. Since Mr. Pine kept everything from shoelaces to pickles for the convenience of North Shore homes, one had to navigate the aisles with some caution. Looking about, Abbie discovered Hannah down by the counter of glass candy jars. She hurried toward her friend, brushing a cracker barrel with her hoops, almost stepping on the cat in her eagerness to see Hannah.

Mr. Pine, his scoop filled with nuggets of horehound that he was pouring into a bag on the scale, saw her before Hannah did. " 'Afternoon, Miss Abbie. Your mama ordered a set of molds for you from New York, so now you can make some of those pretty wax bananas and peaches."

Abbie suppressed a sigh. Mama was forever encouraging her artistic talents in ways like this. She could never understand that her daughter disliked prissy parlor arts.

Hannah had turned at Mr. Pine's words, her round blue eyes bright with excitement. "Abbie, I've been dying to run over and see you, but Aunt Varina has kept me busy. What luck to meet you here. Wait till you hear the news!"

Abbie hushed Hannah with a warning finger. "My news first, or I'll explode." Then she smiled at Mr. Pine. "I'll take everything along, thank you. And I wonder if you can match this rose wool Mama wants. She'll skin me if I don't have it for her when she gets home from her trip." From her knitted reticule Abbie pulled out a strand of wool and handed it to Mr. Pine. While he matched its color, she turned again to Hannah. "Guess what! Lorena Emory is coming to live with us."

Hannah shook her head blankly and her bonnet slipped back from the ruffled brown wings of her hair. "Who's Lorena Emory?" she asked, good-naturedly permitting her own news to take second place to Abbie's.

Mr. Pine, always ready to reminisce, didn't give her time to answer. "I remember when Abbie's ma was Rosa Emory. Her family used to come up here summers all the way from Charleston. Guess that's when your pa met her and married

A Day of News 3

her, wasn't it, Abbie? But of course she's a regular Yankee by now."

Abbie smiled at the thought of her soft-voiced Southern mother being called a Yankee, but she wanted to stop Mr. Pine's reminiscing before it really got under way.

"Lorena's my cousin," she reminded Hannah. "Her father is Mama's brother. You know Mama went South a few weeks ago on a visit home. Now she's bringing Lorena North to spend a few months with us. Lorena's mother died some years ago. She's seventeen—just my age. So the three of us will have heaps of good times."

"Kinda early for them Southerners to be coming North, ain't it?" Mr. Pine asked. "They don't usually start up here till June. When'll she be arriving?"

Abbie glanced at the big lithographed calendar on the wall behind his head. "April 10, 1861," it read. "She should be here any day now. There's a lot of war scare down in Charleston and I guess Uncle Benton thought she'd be better off up here. He's bringing them North."

"Humph!" said Mr. Pine, obviously disgusted. "I should think her pa would be worried. All that secession going on. States dropping out of the Union. Illegal, that's what I call it! But we got a new President now. With old mealy-mouth Buchanan out, Mr. Lincoln ain't going to stand for more nonsense. Abbie, you can tell your pa for me that our boats sneaking out of New York harbor like they did means they're going down to relieve Fort Sumter and he can mark my words."

Hannah nudged Abbie as a signal for escape, less Mr. Pine launch himself into a political discussion, and the two girls completed their purchases.

Outside again, they followed the walk along the Shore Road, their footsteps making a hollow echo on the raised planks. Already the banks sloping toward the bay showed patches of pale green, and the trees on either side of the road were faintly nubby with the promise of spring.

"Whew!" Hannah said, hurrying her shorter stride to keep up with Abbie. "Mr. Pine's a dear, but I hate to get him started. Remember how excited he used to get when the Wide-Awake clubs were campaigning for Mr. Lincoln?"

Hannah was only a year younger than Abbie, but her head came barely to her friend's shoulder. Abbie smiled down at her affectionately. "What are you, Hannah? A Republican or a Copperhead?"

Hannah's parents had died in a yellow fever epidemic when she was a baby; but, despite her stern raising by a widowed aunt, Hannah had grown up carefree and good-naturedly resistant to causes and crises.

"Me? Heavens, I'm not anything! I like everybody."

Abbie slipped a hand beneath Hannah's fringed shawl and gave her arm a squeeze. "That's what's so nice about you. When everybody else is ranting and raving, you stay neutral and happy and calm."

"Only because I'm a nitwit and don't think about serious matters," Hannah said cheerfully. "Oh, goodness, I've let you sidetrack me miles from my news. I'll bet you'll be more interested in this than in your cousin Lorena's coming."

Abbie was aware of Hannah's sidelong glance and she tightened her grip on the other girl's arm. "You look like the cat with her nose in the cream. Better tell me quickly. I know you're dying to."

"All right, I will. Abbie, the McIntyres are back in our neighborhood. Aunt Varina's over there helping them settle in now."

The McIntyres! This *was* news. There were four Mc-Intyres, but to Abbie there would always be one who mattered more than his mother, or father, or brother. Their house was across the brook and meadow beyond Sailors Snug Harbor, and before Mr. McIntyre's business had taken him South to Atlanta six years ago, the two boys and Hannah and Abbie had been inseparable friends.

"Douglas must be eighteen by now," Hannah said, with the same sly look at Abbie. "I wonder if he's as handsome as he used to be."

Again Abbie caught the look. "And if his brother Stuart

is still as homely," she said, shutting Hannah out of any private thoughts she might have about Doug McIntyre.

Hannah, for all her gentle ways, could not be easily deflected when her curiosity was aroused. "I remember how sweet on Doug you used to be."

"I was only a child," Abbie said loftily. "Walk another block with me, Hannah. You can make up for it by running all the way home."

"Which won't please Auntie one bit," Hannah protested, but she gave in nevertheless and walked on at Abbie's side.

"Why are the McIntyres back?" Abbie asked. "Are they going to live on the island again?"

"I guess so. They never sold their house when they went South, you know. Aunt V. had a letter from Mrs. McIntyre just before they returned. It seems Mr. Mac began getting into fights with the Southern gentlemen he had to work with, what with all his sympathies being with the North. And you know how peppery he is. So he got upset and had a heart attack and has to be kept quiet and happy. The South is no place for him just now. Auntie says Mrs. McIntyre loved it down there and hated to come home. And the boys were going to Southern schools. But there wasn't anything else to do."

"I'm glad they're back," Abbie said. She would give Hannah that much of an answer to her unspoken question. "Well, you'd better run for home now. Come over soon— we're getting things ready for Lorena."

Abbie walked on more slowly after Hannah had hurried off. What fun those old days had been. She had always loved to run and play outdoors, to climb Staten Island's hills and roam through the woods. Red-headed Douglas McIntyre had been a wonderful playmate. He had always been as ready for adventure and action as she, and he'd never minded a be-skirted little girl tagging along.

She turned up Bard Avenue slowly, still remembering. There was a cave up there in the woods. Well, almost a cave. It was a shallow opening in an outcropping of the serpentine rock that made up the island's backbone. Doug's

younger brother Stuart had invented the game of the
Highland clans in which the cave had figured. Together
they'd worked out a secret code by which they sent
messages to one another, with the cave for a post office. In
those games Doug had always played the hero, she the
heroine, and Stuart the eternal villain.

Stuart had made a most convincing villain. He had a bit
of his father's temper when he really got mad. She could
remember one time when Stuart had slapped her good and
hard—for what reason she had forgotten. She'd slapped him
back and pulled his hair too, and they'd indulged in a cat-
and-dog fight right out on Bard Avenue, where everyone
could see what a tomboy gentle Rosa Garrett's daughter had
become.

Abbie could still recall the disgrace of that fight for both
Stuart and herself. That a young gentleman of ten should
fight a girl was unheard of, and that a young lady should use
her fists and nails and kicking feet to fight back was enough
to cause any mother to send for the smelling salts. Rosa had
done nothing of the kind. She had sailed down from the side
veranda in a hurry and, with her two little hands that were
accustomed to delicate embroidery, she had separated them
and held each by a collar as they kicked and screamed at
each other. Then, quite calmly, she'd knocked their heads
together with a good bang that jarred sense into both of
them. She'd sent Stuart packing for home and her daughter
up to bed.

Abbie laughed softly, remembering that day. At least the
fight had been a draw. Stuart hadn't beaten her, as she had
found occasion to remind him in later months. The one
thing she had always been thankful for was that Douglas
had not been around to see what a hoyden she had made of
herself.

Someone fell into step beside her just then, bringing her
back from long-ago days. She looked up to find that her
companion was the island's somewhat eccentric eye specialist, Dr. Samuel McKenzie Elliott.

"Good afternoon, Abbie," Dr. Elliott said. "I see you've

stopped for the mail, so I presume your father has not yet seen the *Richmond Gazette*?"

"No sir," Abbie said. "I'm taking it home now. Is anything wrong?"

"Wrong! Hah!" Dr. Elliott drew down his heavy eyebrows fiercely.

"How did your race come out this morning?" Abbie asked, to get him away from the depressing news in the paper.

Dr. Elliott cheered up at once. His morning races with the eight o'clock ferry still amused the neighborhood. When the boat passed the foot of Bard, Dr. Elliott would be ready in his buggy and would race the boat to the next landing. It was easy enough to beat the boat with a fast horse, but Dr. Elliott was always interested in his margin of victory.

"The *Flora*'s a good fast boat," he chuckled, "but we left her behind on the bend. And we'll do better tomorrow."

As they reached the Garrett house Dr. Elliott paused to raise his hat politely. "Remember me to your father, Abbie. I may stop by to see him later."

He continued uphill without explaining what he meant; and Abbie, still busy with her own thoughts, was not curious. More than anything else she wanted to get upstairs to her own room where she could think without interruption about the coming of the McIntyres.

Her father was not yet home, so she left the mail and papers on the desk in his study. Papa's working hours were not the happiest in his life, she sometimes suspected. He was in partnership as a lawyer across the bay in New York, but if it hadn't been for the senior partner the pleading of cases wouldn't have prospered very well. Her father wasn't exactly a lawyer sort of person. He liked best to read and think and write little essays that sometimes appeared in magazines and papers. Some day, she knew, he would write a fine book.

Downstairs, between the parlor and the study, was the big, sunny sewing room where her mother spent so many busy hours. Abbie had not acquired any liking for needle and sewing machine, but she loved the room because it was so much her mother's. She went into it now, sniffing the delicate odor of rose leaves from a potpourri jar on a whatnot shelf. The fragrance would forever remind her of Rosa Garrett. Abbie left the hank of wool near the sewing machine and then tiptoed into the hall.

A slamming of pots and pans from the direction of the kitchen told her that Mrs. Coombs, the cook and housekeeper, was well occupied. Softly Abbie scurried upstairs, not wanting to be caught and sent on further errands.

Abbie's was the corner room upstairs, just above her father's study. Stepping inside, she closed the door and leaned her back against it. The light of late afternoon lacquered the room with a golden hue that was just right for dreaming.

2

The Cave

For a moment Abbie stood with her back against the door, breathing quickly from her run upstairs. Then she went to the bed and dropped her package of wax and molds on the star-patterned quilt. With a quick gesture she loosened the ribbons and hung her bonnet upon the acorn knob of a bed post.

The gold and black dressing glass her sea captain grandfather had brought from China gave back her reflection. She stared at it curiously for a moment, itemizing, trying to see herself as a stranger might see her. A girl with wide dark eyes like her mother's—her best point. A nose that was unimportant, and a mouth that was definitely too big. The chin belonged to her great-grandmother McLeod, whose portrait hung over the mantelpiece in the parlor. It was the chin of a girl who possessed more determination and spirit than was always good for her. The face as a whole was more striking than pretty, yet suddenly, foolishly, Abbie Garrett longed to be pretty.

If only her hair were right, she thought, perhaps the rest

9

wouldn't matter so much. Some months before when she'd had diphtheria, her long hair had been shaved right to her scalp. It was only a couple of inches in length now and had grown in thick and curly, so that it tumbled into soft ringlets like the hair of a child. Until this moment Abbie had reveled in the freedom it gave her. But now she wished for hair that would lie in flat, smooth wings, drawn back from a center part and caught into a snood on the nape of her neck. This was the style most favored by *Godey's Lady's Book* and was the way her mother wore hers. But you couldn't get anything but a baby effect with the curly brown mop on Abbie Garrett's head.

She ran her hands through it despairingly and turned to the maple chest of drawers against the wall. Despite rubbing with candle wax, the bottom drawer always stuck, but, by tugging at the brass pulls, she managed to get it open after a jerk or two.

In this drawer she kept her most prized possessions. Even Mrs. Coombs, who was given to turning things inside out in her cleaning, understood that it was never to be opened and tidied by anyone but Abbie herself. Now she scrabbled in the bottom under a layer of sketchbooks and drawing paper until her fingers found what they searched for. Carefully she drew out the flat, paper-wrapped parcel and laid it on the floor. When she turned back the protecting brown paper the sketch of a boy's head lay revealed.

She knew well enough that it wasn't a good likeness. She had sketched it two years ago from a picture that had not been clear in the first place. Nevertheless, there was the look of Douglas McIntyre about the face. Anyone would recognize his wide forehead with the thick, faintly curling locks above it. She couldn't capture the bright red hue of that hair in a pencil sketch, but that was something her memory easily supplied. She had managed to catch his straightforward gaze at least, and the clear-cut line of his nose. The mouth had never come right and it spoiled the whole picture. Sometimes it looked familiar to her, but in the next moment she had to admit that it wasn't Doug's mouth at all. The lips of the sketch had a wry look to them, while she best remembered Doug's ready, open smile. However, the right mouth was one she had not the skill to draw, so after her fifth attempt she had let that troubling part of the drawing remain as it was.

She propped the picture against the open drawer and knelt in the midst of billowing hoops to study it. Of course Doug probably wouldn't look like this at all by now. When she had tried to make him older in the drawing, her own memory of his twelve-year-old face crowded in to defeat her. But this was the nearest she had been able to come to owning a picture of him. Mrs. McIntyre had sent the original to Hannah's aunt, Varina Phillips, and Hannah had borrowed it secretly for Abbie to copy.

"I'm glad you're back," she told the picture softly.

He wouldn't have changed, she knew. He'd still be fun. He'd still be the adventurous leader. . . . A whimsical thought seized her. Would he remember the cave up there in the woods and the game of the clans? Would he remember the code they'd used? But of course he would! Didn't she remember it perfectly herself?

She tore a corner from a scribbled-on sketch pad and fished a pencil from a box in the drawer. Pushing aside the rag rug, she rested the bit of paper on the floor board and began to write. The symbols of the code came as easily as they had in the past and she finished the brief note quickly. Then she put the picture away in its hiding place and shoved the reluctant drawer shut. The picture wouldn't matter any more, with the real Douglas McIntyre home again.

Now for the next step in her quickly evolving scheme. One thing was certain sure—she couldn't go climbing through the woods in a hoop. She pulled up her brown merino skirt and white petticoats and loosened the hooked band about her waist. The tapered circles promptly collapsed on the floor and she stepped out of the hoops hastily. From an upper drawer in the dresser she took a band made of elastic, a thing that the ladies called a "page." When her skirts were draped over the band, they were considerably shortened and she was able to move more freely. What a nuisance it was to be a lady, Abbie thought for the hundredth time. No one would ever convince her that hoops were anything but a foolish style.

She folded the note and tucked it into her knitted mitten, pulled her shawl more tightly about her shoulders, and tiptoed down the back stairs. Mrs. Coombs did not see her as she sped past the kitchen door. Out in the back yard Jamie, the Garretts' combined coachman-stableboy-handyman, was giving one of the bays a currying. He looked around at the sound of her step on the gravel walk, but she waved at him and he went stolidly on with his work. Jamie would keep his own counsel. Mrs. Coombs said he didn't talk much because he had nothing to talk about, but Abbie sometimes suspected that Jamie was what Mama called a "deep one," who thought wise thoughts he didn't trouble to put into words.

At least she was grateful now for his indifference. She let herself out the back gate and hurried uphill, picking her way as best she could among the muddy ruts of the street. At least she could move comfortably and quickly now, and when the pathway cut off into woods that mounted clear to the crest of the hills, she was glad for spongy grass beneath her feet.

The cave was no more than a ten-minute climb away, but she hurried so that she was breathless when she reached its hidden entrance. Since children had stopped using it for their games, bushes had grown thick and heavy across its mouth and it was a better hiding place than ever. Even now when the bushes were only beginning to leaf, the entrance was hidden.

Abbie parted the intertwining guards and stepped into the small cleared space where a floor of stone gave little encouragement to sprouting seeds. The sun had dropped toward the New Jersey hills and in the fading light she could manage a last quick reading of her note. She translated it aloud as she read it softly.

Dear Douglas:

It is wonderful to have you home again. Staten Island has been lonesome for you. Do you remember the fun we used to have—the games we used to play? If you come to this old hiding place, I'll know you haven't forgotten. Welcome home!

Abbie

For a moment longer she stood there, note in hand. Surely he would remember how he'd played the role of Sir William Wallace, hiding in this highland cave while she, as brave and beautiful Lady Wallace, had refused to betray her husband. He would remember how many times she had gone to her death at the hands of the villainous English Governor Hazelrigg—who was Stuart, of course. He couldn't forget being Robert the Bruce, being crowned King of all the Scots, or of fleeing the country as Bonnie Prince Charlie.

Abbie stopped and wriggled through the entrance to the cave. It was strange how shallow and small it seemed now. Memory had given it greater dimensions. Smiling to herself, she groped for the spike of rock shoulder-high on the cave's wall. There, she had it! She wedged the folded note behind the spike and backed gingerly out of the small space. Then she turned and hurried down along the path, glad of her comfortable, elastic-sided boots that made walking on such uncertain ground fairly easy.

No one seemed to have missed her at home. Jamie was stabling the bays and gave Abbie no second glance. A look through the kitchen door showed her that Mrs. Coombs, floured to the elbow, was deep in biscuit-making and too occupied to notice comings and goings. Abbie was about to run upstairs when she saw the gleam of lamplight through the curtain of painted bamboo beads that hung in the doorway of her father's study. So Papa was home. She paused outside the curtain, wondering whether to go in, or to run straight upstairs to remove all telltale evidence of her walk through the woods. Just then her father spoke and the solemn note in his voice arrested her attention. She could not tell who was with him, but his words came to her plainly.

"So now they've tried to fly the palmetto flag of South Carolina right here on the island. Listen to this in today's *Richmond County Gazette*:

> The war has commenced. The people of Richmond County, a considerable portion of whom do business in Virginia, and are far removed from the influence of "Northern prejudices," on Friday last gave evidence that they were no Disunionists, and would tolerate no insult to their flag or to their patriotism. A schooner from Charleston, S.C., ran into Tottenville, having the palmetto flag flying, and continued to display it after she had anchored. Some of the people then insisted that it should be hauled down, and the Stars and Stripes hoisted in its place. This the Captain refused, but refused with so much insolence and abuse that the ire of the remonstrant was excited and he gave the Captain a severe beating. What became of the flag we did not learn.

With lamplight in the room beyond, she could see her father plainly through the bamboo curtain, but his listener was not in view. She started past the door when a voice stopped her; a cheerful young voice which made light of the incident.

"But, sir, why shouldn't a schooner from South Carolina fly the palmetto banner wherever she docks? That's the flag the state has adopted."

Abbie scarcely heard the words, for listening to the sound of the speaker's voice. The man in the study with her father was Douglas McIntyre. And suddenly Abbie was filled with panic. She knew without the slightest doubt that she had behaved like a foolish, romantic little girl in hiding that note in the cave. The voice she had heard from the study was not the voice of the boy she remembered, for all that it was recognizable. There was a hint of Southern drawl that had not been there before. For the first time she realized that Douglas had grown up and that she did not know him at all. He was a stranger whose reactions she could no longer prophesy as she had been able to in the old days. How he might react to that note was something she did not care to risk in case he happened to find it.

This time Mrs. Coombs saw her as she went by the door and called after her. "Where you going, Abbie? Dinner in a half hour, you know."

Abbie gave her a vague answer, and hurried outside and back up the hill as fast as she could go. She wasn't reasoning now, or figuring things out. She was acting on emotional impulse. Douglas was a young man and she wanted him to see her as a young woman—not as a foolish child. Thank goodness, there was still light enough to find the path, or she would have had to wait till morning.

She made the last upward turn panting and then came to a startled halt. Someone had reached the cave first. A tall, slender young man stood full in her path. His back was toward her and for a moment she thought that somehow Doug had managed to race her up the hill. Then she saw that this young man's hair was sandy, not bright red, and when he turned as a twig cracked beneath her foot, she found herself looking into the amused gray eyes of Stuart McIntyre. In his hand he held the note she had written to his brother Douglas.

For a moment the two stood staring at each other. Then Stuart laid the bit of paper over his heart and made her a mocking bow.

"Miss Abigail Garrett, as I live and breathe. Funny— I've been thinking of you all along as a tomboyish nuisance of a little girl—and here you are grown up. A real young lady."

Stuart had always possessed a talent for making her furious and she saw that he had not changed in that respect. But now she was a young lady and she mustn't give way to anger. How careless she'd been not to take Stuart into her calculations when she had written that note to Doug. She simply hadn't thought that he might be the one to come first to the cave. In fact, once the whim about the note had seized her, she had forgotten Stuart completely. She strove now for dignity—such dignity as her mother might have displayed under the circumstances.

"Hello, Stuart. Welcome home. May I have that note, please? It's not for you, you know."

His mouth was solemn, but his eyes teased her. "I have already discovered that it isn't for me. By reading it, my dear Abigail. Remember the rule? Whoever found a note could read it if he knew the code. And I am wounded to the depths. Here was I—retracing old steps, dreaming old dreams . . ."

"Give me that note," she said, her patience dissolving, as Stuart had always been able to make it dissolve.

She stepped toward him, her hand out, but, though she had grown tall, Stuart was taller, and he held the note high out of her reach.

"This billet-doux is no longer your property, my dear young lady. You have no right to request its return."

"Stop talking like a silly book," she cried. "I wrote it and I want it back."

He reached out with it gently, tantalizingly, and just tweaked the end of her nose with its edge, then pulled it swiftly out of reach again. Abbie found that she was trembling with anger. She flung herself at him, snatching for the note, but he sidestepped easily and she'd have fallen into the bushes if he hadn't caught her by the arm and pulled her back.

"The same old Abbie!" he laughed. "Appearances are deceptive. You really haven't grown up one bit, have you? You know something—just this morning I was thinking about the time you nearly gave me a licking right out in the middle of Bard Avenue. You'd have scalped me, I guess, if your mother hadn't stepped in."

Abbie regained her balance and drew her arm from his steadying grasp. It was perfectly true that she'd nearly gone for him in the old way, and the realization shocked the anger out of her. She was seventeen now. She mustn't let him trick her into behaving as she had at ten.

She managed a quivery smile. "That's the first time I've ever heard you admit that you nearly took a licking that day."

"That's because I'm a big boy now and I can take care of myself."

For all his thinness, he had a wiry, muscular look about him that bore out his words. But if he could not be fought, perhaps he could be coaxed.

"It will be dark soon," she said, "and I've got to be home for dinner. Stop teasing me, Stuart. It was silly of me to write that nonsense to Doug. If you won't give it back, please tear it up."

He fell into step beside her on the downhill path. "You almost melt my heart, fair lady. Almost, but not quite. And I don't agree with you that the note is nonsense. Sir William Wallace—or, if you prefer, Bonnie Prince Charlie—is going to be genuinely touched by so romantic a welcome. May I see you home, Miss Abigail?"

There was nothing to do but walk down the hill toward Bard. She had no least notion of how to get the note back, or rid herself of Stuart's company, so she concentrated on moving with dignity, freezing him out with her silence.

But if she had nothing further to say, Stuart had. He rambled on as casually as if he did not know perfectly well that she was seething with indignation. He even dropped his mocking imitation of a character in a novel.

"It's good to be back on the island, Abbie. I'll behave and call you Abbie from now on. I remember how you always disliked Abigail. I wish Doug and Mama were as happy about returning as Papa and I. Doug would have made a perfect Southerner if he'd been born down there. He's much more the Gentleman in capital letters than I am."

"I'm sure he is," said Abbie.

He glanced at her and whistled softly. "Say! Is that the

way you girls are wearing your hair up North these days? All chopped off like that?"

"I had diphtheria," Abbie told him, making her words few and curt.

"Sorry," he said, sounding sincere for the first time. "I wouldn't have teased if I'd realized you'd been ill. It doesn't look bad that way. And it must be as comfortable as a man's haircut."

And as much like one, Abbie thought rebelliously, unmoved by Stuart's softening mood. They'd reached the Garrett house by now and Abbie wondered if it would be any use to try once more to obtain the note from Stuart. But when she started to speak, she saw that he was looking past her toward the side of the house where the French doors in her father's study opened onto the veranda. Through the glass doors—uncurtained to let in as much light as her father wished—Douglas McIntyre was clearly visible.

Stuart grinned impudently and strode toward the veranda steps. Abbie hurried after him, ready to plead now if necessary. But she had no opportunity, for just then her father opened the double doors and Doug stepped out on the veranda, evidently taking his leave.

"I've got something for you," Stuart called to him. "Remember a little girl named Abbie Garrett, Doug? Well, she left a note for you up in the old cave post office. Only I happened to find it first, so I can save you the trouble of going after it."

He ran up the veranda steps and Abbie could only stand there in the yard, frozen into helplessness. For the first time she remembered how she looked. No ladylike hoops, just skirts looped ungracefully over an elastic band; no bonnet with the ribbons fetchingly tied, just her babyish cap of brown curls. The ground was quite solid beneath her boots and there was nothing to do but stand there in light that was not dim enough to hide her completely and endure the sight of Doug McIntyre smiling at her from the veranda.

Even with his back to the lamplight of the study, she could see his wide shoulders, the bigness of him. He wore his red hair in the thick, unshorn fashion of the time, and the lamplight behind him shone through it in a bright aureole. He stood there for only a moment. Then he jumped down from the veranda without troubling about the steps and crossed the yard in long strides to envelope her in a great hug. A completely brotherly hug, she suspected, as her ribs creaked a little and she put up her hands to push him laughingly away. He did not release her completely, but held her off at arm's length, his hands on her shoulders, and murmured over her in wonder.

"Abbie—grown up. It doesn't seem possible. Why, I remember when . . ." he paused and glanced at Stuart. "What was that about a note?"

"Oh, no!" Abbie cried faintly. "Please, Stuart!"

Stuart grinned and handed the bit of paper over to Doug, who accepted it with every evidence of interest.

"Oh, no!" Abbie cried faintly. "Please, Douglas." She was grateful for the dimming light that blurred the marks on the paper.

There was none of Stuart's impudence in Douglas. At the note of distress in her voice, he turned to her quickly.

"You don't want me to read this? Even though you wrote it to me?"

"It's just that it was a—a childish thing to do," Abbie faltered.

"I won't think that," he said. "I'd like to read it. But if you prefer not . . ."

"What did I tell you?" Stuart broke in. "Always the Gentleman!"

Abbie would not have Stuart making fun of his brother.

"Douglas is only being kind," she told Stuart. "That is something you wouldn't understand." She surrendered abruptly. "Go ahead and read it, Doug. I—I won't mind."

The soft Southern slur in Douglas' speech might seem strange to her, but his smile was one she remembered, warm and gay. He turned toward the lamplight of her father's study and she went with him up the veranda steps. Stuart came too and she was aware of his amusement, as if he were a spectator at a comedy.

Roger Garrett sat inside at his carved teakwood desk, the day's papers spread open before him. Abbie noted briefly that her father looked weary and that there were lines of strain about his mouth. But he glanced up as the young people came in and smiled at them.

Stuart went over and held out his hand and Mr. Garrett rose to shake it cordially. "This is a real pleasure, my boy. It is good to see you back on the island. We'll have to have one of our old reading evenings and all get together soon."

Listening, Abbie remembered that, of the two McIntyre boys, her father's favorite had never been the sunny, lovable Douglas, but always the gloomier, more sardonic Stuart. In the old days Papa had talked to young Stuart as if he'd been grown up, and they'd had endless discussions about books, essays, travel, philosophy. Subjects which interested Papa more than did the law.

But Abbie's attention turned quickly back to Douglas. Because Papa disliked the new gas light with which many North Shore houses were now equipped, he would have only old-fashioned oil lamps in his study. In the rest of the house they used either, as they pleased. Doug stood beside the lamp on the desk, the note held to the light, and if Abbie remembered him as attractive as a boy, her heart turned over at the handsome, brave look of him now.

"It's in our old code, isn't it, Abbie? You've remembered it all this time." He smiled ruefully. "I hate to confess that I've forgotten the characters. Abbie, I can't read it. I'm ashamed."

"Give it here," Stuart said. "I haven't forgotten."

But Douglas held the note out of his reach. "Oh, no, you don't! No public readings, Stu. You can furnish me with the code and I'll decipher it myself."

Abbie felt almost limp with relief. She might have known that Douglas would save her any embarrassment.

"It was a foolish way to greet you," she said lightly. "I suppose I forgot that you'd be grown up by now."

"I'm not that grown up," Doug told her. "It's a perfect welcome, Abbie."

She could think of no response and fortunately Mrs. Coombs saved her just then by appearing in the doorway to announce that dinner was ready.

The two boys turned toward the door and Stuart was the last one out. He brushed past her close enough to whisper a farewell under his breath. "Good night, Lady Wallace."

"Oh, you!" said Abbie and felt relieved to let off a little steam.

As she ran upstairs to wash for dinner she suddenly understood why the mouth she had made for Douglas' picture had never seemed right. It had been Stuart's faintly derisive expression she had drawn—not Doug's at all. Now she would know how to make the picture right.

3

Sound of Cannon

Friday was baking day at the Garrett house, so late in the afternoon Mrs. Coombs packed a hamper of good things for Abbie to take over to the McIntyres.

Two days of bright sunshine had dried out the meadow above Sailors Snug Harbor and Abbie could take the path across it with more comfort than would have been possible earlier in the week. Dressed in her green plaid taffeta and a green bonnet with yellow roses under the brim, and with her best cashmere shawl draped about her, Abbie felt herself a decided improvement over the hoyden whom Douglas had seen on Wednesday.

The hamper on her arm was heavy, but she walked with quick, light steps, leaping the narrow place in the brook, hoops and all, without jarring herself or her burden.

As Abbie ran up the front steps of the McIntyre house, Hannah Phillips waved to her from a window and came quickly to the door.

"Ssh!" Hannah whispered, glancing over her shoulder toward the parlor, from which issued the sound of feminine chatter. "If you don't want Aunt Varina to enlist you, you'd better sneak right down the hall."

Abbie smiled. "I don't mind. I have to see Mrs. McIntyre, since I've brought this basket over."

A remembered voice called, "Hannah dear, is someone there?" and a moment later Mrs. McIntyre appeared at the parlor door, plump and pink-cheeked, her dark red skirt billowing fashionably over an exaggerated hoop. "Why, it's Abbie Garrett! I can't believe the way you girls have shot up. Come in, do."

Mrs. Varina Phillips, resplendent as always in black bombazine with white lace collar and her favorite hair brooch, sat upon the horsehair sofa in the parlor, looking as regal as royalty and twice as important. She nodded to Abbie and burst into words at once.

"When do you expect your mama back from the South? Rosa is wonderful at selling tickets and I hope she'll help me with other details too."

"Mama should be home any day now," Abbie told her. "Uncle Benton is bringing Mama and Cousin Lorena Emory North, and I expect they have to wait until Uncle Benton can get away."

Mrs. Phillips opened her black reticule and pulled out a stack of rose-colored tickets. "Then I know you'll be glad to help us, Abbie, since your mama isn't here. We're going to have a boating excursion around the island in a few weeks. It's for the benefit of the New Brighton Free Library—a very worth-while cause."

To forestall further eloquence from Hannah's aunt, Abbie accepted some tickets and proffered her basket to Mrs. McIntyre. "Mrs. Coombs baked today and we thought we'd bring you a few things, just in case you could use them."

"Can we use them! Thank you, Abbie dear. Will you and Hannah take the basket right out to the kitchen, please."

Carrying the hamper between them, the two girls started down the long, dim hall that led from the front of the house to the back. The moment they came opposite the dining room they were raided by a privateer. At least that is what Doug McIntyre announced that he represented.

"You can see my skull and crossbones flying if you look closely enough," he warned them. "Stand and deliver unless you want to walk the plank."

"No planks," Abbie pleaded. She pulled back the white linen napkin that covered the basket and the fragrance of fresh baking scented the air.

Douglas breathed deeply, helped himself to four cookies, and then reached for the basket. I'll carry this away to a safe place, girls. Now you just run on in the dining room and talk to Papa. He's pining for company."

"I don't trust you," Abbie said, laughing as Douglas took the basket out of their hands.

He gave her an odd, quick look that made her wonder if her bonnet strings were untied, or if there was a smudge on her nose. Then he went off toward the kitchen with the captured basket.

Abbie remembered the McIntyre dining room of old. It was a big, sunny room, with a bright-patterned carpet. The big polished mahogany table was perfect for games, and as children they'd had good times in this room.

Over by the big bay window, where the sun shone in upon him, sat Mr. McIntyre, enveloped in a plaid blanket, his feet propped comfortably on pillows and footstool. Abbie remembered him with hair nearly as thick and red as his elder son's, but the years had thinned his fiery thatch and grayed it. There was only a trace of red left in his sideburns and heavy eyebrows.

"Come in, lasses," he boomed and Abbie noted that his voice at least had grown no softer. "It's good to have girls 'round the house again. Come here and let me see how you've grown."

There was a burr in his speech, left over from his long ago boyhood in Scotland, and Abbie had always loved to hear him talk. She came to him now and held out her hands.

"Welcome home, Mr. Mac. It's fine to have you back."

Douglas came into the r...
placing chairs for the girls, on...

"Isn't Stuart home yet?" Mr. M...
boy's been gone for the mail close...

Abbie remembered the tickets Mrs....
into her hand and put on her best saleswoma...
Mac, wouldn't you like to take yourself and you...   on
an excursion trip around beautiful Staten Island? It's   for a
worthy cause and I'm selling tickets." -She couldn't help a
glance at Douglas to see if he was interested. It would be
fun if she could go on the excursion with him.

Mr. McIntyre waggled a reproachful finger at her.
"Somehow the minute a woman comes into the picture a
man begins to part with his money. All right, my lass, I'll
buy your tickets—four of 'em. I guess that will get the
McIntyres out socially to let the island know they're
home."

While the transaction was being completed, Abbie
invited Hannah and Douglas over for the reading evening
the following night.

"Stuart too, of course," she said. "Tell him, will you,
Douglas, if I don't see him before I leave?"

But Stuart came in a few moments later and was able to
accept for himself. Gravely he handed his father the bundle
of papers and mail.

"I took longer than usual because I met Mr. Curtis on his
way home from the boat," he explained.

Something in Stuart's tone sounded a warning and Abbie
looked at him quickly. George William Curtis was the
island's most distinguished man of letters and his words
were worth listening to.

"Well, what about it?" Mr. McIntyre said.

Stuart went on quietly. "Mr. Curtis was over at the
Tribune office all afternoon—so he had the latest news."

They all knew now that something was wrong. Mr.
McIntyre stared at him, waiting.

"There's bad news," Stuart said. "Fort Sumter was fired
upon around four o'clock this morning. News has been

over the magnetic telegraph, though of
it won't be in the papers till tomorrow. The fort is
defending itself, but that's about all they know."

Mr. McIntyre allowed the letter he held to slide unheeded
to the floor, while a choleric flush came into his cheeks.
Douglas started to speak, then broke off and turned away to
the window. Hannah covered her mouth with her hands, her
eyes round with dismay.

"Don't worry about it, Papa," Stuart pleaded. "A little
state like South Carolina can't do much against the big
United States. It's sure to be over quickly now that they've
fired on our flag."

"Will it be over quickly?" Douglas asked without
turning from the window. "You know the sentiment in the
South, Stuart. You know the strong feeling against the
North."

Mr. McIntyre seemed not to hear either of them. His right
fist clenched the arm of his chair and he shouted one
explosive word, "War!"

That was enough to bring the two ladies running down
the hall from the parlor. Mrs. McIntyre, plump and fluttery,
bent over her husband, beseeching him.

"Dear, you mustn't get excited. What is it—something in
the papers? You know you can't believe what those horrid
papers say!"

He pushed aside her soothing hand. "George Curtis says
Fort Sumter has been fired upon and that means war. With
that wishy-washy Buchanan out of the way, we should be
taking action. Now we can set down this insurrection in
double-quick time and get the states back together where
they belong."

"The whole thing is ridiculous," Mrs. Phillips shrilled.
"If the Southern states want slaves, they should have them.
Who are we to tell them what to do? Might be better for the
country all around if everybody kept slaves."

"Madam," said Mr. McIntyre loudly, "you are a fool!"

At this breach of courtesy, Mrs. Phillips fled from the

room, dabbing at her eyes with... though Abbie suspected there w...

Mrs. McIntyre, torn between conce... should be kept calm, and loyalty to an o... been treated discourteously, hesitated a ... gestured Stuart toward his father and hurried ... Varina.

"Mrs. Phillips might have a point at that, sir," Douglas said. "I mean the South thinks the North has been trying to push her around and this is her answer."

His father looked as if he might explode. "I don't want to hear a son of mine talk such bosh."

For a moment Douglas stood his ground, then his normal good nature and optimism came to the fore. "I'm sorry, sir. I hope Stu is right and this is just a flare-up that will be over soon. It's a matter of differing viewpoints. If anyone can reason with the South, it should be Mr. Lincoln."

His father's indignation turned in a new direction. "Lincoln's still an untried country bumpkin. He's done nothing so far to show a mind of his own. I'd rather have seen Seward nominated at the Republican convention."

Abbie had ceased to follow the talk. At news of trouble with the South her thoughts had turned at once to her mother. Would this mean any change in her mother's trip home? Where was her home, if it came to that? No one knew better than Abbie how much her home state of South Carolina meant to her mother. Not all her years in the North had managed to sever Rosa Garrett's ties with home, or change her love for the South and its people. For all that her love for her family was deep and true, the North had never become more to her than an adopted country.

Abbie longed suddenly to get back to the house, where she could talk to her father. He was the wisest, calmest person she knew. He would be able to reassure her, to answer her muddle of questions.

Mr. McIntyre still muttered, but Stuart had succeeded in reminding him of doctor's orders, and the unhealthy flush was fading from his face.

...orgotten her presence and Abbie spoke hesi-
...ly. "If you don't mind—I just came over to say hello,
Mr. Mac. Now I'd better get home and see if Papa has heard
the news."

He nodded at her. "Of course, Abbie. It's been good to
see you again. I'll expect you to come bouncing in often
now, just the way you used to do."

She smiled and hurried off to say her good-bye to Mrs.
McIntyre. Mrs. Phillips and Hannah had already gone.
Douglas came to the door as she was about to leave.

"I'm aiming to see you home, Abbie," he said. He
appeared to have shrugged off the gravity of that moment in
the dining room and was his old, easy-going self.

She thanked him, feeling oddly shy. For some reason she
was constrained with him the moment they were alone. She
walked sedately at his side along the meadow path, a
ladylike hand on her skirts to keep her hoops behaving,
trying to move in the graceful manner she so admired in her
mother.

"You've grown up, Abbie," Doug said. "Somehow I
can't get used to it."

Abbie tilted her bonnet to allow a view of his face.
"Don't you like growing up, Douglas?"

"I like it all right." There was warm laughter in his
voice. "But somehow I just don't believe in it. Abbie—race
you to the brook!"

She caught up her hoops, set the toe of her boot on an
imaginary line, and was ready to go in an instant. Then she
remembered herself in time and straightened to look at him.

"That was a trap, Douglas McIntyre, and I won't fall into
it. I'm seventeen and too old for races."

He laughed out loud. "You're not too old to hide notes in
a cave."

"Oh, that!" she said tartly and swung ahead of him along
the path.

But he caught her hand in his and would not let her go. "I
deciphered your note, Abbie. I'm sorry I didn't get to the

cave before Stuart found it. Anyway, I like your writing it. I like knowing you've missed me on Staten Island."

She could find no words to answer him and they walked on together in silence. She knew he was no longer teasing her and she felt completely happy in his company. When they reached Bard Avenue and crossed the street to her house, he paused outside the gate.

"Abbie, may I have the pleasure of your company on this excursion party Mrs. Phillips has planned?"

This was something she had hoped for. "Of course," she said. "I'd love to go with you."

Afterward, walking up the steps alone, she wondered if she had been too ready with her acceptance. In novels the heroine behaved more coyly, always promising to tell her eager beau her decision later. Oh, well, never mind foolish novels!

She pulled off her bonnet as she crossed the veranda and shook her short curls free from its restraint. The French doors of her father's study stood ajar and she could see him reading at his desk. He looked up in greeting as she stepped into the room, and she recalled the grave news she must tell him.

"Papa, Fort Sumter has been fired upon. Mr. Curtis had the word right from the *Tribune* office."

Her father closed his book quietly. "Yes, I know. The news reached us before I left town. I've been afraid of this. How foolish can men be?"

"Mr. McIntyre says we'll put the whole thing down in a hurry. He called it an insurrection."

"I hope he's right. If it is war neither side will win."

"What do you mean, Papa?"

He left his chair and crossed the room, to stand beside a window, looking out into the dry browns of the garden, so that Abbie was reminded of the way Douglas had stared out the dining room window at the McIntyres'.

"I don't believe the North can ever really win a war with the South. If we beat them they'll hate us forever. We could never live as united states again. There are fools in both our governments bringing this about."

"But what about slavery, Papa? Shouldn't all those poor colored people be freed and . . ."

"Slavery's wrong and it will go. It will go because it's morally wrong, and it will go because the weight of a slave economy is ruining the South. There are Southern men who already realize that. Not all of them are for slavery by a long shot. I've been reading a fine book called *The Impending Crisis* by a North Carolina man, Hinton Rowan Helper. And of course your Uncle Benton freed his slaves a good while back."

"But they've fired on us, Papa. They've attacked us!"

"Hotheads. People who can't see beyond their own noses."

Abbie went to stand beside him at the window and slipped her hand through the crook of his arm the way she had done so often as a little girl when something troubled her.

"Will Mama be all right?"

"Of course." He patted her hand. "Benton Emory is a man of good sense. He will bring her North at once—if they haven't already started."

"I—I didn't mean that exactly. You know how Mama loves the South."

He nodded. "It will be hard for her. We can't expect her to stop loving her home and her people. But she'll come back to us. You know that."

The clock on the mantel struck the hour with a soft bonging sound. It was nearly supper time.

"Everyone's coming for a reading evening tomorrow night," Abbie said. "Hannah and Doug and Stuart. It will be like old times."

Again her father nodded, but he did not turn away from the window and she went quietly out of the room. Would anything ever be really like old times again, she wondered, climbing the front stairs. Could a person ever go backward through the years? Probably not, and probably it was better that way. Only it shouldn't be the firing of a cannon that kept you from going back, the way those Sumter guns might keep the whole country from old ways and old times.

In the upstairs hall she went to the front of the house and opened a door. Inside, the shutters were closed, but through the filtering of dim light she could see the welcome which was evident throughout the room. The oval rag rugs were new, and so was the Boston rocker with its high, stenciled back. The bed was old, but comfortable; and the quilt which covered it was a family treasure—one Great-grandmother McLeod had made. Once, long ago, this room had belonged to Abbie's small brother. But it had been used for only a few short years before a scarlet fever epidemic had taken him away. Now it waited for a new occupant—Lorena Emory.

Abbie closed the door softly and went back to her own room. As she poured water from the china pitcher on the marble-topped washstand, she wondered about Lorena. What would the firing of those guns mean to a Charleston girl? Would she be willing to come North now? But surely, being Uncle Benton's daughter, Lorena wouldn't be one of those hot-headed Southerners who wanted to fight the United States.

Abbie washed her hands absently with her favorite rose-geranium soap and went downstairs to supper.

4

Reading Evening

By Saturday evening all Staten Island buzzed with news of the guns that roared in the harbor of Charleston. Rumors flew one way, then another, and tension mounted; but no one knew what was really happening.

It was in this disturbing atmosphere that the Garretts held their reading evening. The night had turned cool and a drizzle streaked the window panes of the parlor, making the red spears of fire in the grate seem all the more cozy. Abbie had set chairs in a half circle around the hearth. Above the mantelpiece the oval-framed portrait of Great-grandmother McLeod looked down serenely.

Mr. Garrett's easy chair was in the center, and he had made himself comfortable with an oil lamp on the table beside him. While Hannah cracked nuts busily, a big bowl in her lap and a saucer for the meats beside her, Douglas, his face ruddy in the firelight, knelt before the hearth rattling corn in a long-handled popper.

"This is one thing I missed down South," he said. "Popcorn and cold nights and a hearthfire."

"What are you boys planning to do with yourselves now that you're back North?" Mr. Garrett asked.

Douglas looked up from the corn popper. "More school, I expect, sir, when Papa makes up his mind where to send us."

Stuart reached out to loot Hannah's saucer of nut meats. "I want to get a job," he said, chucking walnuts lazily into his mouth.

"Do you still write, Stuart?" Mr. Garrett asked.

Stuart, whose cocky self-confidence seldom left him at a loss, was suddenly hesitant. "I still do a bit of it. Nothing much."

"Don't you believe him, sir," said Douglas. "He's always at it. He has even written a full report on the state of the South in the months before we left."

The corn began popping wildly at that moment and Doug gave it his full attention, missing the grimace Stuart made behind his back.

"I'd like to read that report," Mr. Garrett said quietly. "That is, if you wouldn't mind, Stuart."

"If you like, sir." Stuart hesitated. "But it would be for your eyes only, if you please."

"Who else would be interested?" Abbie asked tartly.

"You," Stuart told her, and reached again to the nut saucer.

Abbie sniffed and gave her attention to mixing melted butter into the popcorn. When everyone was provided with a bowl of corn, a handful of nuts, and an apple, they all settled down to listen to the reading.

Mr. Garrett had selected George William Curtis' *Prue and I*. It was not exciting reading but it was pleasant, and somehow it was reassuring to read of quiet things tonight. Here, for a little while, the dark and the cold could not crowd in, the guns of war could raise no echo.

When the doorbell clamored suddenly, they all started and looked at one another. Certainly the ring of a doorbell was not alarming, yet concern was so close to each that they tensed easily.

Mr. Garrett nodded to Abbie. "Will you get it, please? Mrs. Coombs is probably napping. If it's a visitor, invite him to join us."

Released from the spell that held her, Abbie flew to the door and pulled it open. The light from the gas jet in the hall fell upon her mother's pale face, upon a girl behind her in a cherry red hat, and upon a tall man coming up the steps. Beyond, in the muddy street, the driver of a cab was clucking to his horse as it turned from the curb.

At Abbie's cry of greeting, her father came to the door and suddenly everyone was crowding into the hall, talking, laughing, asking questions without waiting for an answer. Rosa Garrett lifted cold little hands to her daughter's cheeks and drew her face down for a kiss. "I've missed you, honey," she whispered. Then her husband's arms went around her and even as she tilted her head for his kiss she pulled Abbie close to them both, so they were all together for a moment. The old feeling of everything being right because her mother was home swept warmly through Abbie. Her eyes were bright with happiness as she turned to greet the others.

She had a dim recollection of a childhood meeting with this tall Uncle Benton who was her mother's brother. As she took his extended hand, he drew her around to face the girl in the cherry red hat.

"Abbie, this is my daughter Lorena. I hope you'll be friends."

Abbie held out both hands to Lorena, who looked a little solemn and lost among all these strangers. Even in the light of the single hall jet Abbie could see how pretty her cousin was, with delicate features and eyes that were almost sea green. Her hat, tilted saucily over her forehead, uncovered the heavy blond chignon on the nape of her neck, and she looked very much the young woman of fashion. There was the slightest moment of hesitation, due to shyness no doubt, before Lorena gave her hands into Abbie's for a welcoming squeeze. Then Abbie helped her out of her wool mantle and led her into the parlor to meet her father and Hannah and the boys.

There was something arresting about Cousin Lorena as she stood in the middle of the Brussels carpet, a bright figure in cherry red satin, her cheeks pink with some inner excitement, her eyes snapping. She didn't need to say a word to catch admiring attention. She simply stood there in an electric silence and people looked at her because they could not look away.

Papa shook hands with Uncle Benton, and brought him into the parlor to his own favorite easy chair, asking the while if there was any news of Sumter. Mama turned to the fire, seemingly to warm chilled fingers, but Abbie had the feeling that she was troubled by the question and what the answer would be.

"There is news," Uncle Benton said wearily, leaning back against the chair with his eyes closed. "Whether it is good news or bad, I can't say."

"Oh, Papa!" Lorena cried, whirling about in her red skirts. "You know it's wonderful news." She faced the others defiantly. "Major Anderson has surrendered Fort Sumter to General Beauregard. The South has won a glorious victory."

There was a moment of stunned silence before Uncle Benton spoke dryly. "Considering that reenforcements never came to Anderson's aid, and that the men in the fort were out of food and supplies, I'm not sure how great a victory it was. But at least we understand that no one was killed in the fighting on either side."

Mrs. Garrett turned away from the fire, once more in control of her emotions, though Abbie could see the tight line of her lips.

She touched her daughter's arm gently. "Abbie dear, Lorena will want to be shown to her room, I'm sure. Roger, you'll take care of Benton? Douglas, Stuart, do you suppose you could help us upstairs with our bags?"

The boys moved willingly to do her mother's bidding and Abbie found herself leading Lorena up the stairs, with

Douglas and Stuart following loaded with wraps and bags. Abbie ran ahead down the hall, opened the door of Lorena's room and lit a gas jet, while the boys set her things down outside the door. Lorena picked up her mantle and whisked her bags quickly inside the room—then barred the doorway with her own bright person. Her chin tilted triumphantly and her gaze sped from one to another of the three who stood watching her helplessly.

"This is only the first time we've licked you," she said. "We'll do it again—and as many times more as necessary!" And with that she whirled into the room, leaving the others to stare after her.

"Well, for goodness' sake!" Abbie cried in astonishment.

Doug chuckled delightedly. "Typical Southern spitfire," he said. "You're going to have a war on your hands right in this house, Abbie."

Stuart started downstairs without comment and Doug followed him. Abbie let them go, hesitating outside Lorena's door. Then she tapped resolutely on the panel.

"Who is it? What do you want?" Lorena called.

Abbie went into the room, forcing a smile to her lips. There were rules of hospitality, after all, whether Lorena meant to behave like a guest or not. Besides, she did want to be friends with this new cousin.

"I've been looking forward so much to your coming," she told the other girl gently. "It was fun to fix this room up for you. I hope you'll like it. If there's anything you want . . ."

Lorena broke in upon her faltering words. "It's so cold, so dreadfully cold." She shivered and rubbed her hands together, looking less arresting now, and more like an uncertain little girl a long way from home.

"Of course you're cold, after your warm Southern climate. I suppose things are already green and blooming down in Charleston. Look—" Abbie pulled open a drawer and took out something soft and blue—"this was a shawl that belonged to Grandmother Emory. I thought you might find it warm and—a little bit like home, since she was your grandmother as well as mine."

She put the shawl gently around Lorena's shoulders and was surprised to see the shine of tears in her cousin's eyes.

"Thank you, Cousin Abbie," Lorena said. "I—I think I'll go right to bed. That's one place that's sure to be warm. I want to be up early in the morning."

"Why don't you sleep late tomorrow?" Abbie suggested. "I know how tired you must be."

Lorena blinked back her tears. The momentary softness had vanished. "I must be up early before Papa leaves. I've got to make him take me back home with him when he goes. I don't want to stay here with all you Yankees."

Abbie stared at her in astonishment.

"After all," Lorena went on, "every one of you up here is my country's enemy. Why should I want to stay among you?"

Abruptly Abbie recovered the power of speech. "There isn't any 'my' country, or 'your' country. There's only *our* country." She gave Lorena no opportunity for reply but went out of the room, pulling the door firmly to behind her.

She seethed with annoyance all the way downstairs. What Lorena needed was a good spanking and it was too bad she was too big a girl for Uncle Benton to wallop.

Stuart and Douglas were at the front door, about to leave. Apparently the reading evening was to be postponed. Mrs. Garrett was there, bidding them good night and Douglas smiled at Abbie over her mother's head.

"Don't you let your Cousin Lorena upset you. Lots of girls I knew in Atlanta behaved just like that about the North. It's sort of catching, I reckon. But she'll cool off up here. Southern girls are really pretty nice when you get to know them."

At the moment Abbie wasn't so sure, but she was grateful for Doug's cheerful encouragement.

"Douglas ought to know," Stuart said. "Personally, I think he likes most any kind of girl."

Abbie felt a quick flash of displeasure which surprised her.

"But none as well as Abbie," Doug said quickly. "Don't you let your daughter pay any heed to Stu, Mrs. Garrett ma'am."

"I won't," Mrs. Garrett promised, but she looked as if she could not rise to this by-play much longer. So Abbie hurried her good nights to the boys and closed the door after them. The moment they were gone she slipped an arm about her mother's waist, marveling once more at how she had grown so much taller than this little woman who had once held her on her lap.

"Lorena was horrid, Mama," Abbie said. "She hasn't any manners at all."

Mrs. Garrett shook her head in reproach. "Try to understand her, Abbie. This isn't a time when people remember their manners. If manners were all we were going to lose—" She drew Abbie down the hall to Mr. Garrett's study at the rear of the house. "Uncle Benton and your papa are in here. Perhaps we'd better join them for a little while."

"Just so *you're* back!" Abbie whispered as they went through the door together.

The two men rose as they entered. Mr. Garrett drew up a chair for his wife and Abbie watched the grave look he turned upon her. Uncle Benton was equally solemn and she knew they must have been talking about Fort Sumter and what its loss meant to the North.

"There will undoubtedly be a proclamation from President Lincoln at any moment," Mr. Garrett said. "I hope he will turn back in time from the course of war."

"He can turn back only if he lets the seceding states go," Uncle Benton said.

Abbie, watching her uncle, saw that his eyes were as bright as Lorena's and his thinning hair nearly as fair. But there the resemblance ended. He had deep grooves running down his cheeks about his mouth and he did not look like a man who would smile a great deal. Yet there was both a gentleness and a strength about him, so that she felt an immediate affection for Uncle Benton, while she had felt none at all for Lorena.

"That's what I'm afraid he won't do," her father said. "He'll never let the Southern states go. He stated quite plainly in his inaugural address last month that he would not recognize the power of any party to break the contract of the Union."

Uncle Benton nodded. "A fine speech. I read it. Until last year I've hoped that somehow the Union would hold together. But there's no hope left now. The only way war can be averted is to let the South break away and become a nation by itself. I don't want that, but with the temper of the South what it is, it's the only way to peace."

Abbie stole a glance at her mother. Mrs. Garrett sat straight in her chair, her flowered amber silk making a graceful circle about her. There was a pallor in her cheeks and her lips were faintly gray. Mr. Garrett watched her covertly, too, and when he spoke Abbie felt that his words were directed at his wife.

"I have always hated war," he said gravely. "I would do anything in my power to avoid it. But if we fight, then I must stand with the Union. However, I ask no one else to stand with me. I respect the right of every individual to make his own choice."

Abbie spoke quickly, without thought. "I'm for the North, of course, Papa."

"Not the North," her father said. "The Union. The whole United States, binding North and South together in a strong, free country."

She repeated the words after him softly and a tingle went up her spine. "The whole United States."

Her father glanced at his wife again, then turned to Uncle Benton. Lorena's father roused himself in his chair and stood up.

"It's been a wearing day. And I must make an early start tomorrow. I believe I'll go to my room. Good night, Rosa, Roger."

Mr. Garrett rose and took the other man's hand in a warm clasp. "I know you've thrown your weight against secession from the first, Benton. But what will you do now?"

Uncle Benton sighed deeply. "I don't know. I suppose I must stand by my own. It depends on what step President Lincoln takes. At least it is a relief to leave Lorena here with you. She may not be easy to handle at first, but she's a sunny child by nature. She will adapt herself to the idea of staying indefinitely, instead of for the few months we'd planned. And I'll be free to do whatever I have to do without concern about her. Her two young brothers are still in school, but a growing girl is a more difficult problem."

He told them all good night again and went out of the room. Abbie suspected that he had left them on purpose so that Mrs. Garrett might be alone with her family. When Uncle Benton had gone, Mr. Garrett touched his wife's shoulder tenderly.

"You're weary tonight, my dear. We've needed you here for so many matters which only you know how to handle. Tomorrow, when you're rested, we can set some of these to rights. But let's leave political matters for another time."

His wife looked up at him, her eyes darker than ever in her white face. She spoke like someone in a dream. "You don't know what it was like in Charleston, with everyone screaming against the North. People I've known all my life changed overnight. There are only a handful of men like Benton. They're overpowered by the others. They—they hate us down there. They want war."

There was one word that mattered more than the others, Abbie thought, relief rushing through her in such a wave that she realized for the first time what she had been dreading. Her mother had said "us." She was throwing her lot with the Union—no matter what. No—she was throwing it with her family.

Roger Garrett slipped an arm about her. "It will be hard for you, my dear. We know that. But we'll understand, Abbie and I."

Abbie nodded, her throat choked. She turned away, to

allow them this close moment together, when her mother needed comforting arms about her. On her father's desk was spread a copy of the *Tribune* and Abbie realized that it must be one Uncle Benton had bought in New York. She picked it up and carried it into the hall beneath the light in order to leave them alone. Since news never appeared on the first page, she opened it to the inner section. One column caught her eye. Its heading was not large, but it was arresting.

WAR BEGUN!

The Jeff Davis rebellion, claiming to be the Confederate Government of the Seven States which profess to have seceded from the Federal Union, commenced formal war upon the United States by opening fire on Fort Sumter at 4 o'clock yesterday morning.

Somehow, the words in cold print made what had happened seem real for the first time. The South had broken away from the North and a war for separation had commenced. Upstairs in the front bedroom their own household sheltered one thorough-going little Rebel who would never be content to cast her lot with that of her Northern enemies. It might be better, after all, Abbie thought, if Lorena Emory went home with her father tomorrow.

5

Rebel in the House

Usually the Garretts slept late on Sunday morning, rising leisurely to eat a hearty breakfast of Mrs. Coomb's pancakes and brown sausages. Shortly before eleven Jamie, the coachman, would harness the two bays to the family rockaway and drive them to church.

This morning, however, the usual program was interrupted. Uncle Benton had to catch an early ferry as the start of his trip south. The unrest and uncertainty of the political situation made him all the more anxious to return home as soon as possible. Abbie had hoped that Lorena would be so weary she would sleep through her father's departure. That would have been a more comfortable solution for them all. But Lorena was up as soon as the first one stirred and she was dressed and downstairs before the others.

She and her father had some time together in Mr. Garrett's study and it was evident when they came out that Uncle Benton had taken a firm stand with his daughter. Lorena went upstairs, her eyes red with weeping, and the rest of the family sat down in the dining room for breakfast.

The weather had cleared and morning sunshine poured through the French doors, making the big room bright and cheerful. But despite the cheer lent by the room itself, the group around the oval table was not a happy one.

Once during the meal Uncle Benton made a direct appeal to Abbie. "You can help Lorena more than anyone else," he said. "Don't let her anger you, or prick you into quarreling with her. I'm afraid she will try hard enough. She has grown up with notions about Southern chivalry and courage, and she has our unfortunate conviction that Southerners are the superiors of any other people on earth. That's one reason I want her to have a change of scene. If every Southerner could come North to live for a while, and every Northerner could go South, perhaps we'd get over the idea that we're two different species and that somehow the other fellow is to be looked down upon."

"Goodness!" Abbie cried. "I live in the North and I don't look down on other people in the country."

"That's because you're your father's daughter," Uncle Benton said. "I'm afraid I haven't succeeded as well with Lorena. Abbie, will you try to help her? She has been out of my hands so much since her mother's death. Other influences than mine have set her pattern of thought. It is a pattern I hope to see change. You don't know how badly she needs your help. She doesn't know herself how much she needs it."

Abbie poured more syrup than was necessary on her second helping of pancakes in order to delay her reply. How could she make such a promise? How could she make friends with Lorena, try to help her, when Lorena so obviously did not want her help or friendship?

In the face of her troubled silence, Uncle Benton turned to his sister for aid. But Rosa was in some faraway place of her own. She made assent with her lips, spoke the necessary words, but it was clear somehow that the thought was not reaching her, not getting past the turmoil that recent events had bred in her. Last night she had sided staunchly with her husband, but some inner misgiving and uncertainty must have risen in her since then.

"All right, Uncle Benton," Abbie said at last. "I'll try. I don't think she wants to be friends, but I'll try. I'll have Hannah help me, and the McIntyre boys. Maybe we can make her see how useless it is to go on hating us."

But later when Lorena came downstairs to bid her father good-bye, her eyes stormy, every look breathing defiance, Abbie wondered how she could ever be won. Perhaps she couldn't be, any more than the South could be won. Maybe she could only be conquered as perhaps the South must be conquered. Well, she—Abbie Garrett—was not the one to do that, she decided grimly. Since she had given Uncle Benton her promise, she would try every friendly means possible to approach the girl, but beyond that . . .

Papa himself was driving Uncle Benton to the landing in the buggy, so the rockaway would be left clean for church. Farewells were said at the door and for a moment Abbie thought that Lorena might break down completely and cling weeping to her father like a little girl. But Mr. Garrett stepped in to put a firm arm about her shoulders. Lorena, her lips quivering, looked up startled to meet Papa's steady gaze. Something in his eyes must have made her a little ashamed of herself, for she steadied and released her father from her clinging grip, watched him go down the steps without further objection.

"That's the girl," Papa approved, patting her shoulder. "We'll work things out, Lorena. It won't be as bad as you think living with us. Abbie has always wanted a sister."

Wordlessly, Lorena let them go and watched from the veranda as the buggy went swaying out of sight down the rutted street.

Mrs. Garrett spoke impartially to both girls. "You'd better get dressed for church, so we'll be ready when Papa gets back from the landing."

Church was a special time that Abbie looked forward to every week. At present the community had no regular minister and George William Curtis had given his time

every Sunday morning to reading great sermons that had
been preached in other churches.

After Mr. Garrett returned from the ferry, it appeared that
there might be difficulty about getting Lorena to go to
church with them. But again Papa quietly expressed the
wish that she attend, and after a moment's resistance Lorena
surrendered and agreed indifferently to accompany them.

The four-wheeled rockaway was roomy, so the four of
them were comfortable enough, in spite of billowing hoops.
It was a good thing hoops bent in a reasonably pliable
fashion, Abbie thought, as the three ladies fitted themselves
into the back seat, while Papa took the front one facing
them. Jamie made a make-believe flick with his whip over
the back of the bays, and they got off to a good trot.

When they reached the church, Abbie looked around at
once for the McIntyres. Mr. and Mrs. McIntyre were not in
sight, but she saw the boys at once and smiled a greeting.
Doug cocked an amused eye at Lorena and then looked
questioningly at Abbie. Abbie gave the faintest shake of her
head, while Lorena looked through him as if he had not
been there. Oddly enough, it was Stuart who fell into step
beside Lorena as they went up the walk. He gave her no
more than a quiet good morning and seemed to expect no
response, but he walked beside her right into the church.
Stuart was certainly unpredictable, Abbie thought. He could
be bitter and cutting one moment, and then the next he
would turn around and be more thoughtful than anyone else.

With Lorena off her hands for the moment, Abbie kept
closely to her mother's side. Everyone was coming up to
welcome Mrs. Garrett home from her journey, to ask
questions about the feeling down in Charleston. Had she
been there when the fort was fired upon? Was the South
really anxious for war? What was the matter with those silly
states anyway? Didn't they know they couldn't last a month
fighting a big power like the North? Mrs. Garrett answered
when she had to, but with no more than an I-don't-know,
and then she seemed to retreat within herself. There were
some, Abbie knew, who remembered that her mother was

herself a Southerner and cast questioning looks in her direction. Abbie held her arm all the more tightly and was relieved when they were inside the little church.

George Curtis was a tall, handsome man in his early thirties. There was always a kindliness about him, but there was force too. That morning he read a selection from a sermon—something of Henry Ward Beecher's. Then, after they had sung a hymn of the organist's choosing, he talked to them with quiet seriousness, as one neighbor might talk to another. He spoke of the Union and the danger of letting it disintegrate. He pointed out that when individual groups began to go their own way and refused to see the good of a whole people, then progress was no longer possible.

"In whatever country and whatever case a man may chance to be born, he is born a citizen of the world, and bound by the universal right or law of God. History shows us that the association of men in various relations is made subservient to the gradual advance and advantage of the whole human race, and that all nations work together toward one great result."

The little group in the church listened quietly and with respect, but through the entire period, Abbie was uneasily aware of Lorena beside her, tense and angry. Abbie could feel her cousin's resentment at the words being spoken as if it were a tangible thing. Lorena held the hymnal, but she did not sing. She bowed her head in prayer, but Abbie suspected that she prayed stormily for the Southland she loved and for the thorough defeat of the North. How confusing, Abbie thought, for each side to claim that God was with its cause and against the other.

Fortunately, Lorena did not explode until they were outside again in the bright sunlight of noon. Then, as luck would have it, it was Douglas McIntyre who received the full impact of her wrath. Doug did no more than ask her cheerfully what she thought of Staten Island, now that she had seen it in daylight.

Lorena turned on him with such indignation that Abbie

was thankful they had reached the rockaway and were thus in a group by themselves.

"I hate Staten Island as much as I hate all the rest of the North!" Lorena stormed. "Why don't you let the Southern states go, you Yankees? You have no more use for us than we have for you. All you've done is yelp about how awful we are with our slaves and our cotton money and all the rest. So why should you fight to hold us?"

Doug showed no resentment at the attack. "I don't know why we should," he said frankly. "Honestly, I don't know."

Abbie glanced at him in surprise, but before she could speak, Stuart turned to Lorena.

"Where does all this stop, if we let them go? Suppose Staten Island should secede from the state of New York, or Charleston from South Carolina? Or suppose Georgia wants to leave your Confederacy and then Atlanta wants to leave Georgia? Where do we draw the line? How much or how little can we hold together?"

"That's just silly!" Lorena cried.

Stuart grinned. "It certainly is silly to go back to feudal days. That's the trouble with Europe right now. Do you want us to be like her—dozens of little battling nations?"

Mrs. Garrett heard the heated exchange and stepped quietly between the two, propelling Lorena toward the carriage.

"Good morning, Stuart," she said. "Good morning, Douglas. How is your father? We missed him in church this morning."

And so, while Douglas explained that his father was not feeling well and was being kept home by Mrs. McIntyre, Mr. Garrett helped Lorena up the carriage step and the explosive moment was safely past.

Lorena entered the conversation only once on the drive home. That was when the Garrett carriage passed a Negro woman following the plank walk beside the Shore Road.

"Look," she cried in surprise, "that's the first Negro I've seen since I've come North. I suppose she's an escaped slave?"

"She certainly isn't!" Abbie, still exasperated with her cousin, was emphatic. "Her parents were freed and brought her North when she was a young girl. Her name is Mrs. Hill and she has a very nice confectioner's shop over on Broadway in Factoryville. Everyone likes her and admires the good job she's done in raising her little boy since her husband's death."

Mrs. Garrett put a quieting hand on Abbie's arm. "Lorena doesn't understand about the North. We have quite a few fine Negro people up here, Lorena."

"Northern Negroes are no good," Lorena said. "They're cocky and impudent."

"Do you know any?" Mr. Garrett asked.

Lorena tossed her head. "I've heard enough about them."

"One of these days," Abbie promised, "I'll introduce you to Mrs. Hill and you'll see what nice manners she has and how pleasant she is."

"No thank you," Lorena said curtly and the others let the matter drop.

When they reached home, Lorena returned to her room and could not be coaxed out for one o'clock Sunday dinner. Mrs. Garrett carried a tray upstairs after dinner and the girl must have been hungry enough, for when Abbie tiptoed to her door later in the day, she found the tray there on the floor outside it, with every morsel eaten. At least Lorena wasn't going to pine away.

6

Through the Woods

On Monday, as had been predicted, came the President's proclamation and a call for 75,000 volunteers to serve three months. Boys shouted "Extry!" on the streets and there was no escaping the inevitable now. The war between the states had commenced.

Mrs. Phillips came bustling over Tuesday morning with Hannah in her wake, and Mrs. Garrett sat down with her gravely in the parlor.

Mama looked sweet today in her crisp lavender. A gold locket hung about her neck on a black velvet ribbon and her house cap was crocheted lace trimmed with tiny lavender velvet bows. Mrs. Phillips wore her everlasting black bombazine and upon her bosom the brooch containing a lock of her husband's hair, without which she was never seen. She had never gone out of mourning for Mr. Phillips, though he had died so many years before. Once Hannah had remarked frankly that her aunt liked to suffer, so why take her pleasure away by coaxing her into brighter hues? Nevertheless, it was Mrs. Phillips who now seemed alive and excited, while Rosa still wore her cloak of pale remoteness.

Last night Abbie had spoken to her father about the change in Mama, but he only advised waiting.

"She'll come out of it," he said. "Abbie dear, having to cast your loyalties with the North when you're a Southern woman can't be easy for anyone who feels about these things as deeply as your mother does."

Mrs. Phillips broke at once into news about her excursion benefit for the New Brighton Free Library.

"I suppose Abbie has told you all about it, Rosa, but there has been a change in plans."

Mrs. Garrett glanced questioningly at her daughter and Abbie shook her head.

"I'm afraid all the things that have happened made me forget," Abbie explained in apology.

Mrs. Phillips looked her reproach. Jowls were beginning to sag at each side of her mouth and they gave her expression an added lugubrious droop. She waved her hands in her usual nervous way and rushed on.

"Because of all this ridiculous war scare, we've moved the date of the excursion up. We're going to hold it a week from next Saturday. Otherwise I'm afraid too many of our young men will be off somewhere in camp."

"Ridiculous war scare?" asked Mrs. Garrett softly.

"Of course it's ridiculous. My sympathies are with the underdog, of course. I guess I'm just made that way. I'm so sorry for the poor little foolish South. Of course we'll whip her overnight and the whole thing will be over."

For the first time in days Abbie saw a faint pinkness creep into her mother's cheeks. "You really think it will be as easy as that?"

Mrs. Phillips squirmed uneasily in her chair and her hoops creaked as she moved. "Rosa, my dear! I'd forgotten for a moment that you are a Southern woman yourself. You know how devoted I am to my dear Southern friends. It's just that it is foolish for the South to resist a great nation like ourselves. Of course I wish it hadn't happened, and I wish someone could talk some sense into the silly boys who are rushing out enlisting right here in New York. Really, I have no use at all for that Abraham Lincoln. As Mr. McIntyre says, he is an ignorant country bumpkin without any manners at all. Not in the least a gentleman."

Mrs. Garrett edged forward in her chair, her small hands clasped tightly in her lap. When she spoke the remote quality was gone from her voice.

"I will not have you speaking so of Mr. Lincoln in my house, Varina Phillips," she said spiritedly. "As you know, I love every inch of ground in the state of South Carolina and I love my kin down there. But I think they're wrong in trying to break up the Union and I think Mr. Lincoln is doing what is right for the whole country."

Mrs. Phillips gasped and dabbed at her cheeks with a black-edged handkerchief. "Why, now, Rosa . . ." she began, but Mrs. Garrett went right on.

"If you think the South is going to be licked overnight, you're just plumb crazy, Varina. But don't you come here talking against the South *or* the North. Or against Mr. Lincoln, or Mr. Jeff Davis, or—or anybody!"

Hannah's wide blue eyes were almost popping at this outburst from Abbie's usually gentle mother, but Abbie knew that her mother was close to tears and she was glad of it. Tears, if they came, would provide release for the misery she had been carrying around inside her.

Mrs. Phillips rose in hurt astonishment, her black hoops circling her in massive dignity.

"I must say, Rosa," she complained, "I didn't come here to be insulted by someone I had thought my dear friend."

Mrs. Garrett was unyielding. "If you don't want to feel insulted, then you must learn not to say such things, Varina. You know I'll help with your benefit anyway I can. But in this house we are proud of Mr. Lincoln."

Abbie was proud of her mother as Mrs. Garrett showed Mrs. Phillips grandly to the door. Hannah was less pleased.

"Oh, jiminy!" she wailed, pulling Abbie back into the room. "Now I'll have to go home with Aunt V. and we'll never get to talk. Abbie, have you heard how many of our boys are enlisting?''

Abbie shook her head, hating to think about that. It was right, of course, but once more uneasiness filled her. The MyIntyre boys were young, but Doug was eighteen, and at eighteen one might well become a soldier. It was all right to think of other men going, but when it came to Douglas . . . of course he must be patriotic, and yet . . .

"Hannah, are you coming?'' Mrs. Phillips called from the door. Hannah gave her friend's arm a squeeze and followed her aunt reluctantly out of the house.

When they had gone, Mrs. Garrett turned to face her daughter in the dim light that filtered through the glass fanlight over the door.

"Abbie, I was terrible, wasn't I? But I declare, I don't know when anyone has made me so mad.''

"You were wonderful, Mama,'' Abbie whispered. "You told her just the things she needed to be told. I'll bet even Hannah is glad. And you know Aunt V.! She'll be spitting mad for a couple of days then she'll come back as if nothing had happened. But next time she'll say lovely things about Mr. Lincoln.''

Mrs. Garrett straightened her shoulders and patted her little lace cap into place. She had come to life again and the household need no longer feel it had lost its mistress. To Abbie that meant a serious problem could be tackled without further delay.

"Mama,'' Abbie said, "we've got to do something about Lorena. She mopes in her room all the time and she won't answer me if I talk to her through the door. She's got it locked and she only opens it when someone leaves a tray outside.''

Mrs. Garrett made up her mind instantly. She picked up her lavender skirts with a single gesture and ran lightly up the stairs. At the curve she looked back at Abbie, one hand on the banister.

"Put on your walking boots, honey, and get rid of that hoop. It's a lovely day outside. A little cool, but bright and sunny. A walk in the woods is just what Lorena needs. I'll go tell her so."

There was no choice but to obey and Abbie went up to her room to change. She hadn't expected to have the problem of Lorena thrown so quickly back into her own lap. A walk in the woods with someone who disliked you and didn't want to go walking anywhere was not a pleasant prospect. However, she had no wish to argue with her mother, now that this resolute mood was upon her. She wondered, though, how she would ever get Lorena to set foot out of her room, though, let alone out of the house.

Surprisingly enough, and in practically no time at all, Lorena joined Abbie on the veranda where she waited for her cousin. Mrs. Garrett came firmly along behind her, prodding her gently and uttering little chirps of encouragement. Abbie smiled, watching her mother. People thought at first glance that Rosa Garrett was a helpless little thing who probably couldn't do anything more decisive than select a menu for the day. But when it was least expected, she would up and wind people around her pretty fingers, managing the strong-willed as easily as she wound a skein of wool.

"Don't wear her out, Abbie," she instructed as the girls went down the steps, "but make her stretch her legs. Show her some of the pretty places up in our woods."

Lorena offered no resistance, but she offered no help either. She plodded along behind Abbie on the narrow path, refusing to do more than set one buttoned boot after another."

Abbie, remembering her promise to Uncle Benton and seeking for some way to get Lorena to talk, tried to use those boots to start conversation.

"They're the latest thing, aren't they? I've never had a pair that buttoned. Are they trouble to put on?"

Lorena shrugged and made no answer. Plainly she was not going to be tricked into friendly conversation over a new pair of boots.

Abbie, however, had her dander up and was more

determined than ever to make Lorena talk, even if she had
to make her mad to do it. Next she tried the subject of the
coming excursion.

"It will be loads of fun," she said, holding back a branch
lest it slap Lorena across the face. "We'll pack tremendous
lunches, and there'll be two firehouse bands and dancing.
All the young people will turn out."

She glanced back and, fancying she saw a gleam of
interest in Lorena's eye, pursued the subject further.

"Our island's beautiful to see from the water. My best
friend Hannah Phillips is coming, since her aunt is sort of
running the whole thing. And of course the McIntyre boys
will be there. In fact—" she hesitated for just a moment and
then went quickly on—"Douglas McIntyre has asked me to
go with him. But that won't mean you'll be alone."

For the first time Lorena spoke. True, her tone was sharp,
but at least it was better than maddening silence.

"That Douglas McIntyre! He's a perfectly horrid person."

Abbie looked her surprise. "For goodness' sake! Doug's
sweet. He only meant to be friendly to you Sunday."

"I don't like him." Lorena tossed her blond head so
vigorously that the heavy chignon bounced on her neck.
"Stuart is much nicer any time. For a Yankee."

"Stuart?" Abbie echoed. "He's the one *I* think is horrid.
I was sorry about the way he spoke to you Sunday
morning."

"I reckon I deserved it," said Lorena surprisingly. "But
don't misunderstand me, Cousin Abbie. I couldn't really
like any Yankee boys. So I don't think I'll trouble to go on
your excursion. It doesn't sound like nearly as much fun as
parties we have down in Charleston."

Abbie turned away to conceal her annoyance. They had
climbed just above the secret cave by now and near the path
a big slab of rock jutted out of the hillside. Abbie climbed
up to seat herself on its edge, letting her legs swing into
space. After a moment's hesitation, Lorena came to sit
beside her, though she was not so unladylike as to swing her

own legs. She curled up neatly, kitten-fashion, on the rock and stared at nothing.

"You won't have much fun," Abbie told her, "if you mope in your room all the time and pass up a chance of meeting our crowd."

"Your crowd!" Lorena was derisive. "What will your crowd care about me—a Southern girl? What do they know about me, or know about my kind of people? And what do I care about them?" Her words ended on a quaver.

"Mama's your own kin," said Abbie calmly, "and goodness knows she was born and bred in the South."

"I don't mean Aunt Rosa. She'd be all right, except that she's a traitor to the South."

Anger quivered to the very tips of Abbie's fingers at this insult to her mother. She had an alarming urge to take Lorena by her slight shoulders and give her a good hard shaking. But she forced herself to relax and speak quietly, to ignore the word Lorena had used. Just as Uncle Benton had warned, Lorena wanted to make her mad, and she would be the stronger of the two if she resisted the impulse to lose her temper.

"There are others who know the South too," she said. "The McIntyres, for instance. After all, they've been living down in Georgia for years. I guess they liked it pretty well too, except maybe for Mr. McIntyre who has a temper that's too hot for comfort."

Lorena gave her a quick, sidelong glance and then began plucking silently at a bit of grass beside the rock.

Perhaps, Abbie thought, a different approach might be more successful with Lorena—a reversal of present tactics. There was a contrary streak in her cousin and one might be able to win her by heading off in the opposite direction from one's goal.

"After all," Abbie went on guilelessly, "you're probably smart not to go on this trip. You're a Southern girl and there will undoubtedly be boys in uniform. They might not approve of our taking a rebel along on the party. Maybe you're right and you'd be better off at home. Safer."

Lorena didn't say anything right away, but Abbie could almost see her rearranging her notions, rising without suspicion to the bait. She looked as sly as a kitten who has suddenly discovered a mouse hole. Abbie suspected that her cousin might enjoy being a rebel right in the heart of the North. At least this was one way of getting her out to meet the crowd. And of course everyone would be nice to her and she'd find it wasn't so bad to be living up here after all.

When the two girls walked back to the house, the atmosphere was somewhat less strained between them. Even though Lorena had not yet announced that she would go on the trip, Abbie felt there was a good possibility that she would. And when she stopped moping and hiding in her room a more friendly relationship would be possible.

7

A Strand of Moss

In the time that intervened before the boat trip, the island began to change under their very eyes. Uniforms appeared overnight, and a motley lot they were. Everything was seen, from the bright uniforms of the Zouaves, with their baggy breeches and brilliant colors, to outfits that were obviously filling in until such time as proper garments could be issued.

The current of excitement that tingled in the air was almost pleasurable. Each new day became one of anticipation because so many new things were happening, could happen. Monotony was gone, routine shattered, the old quiet days replaced by events more vivid and stirring. Mr. Garrett found it regrettable that this awakening, this uniting for a common cause, had to come because of war. If only people could unite as enthusiastically in quiet times for the keeping of peace. Peace, however, was less dramatic and inspiring than the danger and excitement of war.

So far neither McIntyre boy had gone off to enlist; but, as Mrs. McIntyre confided to Abbie's mother, she was terribly afraid they might and was doing everything in her power to hold them back. If only Mr. Mac wouldn't be so fierce about the whole thing, she complained. He actually wanted the boys to go to war.

Sunday afternoon the week before the excursion was a warm, lazy one. Stuart McIntyre came over with a sheaf of manuscript under his arm and informed Abbie, who met him at the door, that he wanted to see Mr. Garrett, if her father could spare him a little time. Abbie ushered him coolly into her father's study and left him there, since Stuart made it plain that this was a matter between himself and her father.

Lorena had discovered the piano in the parlor and revealed that she played rather well. Often these days the soft sound of music drifted from the Garrett house and everyone agreed that it was a good idea for Lorena to find whatever comfort music could bring her. If only, Abbie wished, she wouldn't play such melancholy tunes. She was there today, her fingers moving over the keys as she played a sad song about a lady who had died for love.

Abbie went looking for her mother and found her lying down upstairs.

"Mama," she pleaded, "it's warm enough outside to sit in the summerhouse. Won't you come out? We haven't had a real visit since you got home."

Mrs. Garrett smiled and pushed herself to a sitting position. "A lovely idea. I haven't had a chance to tell you about my trip South, or show you something I brought home with me."

She got up and opened a dresser drawer. Out of it she took a folded roll of tissue paper. Abbie picked up some cushions and they went downstairs and out the back door to seek their favorite lazing place in the old, vine-covered summerhouse in the back yard. As far back as Abbie could remember, she and her mother had spent summer hours in this particular spot. Sometimes Mrs. Garrett sewed and Abbie read aloud. Sometimes her mother talked about the times when she was a little girl down South, or Abbie confided in her about school or childish troubles. There had always been a secure feeling of sympathy and understanding between them.

Today Mrs. Garrett unrolled the tissue in her lap to reveal a long strand of something dry and brittle and gray-green in color.

"Do you know what it is?" she asked Abbie, holding it up for her daughter to see.

Abbie touched the dry strand curiously. "It's moss. Real Spanish moss from the South. Mama, did you go out to Cypress?"

Cypress was Grandfather Emory's old plantation, where her mother had lived as a child and a young girl. Abbie had heard so many stories about it that it almost seemed that she had been there herself. She held the crumbling moss in her hands and felt that it was something out of her past as well as her mother's.

Mrs. Garrett's smile was wistful. "Benton drove me out there. The present owners are very nice, though the place isn't kept up the way it was in my parents' day. The driveway is disgracefully overgrown, and paint is peeling everywhere. Papa kept the fluted columns around the front porch snowy white always. They're dingy and gray now."

"Did you hate it when you had to come North to live as a young girl?" Abbie said.

"I didn't hate it because I was coming to marry your father. But, Abbie, I think my roots have never been quite pulled up from Southern soil."

Abbie patted her mother's knee. "It must have hurt when Uncle Benton sold Cypress. Did he really have to?"

"Benton never liked plantation life. And of course without our Negro people it could never be kept up."

"How did you feel about that, Mama?" Abbie asked. "Freeing the slaves, I mean."

"It was right, of course. I believe Papa felt that way too, though he just couldn't bring himself to change his way of life and do it in his time. Of course the colored people were an expense and a burden. Northerners seem to think that plantation owners just sit around being waited on. But we had to care for all those people. We took care of their children and their children's children. There could be practically a town out there in the quarters and we were responsible for every soul in it; for clothing and feeding them, and caring for them when they were sick. Most plantation owners didn't want to break up families by selling their people, but sometimes they had to or go bankrupt. That's why the very economy of slavery is weak, quite aside from the moral weakness."

"I suppose there were always cruel owners," Abbie said, "or indifferent ones who mistreated their people."

"Some of them did. I saw a slave market once when I was a little girl and it was a heartbreaking sight. Mama was terribly upset about our going, but Papa took Benton and me to see it, so that we'd know that side of slavery and remember it all our lives. No, we didn't want to go on owning slaves, any of us."

She fell silent; and Abbie, plucking idly at the moss in her hands, felt it disintegrate between her fingers. A soft spring breeze ruffled her short hair and brought the sound of the piano from the house. Lorena was playing "Dixie." Abbie straightened indignantly. That was the song of the enemy. But when she would have risen to go inside and stop her cousin, her mother put out a hand.

"Let her be," she said. "It doesn't matter."

The pleasant spell of the afternoon had been broken for them both. The war had intruded. Suddenly her mother covered her face with her hands and Abbie saw with a sense of shock that her shoulders were moving convulsively. She could not remember a time when she had seen her mother cry and the sight was disturbing.

Abbie dropped to her knees and put her arms about her to hold her tight. "Mama, you mustn't. Oh, you mustn't!"

Mrs. Garrett fumbled for a handkerchief from her pocket. "I can't bear it when I think of this terrible war. What will happen to Cypress and all those other beautiful old places? Part of me belongs down there, Abbie honey. I have a feeling that so much of what I've known and loved is like—

like that strip of moss. Touch it and it crumbles. But when it crumbles, a little of my heart crumbles too."

Abbie could only tighten her arms about her mother's slight shoulders. After a little while the tears stopped flowing and Mrs. Garrett straightened herself resolutely.

"Don't tell your papa what a baby I've been," she said. "It would only hurt him. Honey, I'm so glad he hates war the way he does. I'm so glad he'd never go off to fight. I think I couldn't bear it if he ever took up arms against my people."

"You needn't worry," Abbie reassured her. "We both know how he feels about that."

"Indeed we do." Mrs. Garrett nodded. "Now run along, Abbie, and let me pull myself together before I go back to the house."

Not knowing how to comfort her mother, Abbie obeyed. As she crossed the garden she glanced back and saw that her mother had bent to pick up the strand of moss from the summerhouse floor. Abbie looked away quickly while pain for her mother stabbed through her again.

As she reached the side veranda she saw her father standing at the study door looking after the departing figure of Stuart McIntyre.

"You haven't read his piece already, have you?" Abbie asked.

Mr. Garrett shook his head. "Not yet. He left it with me. But we had a bit of a talk. That's a young man with exceptional possibilities, Abbie. I knew it even when he was a small boy. Sometimes I think I should have been a teacher. I like to work with young people."

"You are a teacher," Abbie told him, glad to turn away from the subject of war. "You've taught all of us. Even Jamie. Yesterday I heard him quoting you to the mares."

Her father smiled. "I hope they approved of my words."

8

Excursion

Mr. and Mrs. McIntyre had decided to go on the trip, though Abbie's father and mother were staying home, having no heart for parties at this particular time. The excitement in the air had not hypnotized them as it had so many others.

On the morning of the excursion the elder McIntyres went straight to the boat in their own carriage, while Doug and Stuart walked across the meadow to the Garretts' to join the girls. Lorena, of course, had decided to go. And Hannah came over early to be part of the group.

When the Garrett carriage reached the landing where the flag-bedecked excursion boat awaited them, the young people hurried eagerly aboard. The boys of the Excelsior Bucket Company band were already tooting away noisily in the stern of the boat, welcoming the excursionists, while the Zephyr Hose Company waited its turn in the bow.

Already the war talk had begun. Abbie heard Mr. McIntyre giving forth to anyone who would listen: "Fellow told me there's been trouble down in Baltimore. Fighting in the streets. If only the attack on Washington doesn't come before we're ready to repulse it.''

She hurried past him down the deck, not wanting to think about the war today, and found Douglas beside her. Following the example of other couples they circled the deck, pacing like ocean-goers.

The Kill was filled with a variety of craft, ranging from tiny sailboats to big clipper ships. Near at hand the nine o'clock ferry for New York steamed past them with a burst of speed. Their own boat was soon churning along toward the open harbor and Abbie found it exhilarating to walk beside Doug with the sea breeze in her face, talking about anything or nothing.

The lunch hour seemed to come in no time at all, and everyone was starved, what with the exercise and the sea air. Abbie had packed a special basket for Douglas and herself and had let Lorena take a separate lunch. Thus she and Doug were able to sit together while they ate, even though they were part of a group.

Abbie felt lighthearted and gay, and her day would have been perfect except for an uneasiness over Lorena. At the moment her cousin was laughing up into the eyes of a tall young officer who stood beside her at the rail. She looked very appealing and sweet, yet from time to time Abbie caught the barbed mockery in the tone of her voice. Lorena seemed to be asking for trouble.

"I wish she'd behave," Abbie murmured to Douglas.

Lorena made a striking picture in her rose-colored satin dress, trimmed with Roman key in wide black velvet. It almost looked as though she were coquetting lightheartedly with the tall young soldier. But Abbie saw the angry flush in his cheeks, the stiff way in which he escorted Lorena to a seat and left her there, clicking his heels together sharply as he bowed. It was not a very military click, for he had not been in uniform long, but there was dignity as well as outrage in the set of his shoulders as he went off down the deck.

"You know what I think?" Douglas said. "I think she

wants to behave badly enough so that she'll be sent back to Charleston."

That was it, of course, and she ought to be stopped. But how anyone was to manage that, Abbie had no idea.

In the afternoon, when the boat turned into the Arthur Kill on the lap home, the dancing began and both young and old gathered in the upper saloon to watch and listen or dance to the music of the alternate bands.

Abbie had gone to few real dances in her life and during her first waltz with Douglas she found herself wishing she had given more attention to learning how to dance well. Later, watching him with Lorena, she could see how inadequate a partner she had made. The polka was a gay one and Lorena was laughing breathlessly as Douglas whirled her about the room. Apparently she had decided to forget her distaste for Douglas today, as least, and Abbie felt all the more irritated by her cousin's ability to put on this flirtatious pretense.

Mrs. McIntyre and Mrs. Phillips sat together at one end of the saloon, while Abbie, Stuart, and Hannah grouped themselves nearby with Mr. McIntyre. Mrs. Phillips was overlooking Mr. Mac's rudeness of two weeks ago, just as she had decided to overlook the scolding Rosa Garrett had given her. Aunt Varina, as Hannah often said, was not one to be easily discouraged.

Douglas' mother watched her handsome older son with pride in her eyes as he swung the pretty Southern girl about the room. Abbie saw her glance briefly at Stuart and sigh.

"What a shame that Stuart has so few of the social graces," she said. "It doesn't seem fair that one brother should be neglected by the fates."

Abbie stole a look at Stuart, who was well within hearing. But if his mother's words had reached him, he gave no sign. His eyes were on the dancers and Abbie couldn't tell, watching him, whether or not he liked what he saw. Impulsively, she spoke to him.

"You haven't asked me to dance once today, Stuart

McIntyre. After all, just because I gave you a licking one time . . ."

His gray eyes turned sardonically upon her and he rose to his feet. "Dear Miss Abigail, will you do me the honor?"

She smiled and put her hand into his. It had been horrid of his mother to speak as she had and the impulse to lessen the sting of those words was strong in Abbie.

"I didn't know you had such a soft heart," he said as they joined the fast-moving circle.

Abbie was grateful for the breathless pace of the polka that made an answer difficult. She hadn't expected him to make so quick a deduction from her action. Stuart's mother had always made somewhat regretful comparisons between her older and younger sons and had never concealed the fact that Douglas was her favorite. In the past Abbie had taken her attitude rather for granted, but now she was older and it made her suddenly indignant.

"You have some qualities Douglas lacks," she told him resolutely when the polka ended and they stood waiting for the next number to begin.

"Of course I have," Stuart said. "But I hadn't expected any young lady to recognize the fact."

The impulse to heal what might have been a wound died as quickly as it had risen. Abbie said. "Don't think I'm wasting any sympathy in your direction. I just wanted to dance."

There was something in the twist of his smile that she did not altogether understand, and she came to the conclusion that Stuart, as always, was an uncomfortable and aggravating sort of person. To turn their talk to safer ground, she sought a new direction.

"Papa tells me you've done an interesting piece of work in your 'Southern Report' that you let him read. He says you gave him permission to show it to Mr. Curtis, who wants to take it to Mr. Greeley."

There was a light in Stuart's eyes she had never seen before. "Just to be read by Horace Greeley is more than I'd ever hoped for."

"Do you want to write so very much?" Abbie asked.

"More than anything else in the world," Stuart said. "Not stories, not fiction. Accounts of real happenings, sketches that try to present real people and show how they live, and what they think and feel."

She had never known that he felt like this. But before she could question him further, Lorena passed them in Douglas' arms. She was laughing up at her partner as gayly as if he had not been a hated Yankee, and Abbie experienced a twinge of resentment. Stuart glanced at them and went back to his old mood of mockery.

"Fraternizing with the enemy," he murmured. He spoke the words so Lorena could hear and she tossed him a bright glance in which there was an odd sort of triumph. Abbie watched uneasily, sensing an undercurrent of something she did not understand.

When the two couples rejoined their elders, they found that their neighbor Mrs. Johnson had come into the group. Mrs. Johnson was always popular with young people because of the good times she was forever concocting.

"Have you heard what our eye specialist Dr. Elliott is up to?" she was asking the others.

"He's trying to raise a regiment, isn't he?" Mrs. Phillips said.

"That's right. He has been given the authority by Secretary of War Simon Cameron to raise a Highland brigade."

"Indeed?" Mr. McIntyre began to pay attention to this woman talk for the first time.

Mrs. Johnson nodded. "The regiment will be called the Cameron Highlanders—the Seventy-Ninth Highlanders. But of course Dr. Elliot is going about the recruiting in his own original way. All his sons are enlisting and his daughter is helping in the recruiting. But more than that, he says he is going to advertise for redheaded Macs with bad tempers. He'll get them too, or I don't know Dr. Elliott."

"Redheaded Macs!" Mr. McIntyre repeated the words as if he relished them and Abbie saw his look move speculatively to his older son's flaming red hair. "There you are, Douglas. That regiment's made for you."

Mrs. McIntyre gave a little cry of distress and was silenced by her husband. Douglas returned his father's look steadily, answering lightly enough. "Why, Papa, you know I'm famous for my delightful disposition."

Everyone laughed and before Mr. McIntyre could return to the subject, Douglas stood up.

"Come along, girls. Let's have a little action. Here we are on an excursion, with the glorious scenery of Staten Island drifting by outside, and we sit in this stuffy cabin and listen to an atrocious band. Stuart, let's get them out of here."

The two boys moved so quickly, rescued themselves and the girls expertly beneath Mr. McIntyre's nose, that Abbie couldn't help but applaud inwardly. For a moment there had been an uncomfortable tension in the air, and she was glad to escape from it.

They all went below, Doug leading the way, with Hannah, Lorena and Abbie following, and Stuart bringing up the rear. Out in the stern of the boat they found the salt air had a tang to it that was reviving after the stuffiness inside. Lorena, who had dropped her previous attitude of aversion to Doug, now hovered at his side, though he paid her little attention. He stood where he could watch the waters of the Arthur Kill churning in the boat's wake as it moved through the narrow channel. On the right-hand shore marshes swept to the water's edge, while beyond rose the heights of Staten Island.

"That was a narrow escape," Douglas said lightly. He spoke to Stuart, almost as if he had forgotten the presence of the three girls.

"It's a temporary escape," Stuart warned him. "Papa has the bit between his teeth now. You're going to have to give him an answer."

Hannah regarded the two boys in bewilderment. "For goodness' sake, what is all this about? I should think a Highland regiment would be just the place for you, Doug

McIntyre. Of course you'll have to go, so why not go with a Scottish regiment?"

Abbie felt like shaking her friend. "Why does he have to go? No one must go who doesn't want to. Papa hates war. He'd never fight. And I'm sure Doug hates it too."

"You make me sick, all of you!" Lorena cried with sudden heat. "I should think it would be obvious, even to you Yankees, why Douglas can't go to war. He couldn't possibly go out and fight against the South. Could you, Douglas?"

Her hand was on his arm; and, as her eyes searched his face earnestly, something began to come clear to Abbie which she had not understood before. This complication was something that had never occurred to her. She had herself felt no strong surge of patriotism over the North's going to war. All the talk at home had been against war, so she'd had no feeling that Douglas should rush into uniform as so many had done. But it had never come to her mind that he might not want to fight because of his sympathy for the South. She turned to Stuart and his grave, troubled look gave her the answer.

"Douglas, tell me you won't fight against the South!" Lorena demanded.

He drew away from her hand—in itself the sort of gesture that was unlike him. "I don't know," he said quietly. "I don't know what I shall do."

But Lorena would not be put aside, "Douglas, honey, you've lived in the South. You've told me how much you like us. You can't want to go down there and kill your friends. Douglas, you can't!"

His tone was gentle and he answered her patiently, but he did not give in to her pleading. "I have to work this out myself, Lorena."

From the deck above came the sudden crash of music played louder than ever and more discordantly. Apparently, the two firehouse bands had been spurred to greater efforts and were now conducting a contest in which the purpose of each was to drown out the other. But the furious sounds did not make the five young people smile, as it might have done earlier. A pall of solemn quiet had fallen upon them.

Lorena posed against the rail, with her hoops spread around her like rosy flower petals. Hannah and Doug watched the shore of the island slipping past, while Abbie stared fascinated at the ever retreating wake of the boat.

Watching it was like watching the past slip away, she thought. Days that could never come again. As she stood there, Stuart took a wad of paper from his pocket and tossed it idly into the water. It disappeared in boiling froth, only to bob into sight again, farther away, rolling along on the water as the space between it and the boat rapidly widened.

That bit of paper was a symbol of her happy childhood, Abbie thought, slipping softly out of her grasp, leaving her to face the confusion and uncertainty of the present and future.

Resolutely she turned her back on the bit of bobbing paper. She wouldn't reach back to grasp it, even if she could. She raised her eyes, to find Stuart's gaze upon her knowingly.

9

House Divided

After the dancing, fresh air, and activity of the excursion, both Abbie and Lorena found themselves glad enough to spend the evening quietly in the Garrett parlor. Mrs. Garrett sat on the rosewood sofa, its carved top rail rising gracefully behind her, her feet up on a small footstool to escape the drafty floor. Her needle flashed in and out of embroidered petals, never idle. Mr. Garrett, seated where the light from the coal oil lamp fell brightly on his page, read the latest copy of *Harper's Weekly*. Lorena had perched herself on cushions in the bay window and had pulled back the lace curtains so she could look out into the moon-shadowed garden.

For all that she was weary, Abbie felt restless tonight. To keep herself busy she had opened the glass bookcase top of the tall secretary in the corner and was rearranging her prized collection of cup plates. She had always thought the tiny pressed glass plates fascinating, with their endless variety of shapes and patterns, and as a small girl she had started saving one of every kind she could get.

Lorena was restless too. She gave up watching wind-blown shadows on the grass and turned back to the lighted room, her gaze wandering to the portrait of Rosa Garrett which hung on the wall between the front windows.

"Aunt Rosa," Lorena said, "how old were you when that portrait was painted?"

Mrs. Garrett looked up from her embroidery. "I think it was the summer when . . ."

"It was the summer you were seventeen," Mr. Garrett broke in. "I'm not likely to forget. Your mother brought you North for the hot months and she had Jasper Cropsey paint your picture. I remember because that was the summer I met you."

Abbie saw the soft look in her mother's eyes. Cropsey was more famous now as a landscape artist and he made his home in England, where artists were more encouraged and respected than they were in America. But in this dashing picture he had caught more than the outward likeness of a young girl.

Abbie glanced from the picture to its model, now intent again on her moving needle. As a girl her mother had been pretty. As a woman she was beautiful. Abbie sighed without knowing it. Lately she had found herself wishing she had inherited her mother's loveliness of face. If she had, perhaps Douglas— But she pulled her thoughts back impatiently from that particular road. She would be herself, and if Douglas could not like her as herself, then he could like whom he pleased. Even if it was—Lorena Emory.

"Something troubling you, Abbie?" her father asked.

She started guiltily, but she could not tell anyone the trend of her thoughts, so she took refuge in the news of the day.

"Have you heard about the regiment Dr. Elliott is raising?" she asked.

"Why, no, I haven't," her father said gravely.

Abbie rattled on, glad to have distracted him from the subject of her private concern. "It's to be a regiment of Scotsmen—the Seventy-Ninth Highlanders. Mr. Secretary

Cameron has authorized Dr. Elliott to raise it. Mrs. Johnson says he's going to advertise for redheaded Macs with bad tempers."

She had expected her father to laugh over this new Elliott venture, but he did not. His attention seemed fixed on the page of his magazine, though Abbie suspected uncomfortably that he was not aware of a word on the page. In the same instant she noted that her mother's needle had paused in mid-air and that Mama was staring across the room at him in a waiting sort of way.

After a long moment Papa looked up from the page before him. His eyes moved to Great-grandmother McLeod's picture over the mantel, but he did not meet the gaze of his wife or daughter.

"Perhaps a Scottish regiment is the one for me," he said.

It was Abbie who gasped. Her mother made no sound, no move. She merely set her embroidery down in her lap and folded her hands over it, as if to still their trembling. Abbie was almost grateful when Lorena broke the tense silence.

"Uncle Roger! You mean you'd take up arms against my father, against Aunt Rosa's people? Oh, I think that would be a monstrous thing to do!"

Mr. Garrett regarded her sadly. "This is not something I want to do, believe me."

Abbie flung herself across the room and dropped down on the floor to lean against her father's knees.

"Then why must you consider it, Papa? You've always been against war. You've never thought we should fight this out in the first place. Let others go who believe in fighting!"

"Sometimes—" her father reached out to touch Abbie's curly brown head, but still his eyes did not meet his wife's—"sometimes a man must do what is necessary even when he believes another way would have been better."

"I think you Yankees are just plumb crazy, all of you!" Lorena stormed. "You think you can lick the South just because you're bigger, but we're braver any day. You'll just go down there and—and—get killed and—"

"Lorena!" That was Mrs. Garrett speaking her name in a

tone that hushed the Southern girl. She continued, her voice hardly more than a whisper, and now her words were directed at her husband. "You have made up your mind?"

Roger Garrett nodded quietly. "President Lincoln has called for men to save the Union. Regardless of my own feelings in the matter, I have a duty to my country."

He gave Abbie's head a pat of affection, then freed himself from her grasp to go over to his wife. She rose to meet him and her embroidery slipped unnoticed to the floor. Abbie expected her mother to fling her arms about her husband's neck, to cling to him, perhaps pleading, even weeping. She would have done so in her mother's place. Anything to keep her father from going into a fight he didn't believe in. Papa couldn't be a soldier. No matter what happened he would never hurt anything, let alone kill another human being.

Roger Garrett stopped within arm's reach of his wife. There he waited, not touching her. For a long moment, while Abbie was aware of the monotonous ticking of the steeple clock on the mantel, Rosa looked up into her husband's eyes, reading his thoughts, his purpose. Then she turned quietly and went out of the room, her taffeta skirt rustling as she walked. They heard her go slowly upstairs, heard a door close softly. Before Abbie's eyes, lines seemed to form in her father's face. He went into the hall and stood looking up the stairs.

Abbie and Lorena exchanged glances, and Abbie could see that even her cousin was moved by the implications of a tragic situation. Then Abbie heard her father open the front door. In a moment she was on her feet and after him, pausing only to snatch up a shawl from the hall rack. She caught up with him as he reached the street. The lamplighter had gone his rounds and radiance from the gas globes lighted the rutted way.

"Papa, where are you going?" Abbie cried, clinging to his arm.

He did not break his stride. "I'm going down to talk to Dr. Elliott. If he can use a man no longer young, I shall enlist in his regiment. Go back to your mother, Abbie. She needs you now."

She could sense purpose in the way he held his head, in the very manner in which he set his feet upon the road, and even though her heart ached she was proud of him. Roger Garrett would never be guided by anything but his own ideals. If the Union needed him, he would go. Abbie put her arms about him and drew his head down within her reach so she could kiss his cheek. Then she released him without a word and ran back up the walk and into the house.

Abbie turned out the gaslight and then went to the lamp on the table. Her hands fumbled absently over the marble base and up the brass standard. Then she saw her mother's embroidery hoop where it lay discarded upon the floor. She picked it up, her fingers smoothing the raised petals of a rose, weaving the needle into the goods. The circle of cloth had the familiar odor of rose leaves that always hung about her mother's person.

Abbie turned out the lamp, leaving only the gas jet in the hall burning against her father's return. Then she went upstairs, carrying the embroidery hoop to her mother's door. She tapped on the dark wood panel, but no sound came from within. Softly she opened the door and looked inside. Moonlight fell upon the rocking chair near the window where her mother sat, moving gently to and fro, her face pale in the pale light.

"You dropped your work," Abbie said matter-of-factly and laid the cloth in her lap.

Her mother's fingers closed upon it without recognition, but she did not speak. Abbie felt a little frightened. Her mother hardly seemed to be in the same room, so deeply had her thoughts turned to inner suffering.

"Mama," Abbie whispered, not daring to touch this white-faced stranger, "don't be angry with him. You know Papa wouldn't hurt you unless it was a matter of honor. I don't want him to go either, but the way he feels it wouldn't be right for him not to go."

Abbie had to bend to catch her mother's answer. "I made

the North my home because I loved my husband. Because it was my duty as a wife to stand beside him. But if he takes up arms against my people, against those I love, that is too much to be borne."

"What can you do?" asked Abbie.

Her mother looked up at her wonderingly. "I don't know. I don't know yet."

"You—you wouldn't go South, Mama?"

Her mother's eyes met Abbie's in the wavering light, but she said nothing. Abbie groped her way to the door and went down the hall to her own room. There could be no talking to this new, strange Rosa Garrett tonight. Abbie had put her fear into words that still seemed to hang in the air. But her mother had given her no answer. Abbie could not even be sure she had heard.

She got undressed quickly and put on her long-sleeved white nightgown. When the light was out and she was in bed, she lay awake, listening to the rustle of the night outside her window. She heard her father when he came up the steps and into the house. She listened for his footsteps on the stairs, for the moment when he would go to his wife. But time passed and he did not come upstairs at all, so she knew he was sleeping on the sofa in his study, as he did at times when Mama had been ill.

As she lay awake, tossing, Abbie remembered a Biblical phrase which Abraham Lincoln had quoted: "If a house be divided against itself, that house cannot stand."

A division had come to this house tonight. What was to happen now? It was a long while before Abbie fell asleep.

10

Abbie Paints

The week that followed would always remain confused and painful in Abbie's memory. Before she recovered from the first shock over her father's announcement, he had enlisted in Dr. Elliott's newly forming regiment and was stationed in training at Palace Gardens near Union Square in New York.

On the cold day when he left Staten Island, Abbie's mother bundled up in warm clothes early in the morning and vanished from the house. She said nothing to her husband or daughter of her intention, and only Jamie, the coachman, saw her leave and told Mr. Garrett later that she had gone toward the Shore Road.

Abbie, listening at her father's side, saw Jamie's plain, usually stolid face twist briefly into a grimace and knew that he too felt the hurt of what was happening. Lorena retreated to her room again, while Mrs. Coombs, out in the kitchen, dissolved into copious tears, so there were only Jamie and Abbie to see Mr. Garrett off.

Jamie drove them to the Factoryville landing and Abbie,

76

fighting tears she mustn't shed, had a last moment of being held tightly in her father's arms.

"Take care of your mother, Abbie," he said. "Remember that she loves us both, no matter what she says or does. I'm not angry with her, and you mustn't be. I've hurt her cruelly and she hasn't been able to make peace between her conflicting loyalties. Understanding between people who love one another has to be big and generous. So we'll wait and give her time."

Abbie knew how big and generous he was as she stood on the landing, waving till the boat was out of sight. Then she let Jamie drive her home again. Papa wasn't really gone, she reassured herself. He was only across the bay in New York. They would see him again before his regiment was sent away. In the time that must pass, almost anything could happen. He might never have to leave New York at all. The war might end. After all, the enlistment was for only three months. That must mean that President Lincoln expected the trouble to be over shortly.

It was late afternoon when her mother returned and Abbie knew by the dust on her shoes, the stickers in her crumpled skirts, that she had wandered Staten Island roads, rested in fields, and, judging by the trembly look of her, eaten nothing the whole long day. At the sight of her coming wearily up the steps, white-faced and bedraggled, Abbie's heart turned over in pity.

She slipped a gentle arm about her mother's waist and led her upstairs, where she tucked her into the big double bed in Abbie's own room. Then she brought her mother tea and a bowl of soup and went away to let her rest.

The house had an emptying ring as Abbie moved through it and the bamboo curtain from China in the door of her father's study hung dismally still. Just to set the beads to clattering life, Abbie pushed through it and went to her father's desk. He had left everything in the order he liked, but in the center of the green blotter was a sheet of paper with a few lines upon it in his own handwriting. Abbie picked up the sheet and read the few words. She knew who had spoken them—Abraham Lincoln, President of the United States.

> Trusting to Him who can go with me, and remains with you, and be everywhere for good, let us confidently hope that all will yet be well. . . .

> Let us have faith that right makes might; and in that faith let us, to the end, dare to do our duty as we understand it.

There was comfort in the words and Abbie knew her father had left them for his family to read. She folded the sheet and put it away in the top drawer of the desk. Later she would show it to her mother. But now the words would be where she herself could come to them for comfort and encouragement.

In the days that followed Mrs. Garrett returned quietly to her role of mistress of the house, but she was changed. She was as gentle as ever but deeply unhappy, and her inner suffering showed in the pinched look of her mouth, the hollows in her cheeks. Lorena showed a surprising sympathy toward her aunt and, for the first time since her cousin's arrival, Abbie found herself grateful to her. Mama needed Southern kin at a time like this and Abbie did not begrudge her turning to Lorena if she found comfort in the other girl's company. Nevertheless, she could not help feeling a sense of loss.

On the Saturday of the week following the excursion, Douglas McIntyre appeared at the Garrett house and invited Lorena to go driving with him. Abbie, who had thought for a moment that he had come to see her, watched them go off, while all the hurt of the last few days came to a fester within her. She knew there was only one thing to release the pent-up confusion and hurt that was the sum of all that had happened to her since war had been declared. She packed her painting things, told Mrs. Coombs she was going to climb to the top of the hill above the house, and set off through the woods, minus hoops and bonnet.

There was a cleared space at the hilltop where the view stretched away for miles. There she set up her easel and the light campstool she had brought and sat down to paint. The day was brightly clear. Sun sparkled on distant Jersey hills and turned the waters of the Kill to rippling light. Abbie mixed her colors, attempting to match the blues of hill and sky, and began dabbling at her canvas.

She worked at first with nervous energy, exaggerating the form of a tree, brightening the colors of her palette so that they were more challenging, more compelling than those of the scene before her. At the end of an hour she flung down her brush, knowing the picture would never come right. Those daubs on canvas had little relation to reality, though working at them had released some of the tension within her.

When she heard the sound of someone climbing through the brush-grown path, she looked about in annoyance, not wanting anyone to see her queer canvas. When Stuart McIntyre came into view, she wasn't sure whether she was relieved or more annoyed than ever.

"Mrs. Coombs told me you were up here," he said matter-of-factly as he crossed the clearing.

Abbie made no reply and Stuart casually examined the picture. She wanted to tell him to go away, wanted to vent on him her emotions of an hour ago; but, she found strangely enough, that feeling had gone out of her, she felt limp and released.

"Interesting portrait," Stuart mused aloud.

The words pricked her curiosity. Whatever those strange forms on canvas might represent, they certainly added up to no recognizable portrait.

"Have you titled it yet?" Stuart went on calmly.

She roused herself to stare at him. "Whatever are you talking about? You can see it isn't anything at all—or meant to be."

"Then I'll title it for you," he said. " 'Portrait of a Lady in Anger.' And very good, too. I am fairly singed by the heat of your brush."

Abbie looked back at the canvas and in spite of herself laughed out loud. "I do believe you're right. Though how anyone else could understand, I don't know."

"That was a good way to let out your feelings," Stuart went on. "Much better than kicking and biting and pulling out handfuls of hair. It's easy enough for anyone to read who knows you. This must have been a bad week for you, Abbie."

She said nothing to that. How bad the week had been was something she wanted to lock away in her own heart, where it could not be viewed by others. Yet Stuart, in his canny way, went right on to share it.

"Your father's leaving was a shock to me, too, Abbie. I suppose my feeling about war has come to me mainly through him. It's hard to understand how he could bring himself to go."

"He had to go," Abbie said shortly.

Stuart let that pass. "Your mother's taking it hard?"

"Don't talk about Mama," Abbie said and there was a sound of tears in her voice that alarmed her. She didn't want to break down and cry before Stuart's penetrating gaze.

"Then," he went on as if she hadn't spoken, "there's the matter of Douglas taking Cousin Lorena out driving this afternoon."

That was none of his business, but Abbie felt too limp to tell him so and tears were still dangerously close.

"Are you going to sit by and let her get away with it?" Stuart demanded directly.

Abbie looked at him again, startled. "What are you talking about?"

He did not answer until he had found a comfortable place on the grass where he could sit cross-legged watching her.

"Miss Abigail," he said, mockingly formal, "you know very well that I refer to the way your lovely Southern cousin has set her cap for my impressionable brother. What I'm interested in knowing is whether you mean to let her get away with it?"

Abbie shrugged. "How can I help it if Douglas prefers Lorena's company to mine? Besides, why shouldn't he? My goodness, Stuart, nobody could set me up beside her for a minute and come away with anything but—oh, you know what I mean!"

Stuart was laughing at her openly now. "Fishing, Abigail?"

She flushed and did not meet his eyes. He went on, his tone more gentle than was usual with him.

"Lorena is—Lorena, and she has some things you lack. But Abigail Garrett has qualities Lorena lacks. Don't forget that. Lorena is one phase of the South. She's its charming, flirtatious, impulsive phase. But you've got both the North and the South in you, Abbie, and that's a good combination. Use it."

"How?" Abbie asked directly.

"Go after Doug yourself."

Abbie tried to make a conventionally shocked sound. "Stuart McIntyre! You know ladies never pursue the opposite sex."

He laughed at her openly. "I know that is the polite fol-de-rol handed out in novels, but I doubt that any lady believes it. If she does, she's fooling herself. I've done some observing, Abbie, and I've noted that in her own subtle way the lady who wants to capture the interest of a gentleman manages to do just that. Oh, she mustn't be bold about it. The fish that is wriggling around in free waters mustn't know what she is up to, but she has to be up to it all the same. Lorena Emory has more wits than you have on that score, Abbie. Southern women know how to be women."

Abbie picked up a brush and prodded it impatiently at her palette. "I won't play games like that! I don't like women who do. I want to say what I mean and do what I believe and not be forever pretending I am what I'm not."

"Most admirable. Some men will even appreciate that directness in you. But not Douglas."

"You mean Douglas isn't direct and honest?" she demanded indignantly.

"Ssh!" He waved soothing hands at her. "Don't get excited. Douglas has all the most admirable qualities there are and I'm pretty fond of him. But in spite of the fact that he likes girls more than I do, he doesn't know much about them. It's because he is simple and sincere himself that he's likely to be caught by a pair of bright eyes and a saucy smile and find himself in serious hot water. You can prevent that if you want to. You like him, don't you, Abbie?"

"All my life I've liked him," she told him simply. She couldn't use the stronger word, but Stuart used it.

"It's because I love him too, Abbie, that I want to see someone stop Lorena."

"But why me?" she demanded. "You've never done anything but fight me, Stuart, ever since we were children. Why should you suddenly be setting me up to—to—"

His sandy eyelashes veiled his eyes and he plucked idly at a stem of wild grass. "Frankly, because you're the only weapon close at hand. Can't you see beyond your own nose, Abbie? What if Douglas decides to get into this fight?"

"He has to do that sooner or later, doesn't he?" Abbie asked, puzzled.

"Since he's Douglas, I'm afraid that's true."

"I still don't understand. You mean it will be hard for him to fight Lorena's people if she becomes too important to him?"

Stuart tossed the grass stem aside and got to his feet with a quick, restless movement. "Don't be a goose, Abbie. Don't you see where he's heading and where Lorena is trying to lead him?"

Absently Abbie mixed colors on her palette, while realization swept through her in a wave of shock. "Stuart! He wouldn't go into the fight on the side of the South?"

"Why not?" He regarded her wryly. "He has practically turned into a Southerner in the last few years. All his sympathies are with the South. But his roots are in the North. The North is his blood kin and its pull is strong too. That's why he's suffering over this, Abbie. Either way he jumps will hurt him to the quick. Yet sooner or later he has to jump. I think it will be worse if he turns against his own kin.''

She understood now why Stuart had come here to talk to her, understood what he was after. She herself was only a spoke in the wheel of his plan—someone to use to save Douglas. She didn't mind, since she wanted to save Douglas too.

"Do you really think I could do it?" she asked softly.

"You've a better head on your shoulders than Lorena, even if hers is a prettier head.''

She let his frankness pass, admitting the truth readily herself. The point was that Stuart thought she could still catch and hold Doug's interest, even with Lorena in the picture. And there was nothing dull-witted about Stuart. Even when she liked him least, she acknowledged that. He was mature beyond his years. With a resolute movement, she turned back to her canvas and made a sharp zigzag across it with her brush full of color.

"Good for you!" Stuart applauded. "Let's retitle the picture.''

Abbie had scarcely been aware of her own action until he spoke. She looked up at him curiously. "What would you pick for a new title?"

" 'Portrait of a Lady Determined,' " Stuart said, and smiled at her gravely.

11

Widening Breach

Despite Stuart's encouragement, Abbie found herself able to make no real progress in the next few weeks. There were, she discovered, some few things she could do to block Lorena. She could plan ahead, where Lorena was guided by impulse and the instinct of the moment. Thus there were times when Abbie managed to be with Douglas and even had the feeling that he was happier in her company than he was in Lorena's. Mainly, Abbie felt, Lorena was trying to turn one enemy into a soldier who would fight for the South, instead of against it, and she was apparently willing to go to any lengths to achieve her purpose.

Now that she understood Doug's quandary, Abbie could sympathize with his problem. Life had never before forced him into making a life-or-death decision. Always duty and honor had been clear-cut distinctions. Robert the Bruce was never troubled by a moment's hesitation as to where his duty lay. He had only one choice—to fight for his beloved Scotland against England, the tyrant. But the boy who had played at being Bruce and Wallace and Bonnie Prince

Charlie was now torn by a choice of courses, neither of which he could bring himself to take.

Abbie knew well enough that Lorena's flirtatious tricks were not for her. She would have felt self-conscious about attempting them. Instead, she offered sympathy, understanding, a quiet, listening presence that asked nothing for herself. And Douglas seemed to be turning to her more and more. Yet when he was beside her, Abbie was aware of the way his attention followed Lorena's bright presence, responding to the beckoning glint of her.

Much as Abbie was concerned with the problem of Douglas, the difficulty in her own home seemed still more impossible of solution. Though Abbie went over to New York more than once to see her father, Mrs. Garrett held back from going with her. In turn, her father would not come home for a visit unless his wife wanted him to come, and the breach between them grew wider.

Once Abbie tried to plead with him to come home and simply take her mother in his arms and hold her close until the resistance went out of her.

"Papa, I know she couldn't hold out against you if you came. I know how much she loves you and needs you."

But her father only shook his head. "That way isn't for me. I have to respect her right as an individual to make her own free choice. When she turns to me again, it must be because she can forgive me for what I must do. If I tried to coax or force her, doubts would creep in later. No, Abbie, I can't do that. Not even if I have to leave town without seeing her again."

To Abbie's eyes her father had never seemed more handsome than he did in the uniform of the Seventy-Ninth Highlanders. His blue state jacket had red facings and he wore a blue forage cap and Cameron tartan trousers. For dress parade those who had them would wear kilts and Roger Garrett had already got his.

But though his shoulders had straightened and he had a new, decisive look about him, the lines in his face were sharper than ever and sometimes Abbie's heart sickened as she looked at him.

At home Abbie related every detail of her visits with him, but her mother only listened in silence.

The budding green of May gave way to the full blooming of June and on Sunday, the second, the Seventy-Ninth Highlanders marched out of New York.

The day before, when sudden word of the regiment's leaving came in a letter from her father, Abbie had her first stormy session with her mother. Mrs. Garrett was working in her sewing room at the time. The sewing machine had been her mother's pride ever since her father had purchased it for her. These days she was making lace-flounced white petticoats for herself and Abbie and Lorena to wear in number beneath summer dresses. Abbie suspected that her mother found the same release in sewing that she herself found in painting.

Abbie read the letter aloud and had the satisfaction of hearing the whir of the machine cease as her mother put her hands in her lap and stared unseeingly at the white goods before her. When Abbie had read to the end she waited a moment for some response from her mother, and when none came she began to speak earnestly.

"We'll go to see him off, won't we, Mama? We've got to be there when he marches away."

Her mother said nothing and Abbie put an urgent hand on her arm. "Mama, you can't let him go without forgiving him."

"He is taking up arms against those I love," Mrs. Garrett said quietly. "How can I go to cheer him on his way?"

"I don't believe you love him," Abbie accused. "And how can he keep on loving you if you treat him like this—if you don't even go to wave him off?"

"Abbie, stop it!" Her mother's voice was choked. "You don't understand. There is something bigger than personal love."

"Not for you!" Abbie cried. "Mama, you must go!"

The chin that could be soft and rounded and was now so

heartbreakingly firm turned from side to side in refusal. "I cannot go, Abbie."

Abbie went to the door, turning back before she stepped into the hall. "Then I'll go alone! I'll be there when his regiment marches."

She started up the stairs to her room, but her mother's voice stopped her.

"Wait, Abbie." Mrs. Garrett came into the hall and stood looking up at her daughter. "Abbie, I can't allow you to go. A young girl among those rough crowds. It would not be fitting. Your father would not wish it."

Abbie turned and came slowly down the stairs. "All right—then I'll find someone to take me."

She went past her mother and out the front door into the bright sunlight. Nothing was going to stop her. She would be there on the sidewalk to wave when the Seventy-Ninth Highlanders marched out of New York. She knew one way to meet her mother's objections. There was just one answer to her problem of the moment—Douglas McIntyre.

She found him working in his shirt sleeves at the side of the house, spading rich dark loam for a new flower bed. He liked to do active, hearty work that set his muscles flexing. Up on the veranda Stuart lay stretched in a hammock, a book propped on his chest as he swayed gently back and forth at the push of one toe against the rail. Both boys had grown restless since their return. Their education, their father said, could wait till the rebels had been licked. The war was of first importance and they would both soon be in uniform. So the days ran by and they found themselves often idle and without purpose.

Doug waved a grubby hand at her as she came around the side of the house, and Stuart called a lazy greeting from the hammock.

"See if that brother of mine is doing a proper job, will you, Abbie?" Stuart said. "Were I able to regard you as a lady of more than ten summers, I'd hop out of this hammock like a gentleman and bid you welcome."

Abbie ignored his banter and went straight to the purpose

of her visit. "Douglas, Papa's regiment is leaving tomorrow. Marching for Washington. Mama said I couldn't go over to New York alone to wave him off. Douglas, will you take me?"

Douglas leaned on his spade, his thick red hair shining in the sun as he looked at her. "Of course I'll take you, Abbie."

She was warmly grateful because she knew this was something it would not be easy for him to do. This was the regiment his father felt Douglas should have marched with. It would bring his own problem all the more acutely to the fore. Behind her on the veranda she heard the thud of Stuart's feet as he rolled himself out of the hammock and came down the steps to join them.

"We'll both take you, Abbie," Stuart said. "Your father has been the best friend I've ever had. I want to be there on the sidewalk when the kilts march by."

And so it was settled. Surely her mother could have no objection to a plan like this.

12

March of the Seventy-Ninth

Mrs. Garrett raised no further objection when she was told of the plan, but of course Lorena Emory would not go.

"When my own father's in uniform?" she demanded scornfully. "Do you think I want to cheer the very men Papa will be fighting?"

The news about Uncle Benton had come only a few days before in a letter to his daughter. Regular mail had broken down between North and South, but letters were smuggled through the lines, or sent by way of Cuba or Canada. Abbie felt sorry for Benton Emory. Like her father, he hated war, yet like Roger Garrett, he too had been drawn into it because of the demands of duty. In his letter he had explained that the entire South had been angered by the way Lincoln had called upon Southern men, in states which had not seceded, to take up arms against their brothers. Uncle Benton himself felt that such an order could not be obeyed. Many who had remained neutral before had now swung to the Southern cause.

Abbie, who had never been happy about her own father's

action in enlisting, found it increasingly difficult to understand the fervor of the feeling both her mother and Lorena had for the South. To them the South was as real an entity as a living woman. They could probably have told you the color of her hair and eyes and how she looked when she smiled. She was a beloved mother to whose defense every chivalrous son should spring, and at whose side every loving daughter must stand. Those who would shed her blood they could not forgive.

Abbie had to confess honestly that she did not feel that way about either the North or the Union. The two names were words that stood for many complex things that she knew her father believed in. But they were not human beings who could bleed and die. Only the men who fought for them could do that. And her own father might be one of those men. Much of her concern was a personal thing connected with him, while Lorena seemed more concerned with that glorious name: "The South."

Sunday proved to be a fine day and Abbie and the McIntyre boys set off for New York in the early afternoon. Abbie had not crossed the bay for several weeks and she was surprised at the changes in the Battery.

On grassy stretches of park where children had played were pitched the white tents of an army encampment. Quiet walks, where ladies and gentlemen had promenaded of a Sunday afternoon, were sentry-guarded, and everywhere a hodge-podge of uniforms was visible.

The three had no time, however, to give these matters more than a passing glance. They went at once to Broadway, where a horse car waited for passengers before starting its long jog uptown.

Douglas put a hand beneath Abbie's elbow and helped her in. The door was narrow and she had to squeeze her hoops through the opening. She settled herself and her hoops in the already filling car, with Stuart on one side and Doug on the other.

The driver took his place on the roof seat in front of the

baggage rail and slapped the reins of the horses. As the car got under way its iron wheels ground over the tracks noisily.

Abbie had said little during the ferry trip and she had no heart for chatter now. Her father's departure and thoughts of the danger that might lie ahead of him left her too disturbed to enjoy what might have been the adventure of the day. Douglas made a determined effort to be cheerful and talkative, but Abbie, though grateful for his intention, could not make an effort herself.

At Fourteenth Street they left the horse car and joined the throngs gathered in Union Square to watch the mustering of the troops. The Seventy-Ninth was already falling into line and there was a kindling of excitement in the crowd. Douglas took the lead and managed to get the three of them near a curb where they could see what was happening.

Somehow Abbie had not imagined what the marching of the regiment would be like. Her father had told her that Dr. Elliott had mustered more than a thousand men into his Highland regiment, but she had not realized what that meant until she saw them lined up abreast there in the street—so many of them, and from a distance all looking pretty much alike. True, not all were dressed alike, for not all of them wore kilts, but there were kilts enough to confuse the eye and, though she searched frantically, Abbie could not pick her father out in the ranks.

When the regiment marched off, with Dr. Elliott, now lieutenant colonel, at its head, Abbie still had not found her father and she was close to tears. When the watchers began breaking up, Douglas left her with Stuart and hurried off through the crowd. When he returned he was smiling.

"I've found out the line of march. We'll get another chance, Abbie. They'll go down Fifth Avenue to the home of Secretary of War Cameron, where the regiment will be presented with a flag. If we can get near the Cameron house we can see the whole show."

It was a short walk and they were there as the crowd began to gather. When the Seventy-Ninth turned down Fifth Avenue, Abbie could hear the skirl of bagpipes and catch the bright flash of tartan trousers and swinging kilts long before she could pick our separate faces. When the regiment halted before Mr. Secretary Cameron's home, Abbie almost slipped off the curb trying to look at the face of every soldier within range.

A thousand men were so many. At attention now, they stood so straight, with their eyes ahead as if they were soldiers of tin, instead of flesh and blood men whose wives and sweethearts and daughters might be crowding the curbs of Fifth Avenue. Big, handsome fellows they were for the most part, these Scottish-Americans who were going out to fight for a new country as once their ancestors had fought for the old. As the handsome silk banner was presented to the company, Abbie was moved as she had not expected to be. Whatever personal reasons might be sending each individual to war, while they stood here in this one great body, with sunlight glancing from their bayonets, there was a greater purpose governing them. These men stood for the preservation of the United States of America.

Abbie tightened her hand on Doug's arm. "How can you bear not to be going with them?"

Doug's eyes were on the soldiers too and he did not answer or look at her, but she saw the flush creep into his cheeks. For the first time she did not mind if she hurt him. Because Roger Garrett was out there in those kilted ranks, she felt that Douglas McIntyre should be too. Perhaps she would have said more if Stuart hadn't spoken.

"You're beginning to sound like Lorena," he said dryly.

In her state of rising excitement his words angered her and she whirled on him. "What about you, Stuart McIntyre? What are you going to do?"

He hadn't the grace to flush as Doug had. He simply gave her a mocking sidelong look. "If and when I ever enlist, it won't be because I've gone giddy and emotional at the sound of martial music and the sight of a uniform. I'll have better reasons. But as I can't see what those reasons would be, I doubt that I'll ever take up a gun in this war. I hope Doug will be equally sensible."

"We don't feel alike on the subject," Douglas said quickly. "But anyway, Abbie, Stu is only seventeen."

"I'll bet there are boys of seventeen right out there," Abbie said. "And in another year he'll be eighteen. What then?"

"I'll figure that out when the time comes," said Stuart and she knew she would get no more out of him.

The sharp barking of orders called her attention back to the troops. Bayonets glinted as muskets snapped to every shoulder. The regiment was about to march again. Bagpipes shrilled their wild note. Two thousand legs swung in unison and the vibration could be felt in the pavement beneath Abbie's feet. Fur sporrans bounced against bright kilts as the Seventy-Ninth marched down Fifth Avenue.

It was then that Abbie saw her father. Discipline had relaxed and all about her the crowd was going wild. There were cheers and shouts of encouragment to "lick the rebels quickly." Girls ran along beside sweethearts or fathers. A soldier here and there put an arm about some dear one in quick farewell. Abbie stepped into the street to walk beside her father in an outside file. He smiled at her and waved a hand at Douglas and Stuart. She saw his gaze search beyond them and knew he was looking for a face that was not there.

"I looked and looked for you," Abbie said brokenly. "I was so afraid I'd missed you. Mama—couldn't come." She could not tell him the truth, but she knew he understood.

"Take care of your mother, Abbie," he told her.

"Oh, I will, I will! Everything will be all right."

He smiled and nodded and then Douglas drew her out of the crowd and back to the curb. In moments Roger Garrett was lost in the pattern of marching men. Abbie stood there limply as the files marched by, heads high and arms swinging. It took a long time for a thousand men to march away, and by the time the last man had passed, the columns were only a blur to Abbie.

"Where will they go now?" she asked.

"To the New Jersey ferry," Stuart told her. "They'll board the train for Washington at Jersey City."

Doug sighed and the sound meant the release of pent-up emotions. There was a tenderness in his eyes as he looked at Abbie.

"You're tired, honey. Let's take her home, Stu."

She knew the term of endearment was only his trick of Southern speech, but it was comforting to her now. The tears she had held back ever since her father's enlistment came into her eyes and spilled over.

"Now isn't the time for crying," Stuart said unfeelingly, but Douglas gave her his own big square of handkerchief and tucked her hand into the bend of his arm.

"You go right ahead and cry," he directed and threw Stuart a look of reproach.

"At that," Stuart murmured, for Abbie's ears only, "maybe tears are a good idea."

She knew what he meant—that she was imitating Lorena by being womanly and tearful—and his suspicion made her so indignant that the tears stopped flowing. Nevertheless, she sniffed convincingly and clung to Doug's arm most of the way home. Maybe there was something after all in this business of being a weak and helpless female. Douglas apparently liked it.

13

Letter from Washington

June was hot and long and during its course Staten Island burst into a buzzing place of military camps. Uniforms were to be seen everywhere and the island began to experience its first trouble with undisciplined soldiers. The *Gazette* carried accounts of drunken assaults on the street, thievery, and vandalism. The old sleepy days were gone and roads bore the new ruts of cannon wheels, the hoof marks of cavalry. Because of the camps, visitors poured in by the hundreds, and on Sunday dust hung like a pall over roads where loaded stages rolled.

Before the month was ended a letter came from Roger Garrett. Abbie brought it home from the drugstore post office, her hands trembling with eagerness, just to hold it. It was addressed to them all, but she would not open it until she reached her mother's side. Surely her mother could not remain unmoved at the sight of Papa's writing on the envelope.

She found her mother on the shady side of the house, on

her knees weeding a rose bed. Abbie dropped down on the grass beside her and held out the letter.

"It's from Papa." She tried to speak quietly, but emotion choked her voice.

For just a second she feared that her mother would not take the letter. Then Mrs. Garrett put down her trowel and held out a grubby hand. Her eyes read every word of the address and even studied the postmark. Then she handed it back to Abbie.

"Read it to me, please," she said.

"I—I don't know if I can read it out loud," Abbie faltered. Then she saw that her mother's eyes were swimming with tears. Quickly she put a hand under her mother's elbow and lifted her to her feet. "Come along then and I'll try. Let's go to our old place."

She led the way to the summerhouse where they had spent happy hours of summers that now seemed so far away. Abbie brushed off the wooden bench and her mother seated herself upon it. Before she sat down beside her, Abbie peered out through the latticework where morning glories grew. Thank goodness Lorena was nowhere in sight. Papa's letter included Lorena in the address, but her cousin could read it later—if she cared to read it at all. Lorena was unpredictable these days, sometimes seeming to adapt to her new environment, sometimes turning perverse and as full of claws as one of the stray cats she had taken to adopting.

The letter began by apologizing for the penciled script. There was no ink available at the moment, but at least there was light to write by. An enterprising member of the company had rigged up a wooden chandelier, suspended from the ceiling, with four tallow candles stuck into it. The table he wrote on was made of two long boards, resting on wooden horses. Quarters were comfortable enough. Each company had a large room with rough stone walls and a smoky old-fashioned fireplace. The camp itself was magnificently situated overlooking for a considerable distance the waters of the beautiful Potomac. He was, as they knew, a member of the Tenth Company, which was composed mainly of Staten Island men.

Thus casually, as if there had been no unhappiness in his departure, Roger Garrett brought himself once more into the heart of his family. He made no mention of the fact that his wife had not been at Abbie's side to wave him off, but he spoke of the pleasure the sight of his daughter had given him.

The letter went on:

> We arrived in Washington at 1:00 A.M. on Tuesday and were marched to our quarters. The enemy is no more than two and a half miles away and at night we can sometimes hear an exchange of shots between them and the nearby Sixty-Ninth. But so far we have seen no action, though rumors of coming battle constantly assail us and the cry of the people here is "On to Richmond!" It is to be hoped that we will not attempt that coup until our military strength is right. At present we are ill-trained and discipline is lax. In my own company there has been much grumbling and even flouting of orders. We are not yet an *army*.

So the letter went, telling them of outward happenings, but dwelling little on things of the spirit, or on the thoughts of the man behind the writing. That, Abbie knew, was not like her father and she sensed that he wrote with constraint.

When Abbie finished reading, she stole a look at her mother. Mrs. Garrett had plucked a morning glory blossom from its vine and was heedlessly tearing the petals into strips. Her eyes were dry now and only by her restless fingers did she reveal emotion.

"We must write to him today," Abbie said softly.

With a quick gesture Mrs. Garrett swept the bits of blossom from her lap and held out her hands to her daughter. It was as if she were the child now, clinging for comfort and help.

"Tell me what to do. How can I find the right way?"

Abbie patted her hands comfortingly. "The right way is to write to him soon. Why don't you come inside and sit at Papa's desk to write? You'll feel better there. Besides, there's something I want to show you. Something he left for us to read. You weren't ready to see it till now."

Abbie led the way into the house and her mother followed readily enough. From a drawer of her father's desk, Abbie took the sheet upon which he had copied Mr. Lincoln's words and laid it before her mother. Then she went quietly out of the room, leaving the beads of the Chinese curtain whispering softly behind her.

14

The Comet

The July day had been hot and sticky and evening was little better. No cool breath rose from the sea to relieve the sweltering island and dampness almost dropped from the air. Lorena had stretched herself limply in the hammock on the veranda, the light from Mr. Garrett's study touching her bright head whenever it moved out of the shadow.

In the study Mrs. Garrett sat writing to her husband, as she did so often now of an evening. Since his first letter had come she had achieved some sort of working peace within herself, though she talked about her thoughts and feelings to no one.

Abbie stood at the garden gate, her arms folded along its top rail, her eyes fixed on the curious phenomenon that had shot into sight in the night sky some days before. Staten Island was buzzing about the spectacular comet nearly as much as it buzzed about the war. The *Richmond Gazette* had even published a piece about it on Wednesday. Abbie had clipped it out to mail to her father.

Now, her eyes fixed on the brilliant comet with its

spreading tail of light, Abbie experienced a stirring of wonder. The eons of time involved made her feel tiny and not very important. The hurts and joys of Abbie Garrett were a puff of nothing beside all that vast movement and mystery up there. Men must always feel that way in looking at the stars. She wondered if her father might be watching the comet too, experiencing something of her own sense of awe and loss of personal importance.

There was a pause in the creaking of the hammock and Lorena called to her from the veranda. "Abbie, there's someone coming."

Abbie withdrew her gaze from the light of the comet to find a more earthly light approaching in the shape of a swinging lantern. As it neared she recognized Doug McIntyre and swung the gate open to greet him.

"You must have been waiting for me, Abbie," he laughed. "I'm here on a special mission. Mama sent me over because Stu wouldn't budge, the lazy dog. Too busy stargazing. I should think he'd know that comet by heart."

Lorena heard his words and sat up languidly in the hammock. "I hope it's an exciting mission, Douglas. I've been dying of boredom all day."

Abbie felt the usual prick of impatience with her cousin. It was true that Lorena was lonely, that she had not even the solace of frequent letters from her father and brothers. Sometimes, from what was written in the few that came through, she knew that others had been lost on the way. Nevertheless, Abbie felt that her cousin would be less bored and unhappy if she would find something useful to do. Abbie and her mother had been out all afternoon working through the sticky heat, scraping lint, making bandages. Mama said she would help the wounded of either side if the opportunity offered, but Lorena vowed she'd never lift a finger to aid a Union soldier, even if he were dying.

"At least it should be *fun*," Douglas said, following Abbie toward the veranda. "Mama's planning a picnic for a week from next Sunday."

"Ugh!" said Lorena and lay back in the hammock. "Picnics! Bugs and grit and messy food."

"You can stay home," Abbie told her curtly. "Come on in and tell Mama about it, Doug. It sounds like fun. We've done nothing at all this summer."

Doug nodded. "She thinks the young—meaning us—should have some normal lively doings, even if there is a war on. She doesn't think it helps a bit to sit around in sackcloth and ashes."

Abbie and Doug went through the French doors of the study to talk to Mrs. Garrett, and Lorena left her hammock to follow them in. Abbie suspected that her cousin would attend the picnic, if for no other reason than because Doug McIntyre would be there.

Mrs. Garrett looked up from her writing and smiled at them. She looked a bit wan and Abbie felt she shouldn't have worked so hard at the hospital in the heat of the afternoon. Yet work seemed to help her spirits and Abbie hadn't the heart to plead with her mother not to spend herself so freely.

Mrs. Garrett listened somewhat absently as Doug explained about his mother's plans for a picnic to be held at Britton's Pond. Abbie suspected that while her mother nodded and gave her agreement to help in any way she could, she was still far away, lost in the letter she had been writing.

When the plans were more or less settled and Doug had gone home, his lantern flickering in the darkness, Abbie gave the comet a last look and then went up to her own room to write to her father. But though she dipped her pen in the inkwell and wrote words across paper, they did not seem to be worth the writing. When the page was half filled she tore it across and dropped the pieces into a wastebasket.

Sometimes she wondered what her mother found to write. Roger Garrett's letters were colorful pictures of camp life and commentaries on human nature. A good part of being a soldier meant being bored and inactive, he told them, yet his letters showed no boredom on his own part.

The more active and unthinking in the company might yearn for excitement, but for Roger Garrett there would always be the interest of an intellectual life that could go on no matter what the outward circumstances. Abbie suspected that her father could make himself busy and content, even in prison—and then shivered at the thought. Prisons were not something she wanted to think about when there was a war going on.

At any rate, she could not write equally interesting letters in return. The main trouble was that everything she thought of to write seem trivial and of no consequence in the face of her father's great adventure. She knew he would never let anyone realize how hard it had been for him to give up his books and the quiet retreat of his study to take up arms against those he could never hate. So how, in the face of his sacrifice, could she write him that one of the bays had gone lame last week, that Mrs. Coombs had a festered finger, that Lorena had fainted when a puppy had scampered under the wheels of a carriage on the Shore Road yesterday.

Abbie laid down her pen, thinking about the incident. It might be too unimportant to write to her father, but it had certainly been startling at the time. She and Lorena had just come out of Mr. Pine's store when it happened. When they heard the yelp of the injured pup, Abbie had rushed out into the dusty street to rescue it and had nearly been bitten for her efforts. What with Lorena's liking for animals, she had expected her cousin to be right at her side. But when she looked back for her help, she saw that Lorena had crumpled into a limp, quiet heap on the grass at the side of the road.

Fortunately, Mrs. Hill, the pleasant colored woman who ran the confectioner's shop, had rushed out of her store to help Abbie with the yelping little dog. Eventually her own ten-year-old son Bobby quieted the dog and carried it away to its owner, promising that a splint would be put on its broken leg so that it would be as good as new. When he'd gone, Mrs. Hill knelt beside Lorena, murmuring over her sympathetically. The pocket of her voluminous black skirt held a green bottle of smelling salts and she waved it a few

times under Lorena's nose. The girl opened her eyes and
looked dazedly into the kind brown face above her, then
cuddled her head onto Mrs. Hill's comfortable shoulder.

The colored woman smiled at Abbie. "This your little
cousin from Charleston, Miss Abbie? I reckon she sort of
feels like she's back home, waking up and seeing me like
this."

Another whisk of the smelling salts brought Lorena
thoroughly to life and this time she managed to get to her
feet. She glanced toward the road with a look of dread and
covered her eyes with her hands.

"The poor little dog!" she moaned. "I—I just couldn't
stand it."

"Well, you certainly weren't much help to the dog—
going off in a faint like that," Abbie said impatiently. "Do
you think you can walk now?"

Lorena tried a few steps, holding onto Mrs. Hill's hand.
"I'll be all right. If you'll give me your arm, Abbie."

Mrs. Hill accepted their thanks and returned to her shop
and Abbie started slowly toward home with Lorena weaving
uncertainly and clinging heavily to her arm.

"I just can't bear to see live things come apart, Abbie. I
can't help it. It always makes me ill. I just faint dead away."

"All I can say is, it was a good thing Mrs. Hill came out
with her smelling salts," Abbie said grumpily.

Lorena sighed. "She looked real good to me when I
opened my eyes. For a couple of minutes I was a little girl
right back home. She knew it too. She understood."

Abbie glanced at her, puzzled. "But you said once you
didn't care about meeting her. Now you sound as if you
liked Negroes."

"Like them? Some of them I love. Why shouldn't I?
Anyway, she isn't the cocky sort I'd expected here in the
North."

"But you don't think of them as people. To you, they're
just slaves."

"That's what you never understand," Lorena cried. "We
take care of them—those of us who have slaves. They're

our people and we're like parents to them. Why, they lean on us in every emergency. They wouldn't know what to do or where to go without us. You Yankees read books like that awful *Uncle Tom's Cabin* and think we all crack whips and chase around with bloodhounds."

Abbie shook her head. "Papa says that parent-child idea might be all right if they were only children. But they grow up to be adults and still have no rights of their own, no lives except what someone else plans for them. Nobody wants to live like that. My goodness! in every other way this is free America. If you really loved them like you say, you wouldn't want to hold them like that. Your father didn't. He said himself that he'd freed his slaves long ago."

"Papa has some funny ideas," Lorena said. "And anyway the point is we Southerners aren't going to have Yankees coming in to tell us what to do. If you'd just minded your own business there wouldn't be any war."

Indignation had revived Lorena. She drew away from Abbie's arm and walked the rest of the way home without support. After that, the two cousins had been farther than ever from understanding each other's point of view.

But now Abbie did not want to write the incident in a letter to her father. She felt that she ought to write about noble, exalting things that would show him how those at home were doing as much as he was. But even scraping lint for the cause was a grubby, monotonous task and nothing to write about in a letter. Besides, the ladies all gossiped and chattered and had a good time, just as if they were at a social.

She took another sheet of paper and scribbled a few quick paragraphs explaining her quandary frankly to her father. What was there of any consequence about which she could write? He was living in discomfort and probably danger, while here at home she was safe and really very little changed by the war, except for the fact that he wasn't home and she missed him so much.

Then she wrote, "I wonder if you were looking at the

comet tonight too?" and closed the letter. It was the best she could manage for now.

Before she undressed for bed she did something she had not done since the day when she had first learned that Douglas McIntyre had come home. She took the drawing she had made of him from its place in the lower drawer and propped it against her dressing mirror to study it.

What a long time ago it seemed—that day when she had tried to capture a remembered face on paper. This wasn't Doug at all. It wasn't simply because the mouth belonged to Stuart—other things were wrong. She had still been thinking of a small boy, while Douglas was a grown man. Since the picture wasn't truly Doug, she was not quite sure why she wanted to keep it.

Before she got into bed she turned off the light and went to lean on her windowsill to look up once more at the spangled sky where the comet broke the pattern. Douglas had said that Stuart had been stargazing too. She wished it had been Doug instead.

15

One Sunday in July

Sunday, July 21, 1861, was the day of the picnic. It was also a day that would go down in history. Though the picnickers knew nothing of the fact, certain curious maneuverings were under way across the Potomac River. General Beauregard, erstwhile hero of Sumter, and General Johnston, in joint command of the Confederates, had massed their armies in Virginia. General McDowell, commanding the Federals, his hand forced by public demand for a march upon Richmond and against his better military judgment, had decided upon a flanking attack.

Beauregard and McDowell had been classmates at West Point and had studied the same lessons of strategy. Thus it was that both leaders decided simultaneously on a turning maneuver. If both had succeeded, they could have exchanged positions. McDowell might have marched his forces straight to Richmond, while the Confederates entered Washington unopposed. But chance was taking a hand that day down near the village of Manassas Junction, across a creek called Bull Run.

On Staten Island skies were blue and the air balmy—a perfect day for a picnic.

In the Garrett household a good part of the picnic preparations centered about Lorena. That young woman had, as Abbie had expected, decided to attend. She had, furthermore, decided to attend in style. A short while before, an English visitor to Staten Island had displayed a new fashion that had become all the rage abroad. It was a feminine adaptation of the uniform worn by the great Italian liberator Garibaldi. Lorena had fallen in love with the costume, and nothing would do but she must have one like it. After all, she pointed out, Garibaldi had lived on Staten Island a few years ago. It was most fitting that the Garibaldi style be introduced to the island.

Since this was the first enthusiasm Lorena had shown since her arrival, Mrs. Garrett decided to humor her. Together, she and Lorena went shopping at Arnold Constable's in New York, and for days afterward the sewing machine hummed and needles flew.

Abbie scoffed at such nonsense. Why should anyone go to such trouble for a picnic? She herself would wear something sensible and cool. No hoops, certainly. However, she got out some crinoline petticoats to wear under her white muslin.

By now her hair was growing to an uncomfortable length. It hadn't been so bad when it was all little curls tight to her scalp, but now it feathered toward her collar, yet was too short to be successfully bound back. Mostly it escaped its pins, fell into her eyes, and looked generally tousled compared with the sleek fashion of the day. By the time she was dressed and downstairs her temper was slightly frayed.

There was no comfort in discovering that Lorena had turned into a glowing beauty. Her bloused red Garibaldi shirt buttoned down the front and had long loose sleeves and tight cuffs. The red pillbox hat which was part of the costume perched saucily on her blond head. A full blue skirt, graceful over its hoops, completed her dress.

This was all probably meant for Douglas, Abbie thought,

looking at her cousin. And how could he resist so gay and feminine a person?

Strangely enough, however, it was Stuart upon whom Lorena lavished her attention from the moment the party arrived at Britton's Pond. Douglas watched her silently, but she seemed not to notice him at all.

Freed for a little while from burdens or worry, they lazed through the day, eating heartily, resting on the grassy banks of the lake, wandering in the woods. Through the long afternoon Lorena bent her attention on Stuart, who responded by teasing her outrageously, without being snubbed for his efforts. Douglas was quieter than usual, watching Lorena as he might have watched the antics of a hummingbird without attempting to come too near.

Late in the afternoon Stuart, having kept news of his own to himself until now, confided it casually to Abbie. "I've been meaning to tell you. Mr. Greeley actually read my piece about the South."

Abbie sat up on the grass, her interest caught. "How nice, Stuart. What did he say?"

"Well—Mr. Curtis reports that Mr. Greeley thinks some of it on the banal side. But there are a few pages he wants to print in his paper. He has asked me to come over to the *Tribune* office on Printing House Square to talk to him."

"Why, Stuart, that's wonderful!" Abbie cried. She started to call the others to listen, but Stuart shook his head at her.

"Restrain yourself, Abigail. No public announcements, please. I haven't been made assistant editor."

She turned away from him, exasperated, but Lorena, who had been listening indolently, backed him up.

"Stuart's right, Abbie. A few little old words on paper aren't anything to shout about."

"Of course not, Treasure," Stuart agreed and dropped back on the grass beside her, his eyes twinkling.

Abbie, knowing well enough how elated he must be, was annoyed by Lorena's words and Stuart's casual air. However, Douglas came up just then to ask if she'd care to go for a walk in the woods. At the invitation, she promptly forgot Lorena and Stuart and Horace Greeley, and happily accepted.

As she and Douglas started up the hill path he caught her hand and held it in an easy, friendly fashion. The path wound through oak and beech and sumac. It was shady and comfortable here, with the cool touch of deep woods. In a few minutes they had lost the sound of human voices, and there was only the whisper of the mill in the distance and the nearby singing of birds.

Abbie felt a little shy, walking along beside this boy she had known for most of her life. It wasn't the familiar leader of childish escapades who held her hand so lightly now. This was a grave young man whom she scarcely knew, yet for whom she felt an almost mothering fondness. She could not enter into the old banter she might once have picked up so easily. He was a stranger and beloved at the same time and she could not talk to him at all.

Their silence did not seem to disturb Douglas. He held her hand as they mounted the steep path and it was as if they were the only humans in the world. Between them silence became a charmed thing—a comradeship that held them together and away from all others.

Douglas finally broke the spell. They had come to a little clearing, where a fallen tree cut across their path. Douglas swung her toward the log seat.

"Want to rest a moment, Abbie?"

She gave no thought for marks of earth on her white frock, but settled herself on the length of trunk as if it had been a parlor sofa. Doug put one foot on the crumbling bark and leaned on his bent knee, looking down at her in a way that was strange and searching.

"You're nice to be with, Abbie," he said. "You're not like any other girl I know."

She had no answer for that and her eyes fell before his steady gaze. She sensed that he wanted something of her, but she could not tell what it was.

He reached out and put a finger beneath her chin, tilting her head. "Look at me, Abbie."

She raised her eyes to look full into his and felt her mouth quiver in a way she could not control.

"You're the only one who doesn't try to pull me or push me," he mused. "You let me alone. No matter what you think, you let me alone. Only that one time when your father's company marched . . ." he broke off.

She felt uncomfortably guilty, since she had not wanted to let him alone. She wanted to sway him just as much as Lorena did, and at Stuart's urging she had even meant to try. But always when the time came she had hesitated, except for the one instance he mentioned. She knew now that it was better not to tug at him. Better for him to come to his own decision, regardless of what others might think.

"I shouldn't have said what I did that day when Papa's troop left," she admitted. "It was the effect of my own concern. Seeing Papa march away, and the flags flying and bagpipes playing."

"You didn't push me even then," he said. "You only asked me how I could bear not to be in it. The words other people have said have made me feel angry and rebellious, but your words made me want all the more to straighten out the confusion I've been in. You can't know what it's been like, Abbie."

She nodded at him gravely. "You don't have to explain. In a different way, it's the same thing Mama has been going through."

He took a few restless steps away from the log. "Sooner or later I have to choose. And either way will be wrong. But I can't stay out."

"There's only one way to choose," Abbie said, her voice soft. "Which cause do you believe in?"

He answered her without hesitation. "The cause of freedom."

Her heart leaped with hope. Freedom meant the cause of the North. The cause of freeing the slaves.

He came to sit beside her on the log. "Abbie, do you

remember those games we used to play as children? Those hero games of Wallace and Bruce and all the rest?"

"Of course I remember."

"I used to be wrapped up in Scottish history in those days. I've never forgotten those wonderful stories your father used to read aloud to us. Afterward we'd turn these hills into Highlands and fight the battles over again. The South is like Scotland, Abbie."

Her eyes widened and she looked at him, suddenly frightened. "What do you mean?"

"Don't you remember how we always took the part of Scotland against England? We believed in Scotland's cause because the Scots were free people and were willing to fight anyone who tried to conquer them. To me the South is like Scotland."

This was something she had not expected. She wondered if even Stuart knew of this turn Douglas had taken in his own mind. She must dissuade him, though she felt helpless to find a way. The worst of it was that there seemed to be some truth in what he was saying. But not the whole truth.

She put her hand earnestly on his arm. "You're mixing things up, Douglas. Scotland was a land apart from England. Britain was attempting to conquer it. But the South is part of our Union, one with us. It isn't the same thing at all. You have to make the choice yourself, Douglas, but you have to make it for the right reasons."

He covered his face with his hands and once more there was silence in the woodlands—a heavy, painful silence. If only she were wise enough to help him, Abbie thought.

"Perhaps you won't have to choose," she said. "After all, the three months' time for the volunteers is nearly up. Maybe they'll all come home soon and it will be over."

"You don't believe that, do you?" Doug asked.

She could only shake her head. She didn't believe it, much as she had hoped it would be so. If the United States needed her father, at the end of his enlisted period, she knew he would re-enlist. And there would be many others like him. In the meantime there would be a new call for volunteers—for a larger number, perhaps, and for a longer time. And the pressure upon Douglas would be all the greater.

"Listen!" he said abruptly, raising his head.

In the distance the sound of a call reached them. That was Stuart's voice. Abbie jumped up from the log, grateful for an interruption, and answered in the high, clear notes she'd used to signal with as a child.

"We'd better start down," she said. "They must be looking for us."

They turned back together. But now he did not swing her by the hand and the early feeling of comradeship had vanished. In a moment or two Stuart appeared around a bend in the path, his face flushed from his hurried climb. At the first sight of him, Abbie knew something was wrong. She slipped her hand through Doug's arm, as if to brace herself against whatever must come.

"We're packing up to leave," Stuart told them. "Papa has been over in town and he just drove up here to tell us the news. There's a big battle going on across the Potomac."

He paused to get his breath, while Abbie and Doug stood frozen on the path before him.

Douglas found words first. "Does he know how it's coming out?"

"McDowell is beating back Beauregard's regiments and it looks like sure victory for us," Stuart said.

They started back down the path to rejoin the others and Abbie tried to force words through her choked-up throat. Early victory would be wonderful, but she could not forget her father.

"Do they know what regiments are engaged?"

"Probably all those stationed around Washington," Stuart said shortly. "This isn't like Sumter. Men are being killed. You might as well face that, Abbie. Your mother's going to need you till word comes through."

Doug thrust his own concerns aside and put an arm gently about her shoulders. "Don't be a brute, Stu. Abbie honey, you mustn't worry. Mr. Garrett has too much good sense to—well, nothing will happen to him. He'll be all right."

She moved away from the sympathetic touch of his arm. If anyone started crying over her she might go to pieces. Stuart was right. Mama needed her now and there was nothing more important than that, nothing else which could be solved in this frightening moment.

But when she reached the lake, she found her mother far from collapse. Mrs. Garrett was efficiently helping the others pack. There was a pallor in her cheeks, and her eyes were bright, but she was not going to break down. Indeed, Abbie was surprised to hear her speak sharply to Mr. McIntyre when he got in her way.

"You hush now, Fergus McIntyre," Mrs. Garrett said, "and keep out from underfoot. You can't make things better by yelling around about victory like that. Even in victory men get—hurt. We don't know what's really happening."

"That's right!" Lorena cried recklessly. "I won't believe your army has licked ours till the fight's over." Mrs. Garrett gave her a quiet look and she subsided. But when she saw her chance she spoke words only Douglas and Abbie could hear. "Everybody knows Yankees are cowards. They either run, or they don't fight."

"Sticks and stones!" Abbie scoffed. "Don't let her prick you, Douglas."

But Doug had winced and turned away and Abbie wished she could give Lorena a good shaking.

Mrs. Garrett held her head high all the way home, but when she reached the seclusion of her own house, her tears came and all the outward courage fell away. Abbie took charge and saw her firmly up to bed in Abbie's own room. Tonight she and her mother would sleep together and try to comfort each other.

There were further problems to be met. Mrs. Coombs, upon learning the news, went to pieces, torn between excitement over victory and concern for Mr. Garrett, so that she was unable to continue her preparations for dinner. In the end Abbie got the meal, carried a tray up to her mother, and came down to find that Lorena had quietly set their places in the dining room. Lorena, however, merely toyed with her food, keyed to excitement and unable to eat.

After dinner Abbie accepted her offer to help with the dishes. Lorena, still gay in her Garibaldi outfit, said nothing more about the battle. But later, when Abbie had tucked her mother under the covers and taken away the uneaten food on her tray, she came downstairs to find that Lorena had gone to the rosewood piano in the parlor and the strains of "Dixie" were drifting through the house.

Abbie took a step toward the parlor and then turned away. She ought to hush Lorena, but somehow she felt too limp to trouble. Let the Southern girl play out her own emotions if she must. Mama was in a room at the back of the house and probably couldn't hear. Anyway she, Abbie Garrett, couldn't cope with one more problem tonight.

She went out to the veranda for a breath of air, only to pause in the doorway, startled. A man was sitting on the steps. For just a moment she thought it was Douglas and her heart leaped. Then he turned and the gas light from the hall fell on his face and she recognized Stuart. Somehow, in spite of a first surge of disappointment, it was a relief to find him there. Douglas would have meant more problems and she wanted no more tonight.

"Hello," he said softly. "I thought you might come out for one more look at the night. I came over to see if there was anything I could do."

She sat down just above him on the top step. "There's nothing, Stuart, but thank you for coming."

They sat for a few minutes looking up at the calm stars. The comet had gone its way and its fiery drama was no longer displayed in the sky. Behind them in the parlor the sound of Lorena's playing became more audible.

"You'd better tell her not to play 'Dixie,'" Stuart said.

Abbie shrugged wearily. "What does it matter?"

"It will matter more and more, I'm afraid. Even your mother's loyalties may be questioned, you know. There are enough people like Papa who go a little crazy with hatred during a war. You'd better stop her."

The last vestige of strength seemed to crumble inside Abbie. She put her head down on her knees and began to weep a little wildly. "I won't do one more thing! Ever since Papa left, I've had to be like a man. Everyone expects me to solve problems and keep everything running and stop things that go wrong. And I can't, I can't!"

If it had been Douglas, he'd have put an arm about her and given her his handkerchief. He'd have offered a strong shoulder to lean upon and given her comfort out of his own masculine strength. Stuart did none of these things. When he spoke his tone was unruffled in spite of her outburst.

"People will always expect things of you, Abbie. That's the fate of the capable and the strong. The thing you haven't noticed is the growing up you've done lately. A few months ago when you hid that note in the cave you were a little girl. Trouble, new responsibility can make a person grow up pretty fast."

"I don't want to grow up!" Abbie wailed. "I don't want to be strong! I want to give up and lean on somebody else."

Stuart rose without another word and walked into the house. She stopped weeping in surprise and strained her ears to listen. But Stuart spoke softly and she could not distinguish his words. The music stopped and a moment later she heard Lorena run defiantly up the stairs. Stuart lingered in the parlor, picking out a tune with one finger—a faulty "Yankee Doodle." Then he returned to the porch and sat down beside Abbie.

"You through crying?" he asked cheerfully.

"Oh, you!" Abbie cried. "Sometimes, Stuart McIntyre, you make me so mad!"

Stuart's sigh was exaggerated. "I have no luck at all with women. I try my best to help, but all I do is rub them the wrong way."

Her curiosity got the best of her. "What did you say to Lorena to make her stop?"

"I just told her she had a spanking long overdue and

she'd better desist from that 'Dixie' business, or she'd get it now.''

"What did she say?"

"Told me to go ahead. She dared me and put her best dimples in her cheeks. So I said, 'All right, young lady, but this isn't going to be a fun-scuffle. You're going to get hurt plenty. And you won't look pretty when I'm through.' So she made a frightful face at me and ran upstairs." He laughed softly.

"I wish she had never come here," Abbie sighed. "She's impossible to live with."

To her surprise Stuart turned to Lorena's defense. "How would you do in the South if your positions were reversed? Don't be too hard on her. Abbie——" he paused and there was a change in his tone——"Abbie, let down a little. You're still going full steam ahead. And there's nothing to steam about now. Be quiet and look at the night."

Somehow his words made her relax a little. Out above the shrubs in the garden, fireflies danced, flicking their tiny lamps ceaselessly off and on. There was a scent of brier rose in the air, mingling with the pungent, salty smell of the sea—all the familiar and beloved odors of a summer night on Staten Island.

It was so peaceful, so calm and lovely a night. Under its spell it was hard to realize that across the Potomac men lay dead upon a battlefield. This garden before her was real. War was unreal, a nightmare from which she would surely awake.

She rose quietly. "I'm going in, Stuart. I'm getting sleepy. Thanks for coming over. Mad as you make me, I think you're good for me."

He said simply, "Good night, Abbie," and stood there on the steps until she had gone into the house. Then he went off across the starlit meadow.

16

After the Battle

The first real battle of the war had ended in a disgraceful defeat for the North. The next few days were filled with uncertainty. Everyone knew that the waters of Bull Run had flowed scarlet with the blood of both Northern and Southern soldiers. But there was no list as yet of the dead or wounded, no way of getting word of loved ones. The papers said the Seventy-Ninth Highlanders had been in the thick of the fight and had suffered heavy losses, but there was no word of Roger Garrett.

One letter to Abbie straggled through; but, after her first surge of hope at sight of her father's familiar writing, she saw that it was dated before the battle and read it with tears in her eyes.

Dear Abbie:

It was fine to know that you were watching the comet too, those nights when we could see it in the heavens. Knowing that, I could feel close to you.

Don't ever worry, Abbie, because the news you

might write me seems trivial to you. A soldier wants to feel that he has not lost touch with home. Through your letters I can follow you and your mother about the house, watch you at your everyday tasks, go with you when you walk abroad, and am reassured because life goes on with you as usual. If I must fight, these are the things I fight for.

Can you for a moment believe that I would resent your safety, or feel indignation because you have not been asked to disrupt your lives in quite the same way that mine has been disrupted? You know better, I am sure. There are sacrifices ahead of you. Perhaps pain. I will expect you to meet what you must bravely when the time comes.

It is true that I do not want to go into battle. There are times when I have dreamed about it at night and have awakened in a cold sweat. This, I believe, is mainly a fear of the unknown. I have tried to dispel these fears by examining the critical situations, the many complexities which might face a man in battle. I believe that in the excitement and stress of the moment much that would terrify, if one regarded it at a cooler, calmer time, will be taken as a matter of course.

Know this, my dear one, and help your mother to understand it. I do not fear death.

Next time you write I shall expect you to regale me with accounts of stubborn weeds in the rose beds, of the disgraceful state of Staten Island roads when it rains, of the carelessness of the ferries in keeping to schedule—in other words, with all the familiar trivia for which I am hungry.

My love to you all,
Your Father

Now he had gone into battle. He had faced the Presence he did not fear. But what the outcome was his loved ones could not know. Somehow the thought that perhaps now he might never be able to read of those homely incidents for which he had asked, hurt Abbie deeply. It was hard to be brave as he had wanted her to be.

"We will go on with everything as usual, Abbie," her mother decided firmly. "That is what your father would wish. Bandages will be needed more than ever now. We'll go to the hospital this afternoon and work as usual."

Lorena, playing idly with one of her stray cats, surprised them. "May I come too, Aunt Rosa?"

Mrs. Garrett held out a hand to her niece. "Of course, my dear. We're happy that you want to come."

Abbie, however, could not accept Lorena's offer as casually as her mother might.

"You mean you're willing to do something to help the enemy wounded?" she asked dryly.

To her surprise, tears welled up in Lorena's eyes. "Southern boys are dying too. Abbie, if you were down there, maybe you'd help make bandages for them. I—I hadn't figured it out that way before."

So Lorena went with them to the hospital that day.

The United States Sanitary Commission had been organized in June. Its purpose was to step in where needed and do whatever the government could not do. The hospitals of the North were not ready for the great tide of wounded and sick that was to engulf them and it was the Sanitary Commission that helped with nursing and supplies, and made an attempt to care for the human needs of soldiers and their families. At its urging women everywhere gave their services in whatever capacity they could. It was under the Commission's banner that Rosa Garrett had enrolled herself and Abbie. Now Lorena joined them to add her hands to those so desperately needed.

At the hospital Lorena kept her eyes on her work and if she was aware of the curious, sometimes hostile glances that sped her way, she ignored them and turned out as much work as the best of the Union ladies. Conversation buzzed around her and often it did not flatter the South. Once or twice Abbie thought Lorena might explode into indignant protest. It was to the girl's credit that she did not, but Abbie had a feeling that it might be wise not to submit Lorena to much of this sort of thing.

After the battle which the North was to call Bull Run and the South Manassas, President Lincoln recognized the need for reorganizing the Union Army. The rout of the Federals had revealed that the soldiers were poorly disciplined, badly trained, not at all ready to fight. Over this demoralized, inadequate army Lincoln put George B. McClellan and it became his task to bring order out of the miserable chaos.

While Lincoln called for more volunteers to serve three years, members of the Seventy-Ninth Highlanders who had been wounded and honorably discharged, or had refused to re-enlist, began to trickle back to Staten Island. But though they made constant inquiries, no reliable word of Roger Garrett could be had. Rumor reached them of his death, or that he had been wounded, or even taken prisoner, but his wife and daughter could not tell what to believe. Mails were slower and more uncertain than ever and a great many letters never reached their destination. Even telegraph messages went astray.

The year had wound its way into August on the day when Abbie came out the front gate and started toward the Shore Road for her usual trip to the post office. She took no more than three steps before she saw the man coming toward her up the hill. Her heart had turned over so many times at the sight of a blue jacket and tartan trousers that she did not immediately believe the testimony of her own eyes.

When the soldier raised his left arm and waved, Abbie stifled a cry and flew down the road toward him. As she ran, she saw that his right sleeve hung empty because the arm was in a sling across his chest.

Her father reached out his good arm, caught her in the circle of it and held her tight, his cheek hard against hers. Her fingers traced the line of his jaw lovingly and discovered the thinness of his face. He, who had always been so immaculate, was unshaven and grimy. But he was here and he was safe. Whatever his injury, he was alive. She held him tight and wept happily against his shoulder.

As they walked back toward home, each with an arm about the other, Abbie told him of the bad time they'd had, not knowing what had happened. He had written when he could, he said, but the letters had apparently been lost like so many others.

Mrs. Garrett came around the corner of the house just as they reached the gate, carrying freshly pulled vegetables in a basket. Abbie called to her in a choked voice and the basket slipped out of her mother's hands. Mr. Garrett reached her in quick strides and she flung both arms about his neck, laughing and crying at the same time, just as Abbie had done.

The news of Mr. Garrett's return seemed to speed through the air, for Jamie left the stable and Mrs. Coombs her kitchen to hurry into the front yard. Even Lorena heard the excited voices and ran down the front steps to hold out her hands to her uncle in welcome.

When he had caught his breath and had time to wash, they all gathered about him in the dining room. Mrs. Coombs cooked up a huge serving of bacon and eggs, brewed savory coffee, and set a feast before him.

A little of the weariness faded from his face as he ate and talked. Mrs. Garrett asked first about his wound. What had happened? How badly had he had been hurt?

He explained without evasion. "A bullet went through my wrist. The doctors say the ligaments are severed and I may lose the use of my hand."

Lorena shivered and turned white, but at least she did not faint.

"You're here," his wife said simply. "You're alive. Nothing else matters."

Mr. Garrett wasted no time in complaints over his wound. There were, he pointed out, so many others more seriously hurt than he. He tried to tell them a little of what had happened that 21st of July across the Potomac.

"Washington went crazy," he said. "When word got around that there was to be a battle, ladies and gentlemen actually drove out in carriages to witness it—as if they were going to a play. They must have expected an exciting scene in which our army would put the Confederates to flight, while they sat safely on the side cheering us on. They didn't expect to have cannon balls whistling over their heads, to have their horses killed or frightened into bolting. Of course these people added to the confusion of the rout."

He paused to eat a few more mouthfuls of food and then continued.

"I was wounded and I don't remember much after that. I must have been coming down with a fever even before the flight started and after I was wounded it got worse. I can remember staggering along in the rout with the others after I'd tried to bind up my wrist. I have a vague picture in my mind of passing a carriage with a horse down between the shafts and a woman in it, standing up screaming. I think I told her to get down on the ground where she wouldn't be such a good target for bullets, but the whole thing is like a dream in my mind. Everything seems to have drifted out of focus. When I eventually recovered consciousness I was in a hospital. And now I'm home."

You could see that the weariness had returned and that he was tired to the very bone. Too tired to finish the food he had been so hungry for. Between them, Mrs. Garrett and Abbie helped him upstairs and then Abbie left her mother to put him to bed.

When she came down again she found Lorena sitting on the bottom step, her head down on her folded arms. At the sound of Abbie's step on the stairs she looked up and there was a stricken look in her eyes.

"Lorena?" Abbie said gently, for the first time putting something of affection into the name. In a quick moment of understanding she sensed her cousin's loneliness here among strangers. Her uncle's homecoming, his account of the battle must have brought her concern about her own father home to her sharply. Perhaps the fighting of a war seemed less glorious to her than her dreams had made it. Abbie bent down to touch her shoulder, to attempt some comforting gesture, but Lorena burst into tears and ran upstairs to her own room.

Abbie looked after her helplessly. How could she deal with a person who was made up of so many quicksilver emotions?

17

Palmetto Cockade

The Confederate States, beguiled into a false sense of power because of their first victory, did not do as well in girding themselves for further fighting as did the disconcerted Union. In the North preparations for war got under way in earnest and McClellan began the task of more than tripling before the year was out the paltry army with which he had started. The Army of Northern Virginia still barred the way to Richmond, but the Army of the Potomac was rapidly drilling its men into soldiers who would not fall into panic at the first sound of cannon. "On to Richmond!" was still the cry, but the army would not be marching again that year.

Staten Island, somewhat to its own surprise, became the scene of considerable gaiety. The faction which might have frowned upon parties during wartime gave itself enthusiastically to the cause of cheering the brave men stationed in island camps. So all through the fall gaslight burned brightly in the big hotels, and some group or other was forever giving a ball.

Roger Garrett received an honorable discharge and settled again into the quiet life he had known before he had gone off with the Seventy-Ninth Highlanders. His strength had returned, though the use of his hand had not, and he went again every day to his law firm in the city. Often of an evening, or over the weekends, Abbie would persuade him to dictate to her the thoughts he might want to capture on paper, and he seemed to take comfort in this. But now and then when she entered his study unexpectedly she would find him working laboriously with a pencil in his left hand, struggling to reach again some proficiency in writing.

More than ever now he seemed to enjoy the visits of Stuart McIntyre. Stuart had gone to work on the *Tribune*. His talk with Mr. Greeley had resulted in a job. Not as a writer, but working with type, learning the process of setting up a paper. He reported to the Garretts that he enjoyed every minute of his new work. When excerpts from his Southern piece appeared in the *Tribune* columns and were later copied by the local *Gazette*, Stuart was obviously delighted. By contrast, Doug's unhappiness took on a darker cast than ever.

Early in December the Garretts found themselves caught up in preparations for one of the many balls being held at the Pavilion Hotel. Hannah's Aunt Varina had proved as zealous in her work for war projects as she had been for charity in peace time. This particular affair was for the benefit of the needy families of men who had gone into the army, and the North Shore had given its ready support.

This would be the first real ball of the season which the two cousins had attended; and Mrs. Garrett, after an admiring look at the gown Lorena had brought with her from Charleston, insisted that Abbie have a new ball gown too. So there had been fittings and much preparation and the feminine excitement proved more contagious than Abbie had expected. The McIntyre boys were taking them, though somehow the invitation had been so adroitly managed—by Stuart—that there was no telling who was to escort whom.

Lorena alternately ignored and then coquetted with Douglas, and Abbie realized that her cousin made him unhappy. There had been an increasing comradeship between herself and Douglas lately and Abbie had the secret hope that in the long run he would turn away from Lorena.

Once he told Abbie a bit grimly that he would have to make his choice about the war before the end of the year. She had tried to persuade her father to talk to him, but Roger Garrett had said that he could not offer counsel on such a matter. This must be something Douglas decided for himself, and Abbie knew her father was right.

The situation at the McIntyres' was more unpleasant than ever. Douglas' father hardly spoke to him now and he was under pressure on all sides to make a decision. But still he held back and would not enlist.

On the night of the ball—December 14—Abbie, turning slowly before the glass in her mother's room, felt that her dress was a success. It was of blue taffeta, draped over her hoops in three graceful tiers. The sleeves were of puffed lace and there was lace ruching over the bosom. At her mother's insistence she had put her short hair up in curl papers the night before, and her mother had combed it in ringlets about her face. Tiny blue velvet ribbons caught it back on each side and gave her less of a shorn look.

Of course she could never equal Lorena's splendor. Her cousin's far more elaborate costume was of white moire and turquoise blue velvet. The neck sloped diagonally and blue velvet flowers followed its line. There were tiny pleats all around the hem, with a piping of blue velvet ribbon. Her spool-heeled satin slippers had come from Paris, and for a final enchanting touch she wore pearls among the long ringlets of her hair.

"You look like the princess out of a fairy tale," Abbie told her frankly and could not help a twinge of envy.

Their elders were not attending the ball, and the McIntyre boys called for the girls in a hired sleigh. Snow lay deep over the island, and the jingle of sleigh bells was now a familiar sound on cold December nights.

While the boys waited for them in the parlor, talking to Mr. Garrett, and Abbie's mother did a last bit of fussing over her daughter's dress, Lorena shut herself in her own room. When Abbie went to the door she called a hurried, "Wait a moment," and there was the same quality of excitement in her tone that had been evident that first night when she had arrived from Charleston, bringing news of the fall of Sumter. Abbie knew her cousin had recently received a letter smuggled through the lines from some friend at home, and now she wondered uneasily what was up. However, when Lorena joined her in the hall, her mantle about her shoulders and closed tightly in front, it appeared that she was stirred by no more than anticipation for the party.

Since her cousin was bundled into her wraps, Abbie got into her own things before she followed her downstairs. At sight of the girls, Stuart shook his head in mock disappointment.

"So! We have to wait to be dazzled until we get to the hotel?"

Lorena, the pearls in her hair shining through the crocheted black scarf she wore over her head, went at once to Douglas and slipped her hand through his arm.

"We're ready," she said. And as simply as that the pairing-off was settled.

As the other two went down the steps, Stuart offered his arm to Abbie. "The penalty of being slow, my girl, is having to put up with me," he said in a tone so low that no one else could hear.

Abbie made a face at him and took his proffered arm. Rosa Garrett gave her daughter a last affectionate pat and Abbie, glancing back, saw sympathy and understanding in her mother's eyes. She had never been able to bring herself to talk to her mother about the problem of Douglas, but in this swift exchange of looks, she saw that she did not need to. Her mother knew.

Abbie smiled at her and went down the path Jamie had cleared in the snow.

"What's up with our Southern cousin?" Stuart asked Abbie, as Douglas handed Lorena into the waiting sleigh.

So he too had noted the kindling of some inner spark in Lorena. Abbie could only shrug to indicate her own mystification, as Stuart helped her into the sleigh after her cousin.

The Pavilion Hotel was built in the style know as "Greek revival." It had once been a palatial private home, but now its wings and rooms and white columns had been turned into an impressive hotel, patronized by wealthy visitors.

Tonight as their sleigh pulled up before it, the Pavilion was ablaze with light. Stuart and Douglas helped the girls out of the sleigh, and the four went up the wide steps and into the foyer of the hotel. The girls sought the ladies' retiring room to be rid of mantles and scarves, and restore their disordered ringlets. As others in the room were doing, they shook out their skirts, smoothed down their hoops, and surveyed themselves in mirrors.

"How do I look?" Lorena asked, and turned slowly about for Abbie's inspection. There was something about her manner that was oddly defiant, almost as if she expected some objection from her cousin. For what, Abbie wondered? She saw nothing amiss with this vision in white and turquoise.

"You look perfect," Abbie admitted. Her attention was caught by a pin of some sort Lorena had fastened among the velvet flowers that banded the diagonal neckline of her gown. "That's an odd brooch you're wearing. I don't believe I've seen it before. It looks almost as if it were made of straw."

Lorena lowered her long lashes. "Do you like it, Cousin Abbie? If you're ready, do let's join the boys."

Douglas waited for them near the door of the ballroom, but Stuart had stopped some distance down the corridor to speak to an elderly gentleman. Abbie could not help but note the lighting of Doug's eyes as he looked at Lorena.

"You're beautiful tonight," he said simply.

Down the hall Stuart shook hands with his elderly friend and turned to join the girls. At once Lorena seemed nervous. She moved toward the big lighted room with its music and dancing couples.

"Don't let's miss a minute of the evening, Douglas!" she cried.

Doug threw a look of apology at Abbie, but Stuart had nearly reached her side, so he hastened to take Lorena into his arms and whirl her away to the rhythm of a waltz.

"Your cousin seems to be in a hurry," Stuart said. "I'd have expected her to wait and let me admire her, even though I hardly count in her scheme of things."

"She's behaving oddly," Abbie admitted. "Though I don't know what's the matter. It almost seemed as if she didn't want you to see her."

Stuart nodded. "I have a suspicious nature. Something is up with that young woman, and perhaps we'd better find out what it is. Will you dance, Abbie?"

Abbie gave him her hand, and he smiled as he led her into the ballroom.

"I haven't had time to tell you, Abbie," he said, "but you remind me of your mother tonight. You look a little like that portrait Cropsey painted of her."

Of all the compliments that might have been paid to her, this was the nicest and she could not help but warm to Stuart.

As they entered the ballroom, she found herself caught up in the color and spirited movement of the scene. Great chandeliers were asparkle with crystal. The gowns of the women, the many uniforms of the men were turned to rainbow hues in countless mirrors, and the air was heady with perfume from Paris. All around the vast room had been set little French gilt chairs where those who were not dancing might rest. Logs burned in a huge fireplace, adding to the color and dancing life of the room. Everywhere there were American flags. Small ones decorated the sides of the room, and an enormous one draped the wall behind the dais where the musicians sat. That one, in particular, was the biggest flag Abbie had ever seen.

She glimpsed Hannah's Aunt Varina in one of the gilt chairs and smiled at her as they circled past. A moment later she caught sight of Hannah, very gay in pink silk, dancing with a New Brighton boy.

"It's beautiful," Abbie whispered to Stuart. "I've never been to a ball at the Pavilion before. Mother says this is the room where Jenny Lind sang. I remember our parents talking about it when we were children."

Stuart nodded, but she sensed that he was less enchanted by the scene than she. He was dancing as if he had some special purpose in mind and she realized what it was as they began to cut closer and closer to Douglas and Lorena. When a break in the music came they were a few yards from the other couple. Lorena stepped out of Douglas' arms, and they could see her clearly.

Stuart said, "So Cousin Lorena *is* looking for trouble tonight?"

"Why? What do you mean?" Abbie asked.

"That thing she's wearing on the front of her dress. Let's get over to them, Abbie."

But before they could reach the other two, the music started up again and Lorena and Doug were swept away around the room. Instead of joining the dancers, Stuart guided Abbie toward the door.

"We'll wait here," he said, "till they dance by again. Then I'll give Doug a signal that will bring them over here. We'd better talk to that young lady, Abbie."

"But tell me why!" Abbie pleaded. "What's wrong with that pin she's wearing?"

"It's a palmetto cockade," Stuart said. "We saw them on visitors from South Carolina when we were living in Atlanta. They're a symbol of South Carolina's defiance of the Union."

Abbie gasped. A palmetto cockade! Someone might identify it at any moment, and at the very least there could be unpleasantness.

"Tempers are getting short up here," Stuart warned. "Union soldiers have died and we're considerably less tolerant of the South than we were last April. Lorena has to behave herself."

"I'll talk to her," Abbie said resolutely.

They stood there waiting, their eyes following the movement of Doug's red head and Lorena's fair one as the two moved nearer to the door.

18

Douglas Makes His Choice

So far no knowing eye appeared to have rested on the ornament which graced the front of Lorena's gown. When the two came near the place where Abbie and Stuart waited, Stuart caught his brother's eye and Doug brought Lorena over to the door. Abbie took her cousin's hand to draw her into the corridor and the boys followed.

"Lorena," Abbie said, "you've got to take off that cockade you're wearing. There may be trouble if anyone notices it."

Lorena returned her look defiantly. "I'll wear what I please."

"I've tried to get her to take it off," Douglas said. "It's foolish to wear a thing like that up here. Suppose some officer recognizes it?"

Lorena's laugh had a tantalizing ring. "I'd love that! I'd just love that!"

Watching her cousin, Abbie was reminded of a child who has been keyed up to the point where he is ready to laugh or cry or fight at the drop of a pin. All this tingling excitement in Lorena could lead to no good.

Stuart regarded the Southern girl gravely. "You might consider that you're here as your aunt and uncle's guest, Lorena. If there is any sort of disagreeable incident tonight, it will only reflect on them."

"I never wanted to be a guest of the North," Lorena said heatedly. She put a hand to the cockade at the neck band of her dress as if she would protect it from any who might reach for it. The cords of her hand were sharply marked, revealing its tension, and her mouth had a pinched look at the corners.

For a moment longer Stuart hesitated. Then he made Lorena a mocking bow and led Abbie back to the dance floor.

"What can we do?" Abbie whispered.

"Nothing, short of ripping the thing off her dress," Stuart said. "We've done what we could, so let's relax and hope no one here tonight will identify what she's wearing."

But Abbie could not relax. She found herself watching faces of those near Lorena for any sign of recognition.

The dancing had stopped and some sort of entertainment was being arranged on the musicians' dais. Douglas led the way to where the girls could seat themselves in two of the little gilt chairs. He stood behind Lorena, while Stuart found a place beside Abbie.

"Someone's going to sing," Douglas said.

His brother groaned. "I wouldn't object to Jenny Lind, but I'm not always enraptured by local talent."

"Hush!" Abbie warned him. "This isn't local talent. I read in the *Gazette* that a singer from the city was coming over and that we could expect an unusual treat."

The singer was introduced and, as she stepped to the front of the platform, the rustling in the room ceased. She was a handsome, dark-haired woman with a somewhat commanding presence. Her first two songs were operatic arias dramatically executed. She had a good voice, but Abbie wished she would omit the elaborate gestures. However, everyone applauded generously and the singer bowed her readiness for an encore. But now the accompanist waited, and a hush fell upon the room as the singer began to speak.

"A dear friend of mine—a lady whose name is known to most of you—has been visiting our splendid encampments around Washington and has been inspired to write stirring new words to a song you all know. These verses will appear in the *Atlantic Monthly* in February and then I am sure everyone will be singing them. My friend, Mrs. Julia Ward Howe, has kindly given me permission to sing this song to you tonight."

She nodded to the pianist. He set his hands on the keys in the arresting chords of the introduction. Why, Abbie thought, that was the music to the John Brown song, which in turn had been based on an old camp-meeting tune.

This time the singer did not gesture. She stood quietly, holding the manuscript of music in her hands, and sang without dramatic embellishment. The song needed none. As she listened, Abbie felt a tingle run through her.

Mine eyes have seen the glory of the coming of the Lord;
He is trampling out the vintage where the grapes of wrath are stored;
He hath loosed the fateful lightning of his terrible, swift sword;
His truth is marching on.

And then the rousing music of the refrain: "Glory, glory, Hallelujah! . . ."

The great ballroom held its breath. Not a chair creaked, not a whisper broke the listening hush through which the music swelled and pounded. When it died away the applause was stormy. Something had come to life in the room that had not been there before. Something almost primitive in its emotional force. Abbie put her hand to her throat and glanced at Stuart. He saw her look.

"There will be Union soldiers marching to that song," he

said quietly. "There will probably be men here tonight who will go away and enlist because of it."

Abbie glanced quickly at Douglas and saw his white face, the distant look in his eyes. Could a song like this "Battle Hymn of the Republic" resolve Doug's problem? Something told her that it wasn't right that it should. Roger Garrett's daughter could not believe that a solution should come from anything but reason.

She reached out a hand and touched his arm gently. "Come back to Staten Island, Doug. That was only a song, you know."

Before Doug could find an answer for Abbie, Lorena left her chair. "There, the music's starting up. Douglas, I can't bear to sit still another moment."

Douglas took her out upon the floor and Abbie turned to Stuart. "It isn't fun any more. When I walked in here tonight every one of these chairs was solid gold, and now they're only made of wood and thin paint."

A buzzing near the door made them turn to see the young captain who had just entered the room. It was obvious that he brought news, for excitement seemed to flare through the groups around him.

"Listen!" Stuart said tensely.

Abbie caught the word "fire," but could make no head or tail of the rest until a woman nearby turned to her.

"Some city is on fire. Captain Spaulding says great parts of it are in ruins."

By the time the dance ended and Douglas and Lorena joined them, the story was sweeping through the room like wildfire itself.

"Charleston!" They heard the whisper. "Charleston is in flames. Our boats in the harbor have set Charleston on fire!"

Lorena Emory, who had been born and bred in Charleston, stopped near Abbie's chair, her lips parted with quick breathing, alarm in her eyes. Abbie reached out to touch her.

"Don't believe it, Cousin Lorena. You know how often such news is only rumor. Why would we burn your cities?"

Lorena looked at her without comprehension. There was just one fact that had swept every other thought from her mind. Charleston was burning. She rushed across the room to Captain Spaulding and thrust herself into the group around him. Abbie stood up in consternation to watch her.

"Is it true?" Lorena demanded. "Is it true that Charleston is on fire?"

Captain Spaulding's look sharpened as he turned to her and Abbie knew why. The captain's quick eyes had noted the cockade.

"It is indeed," he told her gravely. "Madam, I see you wear a rebel symbol on your gown."

There was a gasp from those nearby and there was no telling what might have happened next if Lorena had stayed where she was. But she did not answer Captain Spaulding. Instead, she whirled and sped across the room toward the platform, unrestrained fury in her movement. Fury over what was being done to her home and those she loved; done to them by these hated Yankees.

The musicians on the platform saw her run up the steps, but they had no inkling of what was about to happen and only stared in bewilderment. It was Abbie who saw Lorena's intent and realized what her cousin was about to do. Oh, no—not the flag!

Douglas had started after her, but there was no way to stop her now.

Lorena's hoops knocked over a music stand. She put out a hand and pushed a chair out of the way. It toppled backward with a small crash. People near the platform had seen her and were staring, but Lorena paid them no heed, intent on a single purpose.

Her hands reached above her toward the silken folds of the huge United States flag and pulled at them ruthlessly. While the stunned room watched, there was a tearing sound and the banner sagged, then slid down the wall, its enveloping folds slipping out of Lorena's hands to heap themselves on the floor. Doug, still too far from the platform to get through the throng about it in time, could only watch helplessly.

A soldier nearby was the first to move. He sprang upon the platform, flung Lorena aside with a single sweep of his arm and caught up the heavy folds of the flag. All about the room an angry murmuring began.

What followed happened so quickly that afterward Abbie could not be sure whether anyone gave an order, or if the whole thing occurred spontaneously. In a moment's time every uniformed man in the room was around the platform. No hand was laid upon Lorena once the flag had been raised from the floor, but suddenly two files of men opened between her and the door—a marked aisle of uniforms. What was expected was clear. The murmuring in the room died away and in the tense hush Lorena stood looking down upon the soldiers before her.

Now that her purpose was accomplished, she had gone pale, but her bearing spoke defiance rather than submission as she walked to the steps and came down them. With the same arrogant air she walked between the two long rows of uniforms, a slight girl in white moire with pearls in her hair and a kindling in her eyes.

The men broke their ranks, melted into the crowd, and an excited buzzing hummed through the room. Abbie saw Douglas hurry after Lorena and she and Stuart followed him, pushing their way across the crowded floor. Behind them the orchestra recovered its senses and burst somewhat feverishly into music. Those present seemed to come to an unspoken agreement to forget so shocking an episode, and while there was a hum of voices beneath the music, everywhere couples began to dance again.

The corridor was empty, except for Lorena running swiftly down it. Doug reached her first. He caught her by the shoulders and swung her toward him, and Abbie saw the tears streaming down her cousin's face.

"Don't cry, Lorena honey," Doug whispered.

Lorena stiffened in his grasp and recovered herself enough to push him away. "Let me go, you—you Yankee!"

"I won't let you go," Douglas said calmly. "And I won't let you call me that name. I'm going away tonight. I'm going to get through to Confederate lines."

The sobs died in Lorena's throat and she looked up at him as if she could not believe what she had heard. He bent his head and kissed her lips gently.

Abbie turned to Stuart. "Did you hear him? Stuart, you can't let him do this. You've got to stop him, Stuart!"

He put a steadying hand on her arm. "Easy, Abbie. There's nothing we can do."

"But your brother—your own brother! How can you stand there so calmly?"

"Don't you think I've tried everything possible to dissuade him before this?" Stuart said. "There's no more to be done now. And perhaps it's better for his own peace of mind that he has made his choice."

His words woke an echo in her mind—a memory of that day in the woods above Britton's Pond when she herself had felt that it would be best for Douglas to come to his own decision without influence from others. But now that the moment had come and he had chosen the wrong side, she could not accept his decision as calmly as Stuart was accepting it.

She turned away from him helplessly, numb with shock.

In these few moments Douglas had changed. All the strain of indecision had fallen away and he was more like the boy Abbie had known as a child. As they reached him he spoke directly to his brother.

"There's still time for me to make the last boat from the New Brighton landing."

"Do you want me to go home and pick up some things for you?" Stuart asked.

Doug shook his head. "I don't dare miss the boat. Just give me what money you have on you. I won't need these clothes for long."

"I'll call the sleigh and drive you to the boat," Stuart offered.

Douglas looked at Lorena. "Will you come?"

"Do you think I'd let you go alone?" Lorena demanded.

No one had asked Abbie whether she cared to go, but she followed Lorena at a more sober pace and got silently into her wraps. Lorena was fairly quivering with excitement and she appeared not to notice Abbie's silence. Of if she noticed, she did not care.

By the time they joined the boys again the sleigh was waiting and they bundled into it quickly. The landing was only a short drive and they saw the lights of the boat as they drove up beside the trampled, dirty snow of the dock. There was little time to spare. The ferry men were already preparing to pull in the gangplank, and Douglas ran toward it, with Lorena clinging to his arm, heedless of what slush might do to her Paris slippers. At the gangplank's foot Doug stopped to take her into his arms.

"We're going to be married when I come back," he said gently.

"I'll be waiting," Lorena told him, and now she was holding back her tears, smiling at him proudly.

He turned to give his hand to Stuart, who took it in his own firm clasp.

"You understand, Stu?" Doug said.

Stuart threw an arm around his shoulders. "Of course, Doug. Take care of yourself."

Abbie stood silently by, almost hoping that she would not have to say good-bye to him. If he remembered her presence she might stop being numb and she was afraid to have that happen. But he did not forget her and he stood on no ceremony. He put his hands on her shoulders and kissed her warmly on the cheek.

"Thanks for everything, Abbie. Don't think too hard of me."

She shook her head at him, her eyes swimming with tears, her throat too choked for words. Then the boatmen were calling and he ran up the gangplank and turned at the rail to wave.

"Don't get cold! Go back to the sleigh!" he shouted.

They paid no heed, standing there in the frosty night till the lights of the ferry vanished around a bend of the Kill van Kull.

Bonnie Prince Charlie was gone.

Stuart took both birls by the arm and hurried them to the warm carriage robes of the sleigh. Lorena was keyed up and ready to talk now. She wanted to talk of Doug's heroism as she saw it, of how wonderful he was, but Stuart hushed her a little grimly.

"That's enough, Rebel. You've done enough damage for tonight."

Lorena tossed her head. "I reckon I showed all those Yankees at the ball that no Southern girl is afraid of them. I paid them back."

Abbie found there was a sharp note in her voice when she spoke. "Charleston is still burning."

Lorena gasped. "I—I'd almost forgotten."

"You forget a lot of things," Stuart said. "You forget the injury you do the Garretts with the crazy sort of thing you pulled tonight."

"I didn't want to come here!" Lorena cried defiantly. "And I don't want to stay. I've a good mind to run away and go back to the South the way Doug is doing."

"I'll help you pack," Abbie said dryly.

Lorena sniffed and sought for her damp handkerchief. "You're just jealous, Cousin Abbie, because I took Douglas away from you. Don't think I haven't seen . . ."

"Stop the sleigh, driver!" Stuart called.

The horses snorted at the sudden pull on the reins and the runners squeaked to a stop. Lorena stared in surprise.

"Now then," Stuart went on calmly, "you either stop that right now, Lorena, or you get out in the snow and walk the rest of the way home."

"I won't get out," Lorena cried. "You can't make me. And I'll say what I please whenever I please."

Stuart flung back the robe, reached out and put his fingers firmly about her wrist.

She squealed and tried to pull back. "Stu, you're not one bit of a gentleman."

"That's right, I'm not," Stuart agreed.

"If Douglas were here . . ." Lorena began, but his fingers tightened and she sank limply back in her corner of the sleigh and said nothing more. Stuart signaled the driver and the horses started off again. The rest of the trip was made in silence. Abbie felt like hugging Stuart. She couldn't have borne any more from Lorena tonight.

Lights were burning in the Garrett parlor when the sleigh pulled up at the front gate and she knew her mother and father were waiting. Stuart saw the girls to the front door and then returned to the sleigh for his short ride home. Lorena swept up the stairs to her own room at once, still riding the crest of her rebellion.

When Mrs. Garrett came into the hallway, surprised that the ball should have ended so early, Abbie went straight into her arms as if she had been a little girl. Quietly her mother led her upstairs to her room. She helped with hooks, hung up Abbie's clothes, and tucked her into bed. All the while Abbie poured out a stormy account of the evening.

Charleston was burning. It was thought that the Yankees had fired it. Lorena had gone absolutely crazy and had disgraced them all by pulling down an American flag. Douglas had gone off to war to fight on the Confederate side. And when he came home Lorena was going to marry him.

Mrs. Garrett hushed and comforted and gave no sign of shock, though much of Abbie's news must have disturbed her. She dried her daughter's tears and bent toward the pillow to press her cheek against Abbie's.

"Hush, darling," she whispered. "Don't go on like that. You'll work things out. Everything will stop hurting in time." She sat on the bed, her eyes on faraway things. "Poor Stuart. He's the one who has to go home and deal with his father. I don't know how Fergus McIntyre will take this news.''

Abbie ceased her sobbing. Until now she hadn't thought of Stuart at all. He had been there to take charge, but she had given his own problem no thought. Thinking of it now, she quieted. Her mother bent to kiss her once more, then turned out the light and went softly from the room.

In the darkness Abbie lay still and tried to think. Douglas was gone, she told herself. And when he came back he and Lorena would be married. But none of the words made any real sense. She couldn't make it real until she thought of what was happening across the dark meadow, where lights burned late in the McIntyre house and Stuart must tell his father why his oldest son had not come home from the ball.

19

The Ring

The McIntyres were not in church the next morning, though Abbie looked about for them anxiously. In the early afternoon, right after dinner, she packed a small basket of preserves to take over to Mrs. McIntyre.

"A good idea," Mrs. Garrett said. "And besides, it will give your father and me a chance to talk alone with Lorena. We have decided that except for walks about the neighborhood, she is not to go out in public again unless he or I are along."

When the basket was ready, Abbie dressed in her walking things and set off through the tramped snow of the path across the meadow. At the McIntyres' Stuart opened the door.

"Hello, Abbie. Glad you came. Mama's upstairs lying down, but I think Papa would like to see you."

He took the basket out of her hands and she stamped the snow from her boots before stepping into the hall. There were shadows beneath Stuart's eyes and he looked as if he had done little sleeping the night before.

"You've told him?" Abbie asked. "Is—is he—?"

"I don't know how good a job I did," Stuart said wearily, "but I tried to make him understand that to Douglas—even though he may be wrong—the South's cause is like the cause of Scotland. Looking at it that way, Papa can bear it, even though he can't forgive."

Abbie wished she knew how to tell Stuart that she admired him for his treatment both of Douglas and of his father. But complimenting Stuart was something in which she had had little practice and the words would not come.

He led the way to the dining room, where a wintry sun came through the bay windows, to touch the graying head of Fergus McIntyre. Well bundled in blankets, he was sitting in a Lincoln rocker.

"Hello, Mr. Mac," Abbie said gently.

He looked at her for a moment as if he did not know who she was, and she saw how much he had aged in the last months. This was not the strong, tall man who used to roar around the house until the very dishes rang when he was displeased. This man seemed shrunken and frail and hollow eyed. Then his gaze lighted and he put out a hand to pull her down on a big hassock at his side.

"My favorite young woman," he said. "Sit here, Abbie, and tell me about Douglas. What do you know of this wild thing he has done?"

She talked to him quietly, told him of that day at Britton's Pond—the day of the Battle of Bull Run—when Douglas had walked with her in the woods and talked to her of his feelings toward the South.

Mr. McIntyre listened with his eyes closed and Abbie glanced doubtfully at Stuart. He nodded in answer to her unspoken question. Apparently Stuart felt that what she had to tell might help reconcile his father to Douglas' decision.

"If you can just understand why he had to act as he did, Mr. Mac," Abbie pleaded. "Then you'll be able to forgive him."

He opened his eyes and something of the old spark showed itself. "I can never forgive a son of mine for turning against his country!"

Abbie held his hand tightly. "You mustn't speak words like that. You love Douglas very much. We all love him."

"Yes," he said dully, "we love him." Then he looked at Abbie, his gaze suddenly penetrating. "You do love him, Abbie? Somehow, I've always hoped . . ."

She looked around for aid from Stuart, but he had slipped out of the room.

"Please, Mr. Mac, we must let time take care of that."

"You'd make a good wife for Douglas, my dear." The old man was persistent.

Abbie stood up resolutely. "Stuart said you mustn't be wearied so I'll run along now. But I'll come for more visits. Would you like to be read to, Mr. Mac?"

The suggestion distracted him and he left the dangerous topic of a wife for Douglas. Neither she nor Stuart had dared tell him of the part Lorena had played in this. When Abbie had promised to return and spend an hour or so reading to him, he let her go.

She went into the hall to find Stuart waiting for her at the parlor door.

"I told Mama you were here," he explained. "She has come downstairs to see you for a moment. Abbie, Mama knows everything. She knows about Lorena too. And I'm afraid she has some sort of foolish scheme in mind."

Because of Mrs. McIntyre's headache, no blinds had been opened in the parlor, and what light seeped into the room was thin and gray. She lay propped against pillows on the sofa, and now and then she whisked a bottle of salts beneath her nose. The odor was pungent as Abbie approached her.

"Get a chair for Abbie, Stuart," Mrs. McIntyre said. "Put it here close to me."

Abbie took the chair Stuart brought. As her eyes accustomed themselves to the dim light she saw that Mrs. McIntyre's face was puffy and red from crying. Douglas had always been his mother's favorite son. Yet somehow Abbie could not pity her as deeply as she pitied Mr. Mac.

There was a quaver in Mrs. McIntyre's voice when she spoke, but she hinted at no criticism of her son.

"All along I've been afraid this would happen," she said. "His father couldn't—or wouldn't—see it coming. But I saw it. My heart is breaking because he has gone, but I love him just as much as ever."

"Of course," Abbie said gently, a little embarrassed by her outburst.

Mrs. McIntyre dabbed at her eyes and blew her nose before she went on. "Abbie, I want to do something for my boy. I haven't slept all night for trying to think of something I could do that would please him. Something he would want me to do. Before dawn came I knew what it must be. Your visit today is most fortunate because, Abbie, this is something you can help me with. You'll be doing it for Douglas too. I know he has always been as close as a brother to you—"

"Mama," Stuart broke in, "don't you think you're being hasty about this? Why don't you wait a while?"

His mother went on as if he had not spoken. "Hand me the box on the table, please, Stuart."

For just a moment Stuart hesitated. Then he picked up a leather case from a table and brought it to his mother.

"Open the blinds a little, please," she said.

More light filtered into the room, shimmering over the contents of the jewel case in Mrs. McIntyre's hands.

"These are my few treasures," she told Abbie. "Some of them belonged to my mother, some to my grandmother."

With plump fingers she extracted a slender gold band with a diamond solitaire set upon it. She put it into Abbie's hand and closed her fingers about it while the girl stared in bewilderment.

"This was my mother's engagement ring," Mrs. McIntyre said. "I have always told Douglas that my eldest son must have it for the girl he marries. So, Abbie dear, I want your cousin Lorena to have this ring. I want you to give it to her today."

Abbie dropped the ring back into Mrs. McIntyre's palm as if it had burned her. "Oh, I couldn't!" she cried. "Please don't ask me to."

"Hush! Mr. Mac will hear you!" Mrs. McIntyre sat up and caught Abbie's hands pleadingly in hers.

"Don't you understand? I can't see Lorena myself. If my husband knew about this Southern girl and Douglas . . ." She shivered, leaving the sentence unfinished.

Again Abbie looked pleadingly at Stuart. He came over and took the ring from his mother.

"I think Mama is doing something impulsive, Abbie. She can't even know that Douglas would like this. But that's not your problem. Suppose I see you home, since I have to go over to the *Tribune* office soon. Perhaps we can present this to Lorena together."

Since Mrs. McIntyre seemed so determined, this was probably as good a way as any. The ordeal wouldn't be quite so bad if Stuart were there to see her through.

Mrs. McIntyre accepted the plan and a few moments later the two were walking across the snowy meadow together. Abbie could not help but remember that other time in April—such ages ago—when she had crossed this very stretch with Doug at her side. Life had seemed exhilarating then, as if something lovely were just beginning.

"I'm sorry about this," Stuart said as he helped her across the frozen brook. "Abbie, I'm sorry about a lot of things. I don't think I've done you a very good turn."

She shrugged lightly. "I don't know what you mean."

"I'm talking about that fine scheme of mine to get Lorena out of the picture."

"The only thing wrong with it was that I—just wasn't the right girl," Abbie said.

"I didn't consider your feelings at all at the time. I wasn't concerned with the possibility that you might be hurt."

Abbie managed a choked laugh. "I know. You were pretty single-minded about the whole thing. I knew right along I was a cog in the wheel of your plan."

"That does me no credit," Stuart said. "I can't tell you how sorry I am."

Abbie glanced at him in surprise. She had never known Stuart McIntyre to admit to a mistake before. He looked so grim and angry with himself that she slipped a hand through his arm to show her forgiveness.

"Let's forget about it," she said. "If I've been a goose it's my own fault. Tell me about your work and about Mr. Greeley."

He seemed glad enough to change the subject. "Mr. Greeley's wonderful. I hope you can meet him sometime. He's an individualist, of course. He goes around in a dingy white duster coat and shabby clothes. His spectacles are always sliding down his nose and he wears a wreath of thick whiskers all around his face. His expression is always so cherubic that he looks harmless as a baby. But he was one of the powers that helped to get Lincoln elected—once he'd decided to go over to Lincoln's side. Of course no one on the paper knows which way Mr. Greeley is going to jump next and it makes life exciting."

The rest of the way home they talked about the *Tribune* and Horace Greeley. At the Garretts' the talk with Lorena was apparently over. Abbie's father worked in his study, while her mother sat reading in the parlor. They found Lorena by herself in the dining room writing a letter. She still looked rebellious and had no welcome for them.

Stuart took his grandmother's ring from his pocket and laid it upon the letter Lorena was writing. She stared at it for a moment and then looked up at him questioningly.

"It's for you," Stuart said. "But don't think I'm going to put it on your finger. Mama wants you to wear it because it was her mother's engagement ring. She thinks Douglas would like you to have it."

A smile of delight lifted Lorena's lips. She took up the ring and slipped it onto her engagement finger, moved her hand about so that fire danced in the white stone.

"How sweet and thoughtful of your mama! Of course I'll love wearing it. I must go over right away to thank her."

"You'd better not," Stuart said brusquely. "When the story of what you did last night gets around the island, you aren't going to stand very high with my father. It's hard enough for him to accept that Douglas has gone over to the

Confederate side. So you'd better stay away from our house."

Lorena frowned at him. "Sometimes you're just plain mean to me, Stuart McIntyre!"

"Some day I may be even meaner." Stuart leaned his hands on the table and looked directly into her eyes. "Lorena, are you in love with my brother?"

Long lashes fluttered briefly over green eyes and her lips parted in a startled gasp. "Why—why, of course I am. I've promised to marry him when he comes home, haven't I? Why, Stuart honey, whatever do you think—"

"I'll tell you what I think," he said. "I think you're in love with the South truly and honestly. I think you're in love with the idea of sending another brave soldier off to fight for the South. Especially since he's one who has turned away from the North. But I don't know whether you love Douglas or not. When the time comes, I don't think you'll marry him. I'll give you the benefit of the doubt and grant that possibly you don't know enough about your own feelings. But these are things for you to think about as you wear that ring."

He went out of the room and Abbie hurried after him with only a backward glance for Lorena, who sat looking at the ring on her hand. At the front door Stuart turned with a wry smile for Abbie.

"I suppose I've said all the wrong things, but I had to say them. Have I made things hard for you again?"

"Of course not," Abbie told him. "I'm glad you talked to her the way you did."

Stuart's eyes were grave. "We don't want him hurt, do we, Abbie?"

She shook her head, sudden tears blinding her. She watched Stuart go down the steps and then blinked her eyes clear at the sight of a solemn delegation of five men and women coming up the walk. She knew the identity of each, though they were not close friends. These were dignitaries of the island and she knew that they had come to register a protest over Lorena's behavior of the night before.

20

Eighteenth Birthday

The year moved on through a quiet Christmas for the Garretts. Lorena's action had caused them considerable trouble and embarrassment and there were those on the island who had taken to ignoring them in church, passing them on the street without recognition. Roger Garrett did not mind and Rosa Garrett carried her head high, pretending that she did not see the slights.

Abbie herself might not have minded, for all her anger with Lorena. Like her father, she recognized the foolishness of those who turned their disapproval of Lorena upon the entire family. The real hurt came when Varina Phillips decided to break off all relationship with the Garretts and forbade Hannah to speak to Abbie at all. Since Bull Run, Mrs. Phillips had forgotten her previous sympathy toward the South. Hannah managed to disobey her aunt's orders whenever she met Abbie alone away from home.

Sometimes lately Hannah seemed terribly young to Abbie and she found herself recalling Stuart's words about trouble making one grow up quickly. No real trouble had touched

Hannah and she went right on being her lighthearted self. Now that there could be no more visiting back and forth, Abbie missed her friend's gaiety and bright optimism.

Lorena, at least, seemed somewhat chastened these days. Stuart had brought word from the *Tribune* that Charleston, after all, had not been fired upon by Yankee boats. The North was entirely innocent of causing the fires. They had sprung up and spread through a combination of unfortunate circumstances and, while the destruction was serious, Charleston could not blame the enemy. The truth made Lorena's behavior on the night of the ball seem all the more unjustified. Word from her brothers came through the blockade that their section of town had not been damaged, and even Lorena began to look back on her action with unaccustomed shame. What effect Stuart's words had on her Abbie could not know, but Lorena wore her ring proudly and spoke of Douglas often—as if to disprove his brother's accusation. Sometimes Abbie wondered if she had ever really known her cousin, or understood anything about her.

Abbie's birthday fell on a Saturday early in February. So much had happened in the intervening year that it was hard to believe that she was only eighteen and not several years older. Her mother gave her new sketching pads and paints. From her father she received a leather-bound set of poems by the Brownings. The romantic story of Robert Browning and Elizabeth Barrett had charmed Abbie and she was happy to have the volume. The surprise gift, however, came early in the afternoon, just when Abbie was starting off to pick up the mail.

Lorena hurried down the stairs with one hand behind her back just as Abbie reached for the knob of the front door.

"Abbie, I—here's something—for you," Lorena faltered and held out a small, tissue-wrapped package.

Somewhat disconcerted, Abbie took the small package and began to untie the blue ribbon that bound it. The doorbell rang before she had the wrappings loose, and she opened the door to admit Stuart McIntyre. He noted her bonnet and mantle and nodded in satisfaction.

"Just caught you, didn't I? I was down in the village and thought I might as well bring your mail since I was coming this way. There's something for you, Lorena."

Abbie saw the Canadian stamp on the envelope as he handed it to her cousin. It had been months since a letter had come by its circuitous route from Uncle Benton. Lorena took the envelope eagerly and hurried into the parlor with it to read it by herself.

Stuart fumbled in the pocket of his coat and drew out a package of his own, obviously book-shaped, and presented it to Abbie with a flourish.

"To Miss Abigail Garrett on the dignified occasion of her eighteenth birthday." Then he dropped his play-acting. "I thought you might like to have a copy of this."

Abbie set Lorena's package aside on the hall table for a moment and opened the book from Stuart. It was a beautifully bound copy of Tennyson's *Idylls of the King*.

While Abbie was thanking him, Lorena whirled into the hall, waving her letter excitedly. "Abbie, Stuart! My letter's from Papa and there's word in it about Douglas. Listen!"

Abbie saw that her cousin's hands were shaking as she tried to steady the paper to read the words aloud.

> Yesterday, Lorena, the young man of whom you have written me reached this camp. He has been commissioned as a lieutenant and is with a cavalry group. He appears to be a fine young man and you will be glad to know that he is enjoying the best of vigorous good health. He reports having been in several engagements, though none of great consequence . . .

Lorena's voice broke momentarily, then she controlled it and read on.

> . . . He has come through unscathed and is for the most part in good spirits. I believe he is troubled by something of an inner conflict, which is natural

enough under the circumstances. He cannot be entirely at peace over the action he has taken, though he seems to have moved to the side with which he is most in sympathy. Old ties, however, are hard to break.

He is eager for firsthand word from you and wanted to know from me how you were and whether you had written to me about him. I know many of our letters are lost in these times, for there are long silences between the letters I receive from you, as you report there are between mine. You may be able to reach him at the address which I will place at the end of this letter. No word from you has reached him so far, though he reports having written to you.

Lorena looked up from the page, her eyes stricken. "Of course I'd have written to him if I'd known where to write. How dreadful that his letters haven't reached me."

Abbie, listening, was happy over the news, yet puzzled too by her own reactions. Somehow the hurt she had felt for so long whenever Doug's name was mentioned had faded a little. She could be happy for news of him without feeling the old tug of jealousy and pain. The realization surprised her.

"Do something for me, Lorena," Stuart said. "Will you copy the parts of the letter that concern Douglas, so I can take them home for Mama to see? And of course the address."

"I'll do it right away," Lorena agreed and started upstairs.

Abbie turned quickly to pick up Lorena's package from the hall table. "Wait, Cousin Lorena. I haven't had time to look at your present yet."

Lorena paused halfway up the stairs and Abbie turned back the tissue to reveal an oval brooch of carved coral. She recognized it as one Lorena often wore and knew that it had belonged to their Southern grandmother.

"Your coral brooch!" Abbie said softly. "Lorena, you mustn't give me this."

Lorena looked down at her for a long moment. Then she turned without a word and ran the rest of the way upstairs. Abbie turned to Stuart.

"I can't figure her out. This pin is one of her treasures. Why should she give it to me?"

Stuart shrugged. "Maybe because of mixed feelings compiled of bits of guilty conscience, liking for you, disliking for herself, sense of duty, sentimentality, and goodness knows what else."

"I don't know," Abbie said. "I just don't understand her at all."

"Well, let's not worry about it. Since Saturday is my day off, how about celebrating your birthday by going skating, Abbie? I hear the ice is fine up at Silver Lake."

"I'd love to go," Abbie said quickly. "But, Stuart, do you suppose we could take Lorena along? I'd like to be nice to her after this. I've been teaching her to skate and she isn't at all bad at it. She's never been to Silver Lake."

"Bring her along," Stuart said, looking at Abbie somewhat quizzically. "Be back for you in half an hour."

When Abbie went to Lorena's door, her cousin agreed to go readily enough. Later, as the three bundled themselves into the small sleigh Stuart was driving, everything about Lorena seemed to be dancing with happiness. The change since word had come from Douglas was so marked that Abbie found herself thinking about it on the drive. Lorena's feeling at the moment was surely genuine, so Stuart must be wrong in his judgment of her.

Silver Lake was a lovely, woodsy spot high on the island off Richmond Turnpike. Trees and bushes crowded in to the lake's edge and during the summer it was a favorite place for boating. Today scores of skaters were out on the ice and the three could hear the swish of blades, the laughter of children, the sound of gay voices before they reached the lake.

Stuart helped the girls with their skates and took each by

an arm when they went out on the ice. Lorena was still uncertain on skates and unable to move as expertly as Abbie and Stuart. However, Stuart saw several young men he knew and it was easy enough to find a willing partner for Lorena. Then Stuart and Abbie crossed hands and set out around the pond together.

Abbie had skated for as long as she could remember, and she felt much more at home on the ice than she did on a dance floor. If it hadn't been for the nuisance of full, heavy skirts, she would have been able to skate as expertly as Stuart.

After a few quick rounds to warm up, they settled to a rhythmic pace in which it was possible to skate and talk at the same time.

"Have you noticed how Lorena took the news about Douglas?" Abbie asked. "I mean how excited and happy she seems?"

"I've noticed," Stuart said briefly.

"Maybe you were wrong about her that day. Maybe she does think a lot of Douglas."

"I'm sure she thinks she does."

Abbie was silent for a while after that, skimming along effortlessly, leaning into the turns. Stuart swung her to the side to miss three clowning youngsters piling up on the ice in their path, and Abbie followed his lead, but her thoughts were far away from Silver Lake.

She was still thinking about her own reaction to news of Douglas. For some time now she had been taking her hurt about him for granted. She turned away, wincing if Lorena spoke of him, tried not to think of him herself. But now definite word had come—word that asked about Lorena, not about Abbie. And Abbie Garrett puzzled over the fact that she had not recoiled with hurt, had felt no pang of jealousy or longing. Did what Stuart thought of Lorena apply instead to her? Had she been fooling herself all along in believing that she was in love with Douglas?

"Penny for your thoughts?" Stuart murmured. "I'm beginning to think you're not here at all."

She laughed and gave her attention to equaling Stuart's skill on skates, just to show him how very much she was there. But she did not tell him her thoughts. When they reached the Turnpike side of the lake they found that some boys had built a roaring bonfire on the bank and a number of skaters were crowding about it to warm cold-nipped fingers. Lorena had given up skating for the moment and was there beside the fire, with three admiring young men around her. She was fluttering her eyelashes at all three alternately and behaving to each in turn as if he were the only man on her horizon.

"So you think Lorena's thoughts are all for my brother Doug?" Stuart asked pointedly.

"I don't know," Abbie admitted. Somehow she wanted to be generous to Lorena today. "Perhaps she's just having fun. She hasn't had very much lately."

They climbed the snowy bank, teetering as their blades cut through the white crust. The fire was hot upon their faces and noisy in its crackling. As always, wherever one went these days, uniforms were in evidence. One of the boys talking to Lorena wore blue and she appeared to be teasing him about something.

Abbie turned uneasily from the sight. She had been pleased with Lorena's happiness over her news of Doug. She wanted Lorena to be whatever Doug thought she was.

"How is your father?" Abbie asked Stuart.

He pulled off his gloves and held his hands out to the blaze. "All the life seems to have gone out of him. He doesn't care about anything any more. He doesn't even get angry about the news in the papers."

"Does he mind that you aren't in uniform?" Abbie asked curiously.

"I wish he did," Stuart said. "He'd be acting more like himself. I suppose I'd even be happy to see him angry with me. As it is, he's fading away."

"Would it bring him to life if you enlisted?"

Stuart gave her a long look. "Trying to throw me to the army again?"

Abbie considered that. "It's just that I've been trying to think how I'd feel if I were a man. I've been wondering if I'd enlist."

"Would you, Abbie?"

"I don't know," she said honestly. "There are times when I get excited about the war. I hear a band playing, or see soldiers marching, and I think that if I were a man I'd want to be in there fighting for my country, and I'm angry with those who aren't. But when I think about bloodshed and killing—well, I only know how I feel about such things as a woman. It's hard to know how a man must feel."

"I know how I feel," Stuart said tersely. "Someone has to believe that wars must stop. There are less costly ways to settle differences."

"Papa believes that too," Abbie said. "Yet he went away to fight. Oh, I wish I knew the truth. I wish I could know inside me what was right."

Stuart began drawing on his gloves with sharp, angry tugs, but Abbie could not tell for whom his anger was meant. On the other side of the bonfire Lorena's laughter rang out, lighthearted and clear, and a slow, quiet anger began to burn in Abbie too. But hers was a personal anger. If Lorena proved that she did not deserve Doug McIntyre's love, Abbie Garrett would have a score to settle with her cousin.

Stuart, however, was not thinking of Lorena. "The time may come when the whole thing will be settled without our consent."

"What do you mean?"

"Mr. Curtis says there's talk in Washington about a draft. If the number of soldiers needed can't be raised through volunteers, men may be conscripted."

"Oh, but that's wrong!" Abbie cried. "No man should have to fight unless it's by his own choice."

"They're conscripting them in the South and I suppose wars must be won," said Stuart dryly. He raised one foot and crunched down into the snow with the sharp blade of a skate. "The first enthusiasm has died down up here. There isn't as much patriotism flying around as there was at first, and we just don't have enough men."

"Let's get back to the pond." Abbie held out her hand. She wanted to get away from Lorena's coquetry, wanted to flee from sobering thoughts and be lighthearted again in the old way.

Stuart roused himself and took her hand. Halfway down the bank Abbie paused, looking out over the bright picture spread below—the whiteness of snow and ice, silver of skates, the scarlet of a woolen scarf or striped stocking cap. And all around, like the frame to a painting, winter trees in somber brown.

"I love trees in winter," she said. "You can really see them then. When they're in leaf all that fragile tracery of the branches is lost. Stuart, it's such a beautiful world! Why can't we hold onto that?"

His hand squeezed hers briefly. "Keep seeing the beauty, Abbie. Never forget it's there."

Something in his tone made her turn to him wonderingly. For a moment, searching his face, she caught a look in it she had seen more than once in recent months. A look she did not understand. Then he laughed, and she could not be sure whether he was laughing at himself or at her.

Together they went back to the ice and put an earnest effort into their skating, as if by sheer exertion they could thrust away all matters that troubled them.

21

Soldier in Blue

Later that month came news of the first great victory of the North, the capture of Fort Donelson. In March the funny looking little *Monitor* sailed into Chesapeake Bay to meet the formidable Southern *Merrimac*. Neither vanquished the other, but the first battle of iron ships had taken place.

By the time the usual summer languor had settled down over Staten Island, chances for victory in the West looked imminent. Memphis and New Orleans were in Northern hands and, except for Vicksburg, the Mississippi River was practically open.

"Oh, let it be over soon!" Abbie prayed every night before she got into bed. For two months there had been no word of Douglas and she could not help a sense of foreboding. Lorena was confident that all was well and outwardly, at least, she appeared not to worry.

One Saturday afternoon in July Mrs. Garrett gave a tea for a few ladies who were her good friends. Lorena and Abbie were pressed into service to assist, and Abbie was in the act of passing a plate of ginger cookies to Mrs.

McIntyre, when she happened to look out the front window in time to see Stuart McIntyre coming up the walk. With him was a young man in the blue uniform of the Union army. Without stopping to think, Abbie gave the cookie plate into Mrs. McIntyre's hands and went into the hall, pulling the parlor door quietly shut behind her. When she reached the veranda Stuart was coming up the steps. Abbie glanced from him to the strange young man who remained behind on the walk. The soldier looked away uneasily under her intent gaze and Abbie turned to Stuart.

"What is it? What's happened?"

"Mama's here, isn't she?" Stuart asked. "Abbie, it's news of Doug. Not good news, I'm afraid. Can you find us a place to talk without disturbing your mother's party?"

Abbie stared at him for a moment, her heart thudding. Then she went to find her mother. Mrs. Garrett skillfully drew Mrs. McIntyre from the group and led her to Mr. Garrett's study.

"Bring him in, please," Abbie told Stuart, nodding at the soldier.

Stuart beckoned to the man in blue and he came into the house and followed the others to the study. Lorena, noting that something was up, caught Abbie's elbow questioningly.

"You'd better come too," Abbie said. "There's news about Doug."

She spent no more time on Lorena, but went quickly into the study, leaving her cousin to follow or not as she pleased. Lorena came into the room slowly and found a chair on the far side. She looked shaken and Abbie saw the flash of her ring as she put her left hand to her throat in a trembling gesture.

The young soldier, seen at close range, was white and weak.

"This is Corporal Flynn," Stuart said and mentioned the name of each woman in turn.

The corporal mumbled an acknowledgment, and Abbie saw that his main attention was fixed uncomfortably on Lorena. Stuart found him a chair and he sank into it gratefully.

"Corporal Flynn is from New Dorp," Stuart explained. "Suppose you tell these ladies your story, Corporal."

The soldier—he was hardly more than a boy—managed to take his eyes from Lorena's face.

"I was in the fighting down in Virginia a couple of months ago," he began. "There was a time when we weren't more than ten miles from Richmond, but we weren't strong enough to get through, and McClellan started us on a retreat to the James River. The roads were wretched and we had to go through swamps mostly, with the rebs right after us, so there was fighting all the time. I got a bullet through my foot and couldn't keep up with the others. I crawled up a bank and got behind some bushes, but it wasn't much shelter."

Mrs. McIntyre moved restlessly. "What of my son, young man? You've brought news of him?"

Abbie noted that her cheeks, which had once been so plump and pretty, had hollows in them.

"Let him tell it, Mama," Stuart said gently. "You'll want to know just what happened."

"It was your son found me there, ma'am," the soldier went on. "I had my gun, but it wasn't loaded. He was armed and he wore gray, so I thought my time was come. Out of the corner of my eye I could see his cavalry boots real close to me. I guess he'd lost his horse somewhere."

The self-consciousness seemed to fall away from the soldier as he forgot his listeners and lost himself in his account.

"I put my head down in my arms and just waited and I could hear all the noise and shouts and firing getting farther and farther away till it seemed like it was only we two alone in the world. Funny thing—there was a bird singing up in a tree. I kept thinking it was the last thing I'd ever hear. After a while when nothing happened I looked up and saw that Johnny Reb had sat himself down on the grass beside me and was just looking me over. He was a big fellow with the brightest red hair I ever saw."

"Douglas!" Mrs. McIntyre whispered.

The soldier nodded and went on. "He asked me how bad I was hurt and I knew by the way he talked that things were going to be all right. Reb or no, he wasn't going to shoot me. I told him I'd got it in the foot and couldn't walk.

"He said, 'Where're you from, soldier?' and I told him 'Staten Island,' and it was hard to believe, but he was from Staten Island too. He stood up and looked all around. Then he said maybe he could get me back within shouting distance of my own lines. If he'd left me I'd sure have died in the swamps. Well, ma'am, he hauled me up on his back and headed toward the fighting noises. When he stopped to rest, he'd kind of talk to me to keep my spirits up and make me forget I was thirsty and in pain. He told me his name and about his family and about the young lady he was going to marry when the war was over."

There was a choking sound from Lorena. The soldier looked at her briefly and then away.

"Well, he got me close enough so there were blue uniforms in sight. He put me down on the ground and told me to yell for help and then he started to sneak back toward his own lines. But I guess he didn't take three steps before a shot hit him and he went down like a log right out there in the open."

There were beads of sweat on the young soldier's face and Abbie felt a stab of pity for him, even as she hung tensely on his words.

"Honest, ma'am," he said weakly, "I'd have helped him if I could. But some of the boys in my own company came and carried me away. I tried to tell them about the reb, but they weren't worried about anybody in gray. They had enough trouble on their hands. But I remembered the location. I looked for trees and rocks and tried to get the picture right in my mind. When we got into camp that night I told the lieutenant about it. He was a good sort and he said he'd see what could be done. When daylight came, he and another fellow went back into neutral territory before the fighting started again. He thought he found the place where the rebel soldier was shot. Everything there was like I said.

But the soldier was gone. There was just an awful lot of blood on the ground."

The young man stopped and closed his eyes as Mrs. McIntyre began to sob softly. Lorena left her chair and went over to stand beside the older woman, who seemed to find comfort in clinging to her.

"We're proud of Douglas, Mrs. Mac," Lorena said. "And I think he'd like us to be proud of him."

Abbie gave her a quick look of surprise. She had not expected this sudden strength from Lorena. Then she turned back to the soldier.

"Is that all you ever found out?" she asked.

"Well, later on I heard a rumor. Somebody told me that a red-headed rebel soldier had been taken prisoner. But I never could find out if it was true, or if it was the one I knew. Anyway, I had to come and tell you about what had happened as soon as I could get around again. My wound wasn't bad, but I'd have sure died if it hadn't been for Doug McIntyre."

Abbie and Stuart exchanged glances and she knew they were thinking the same thing. Doug had been true to the code of honor he had held to even as a child. It was like him to have risked his life for the wounded enemy.

Mrs. McIntyre turned to her younger son, as she turned to him so often these days. "What are we to do? How can we find out?"

Stuart nodded his reassurance. "Mr. Curtis will help us. He'll know how to put through an inquiry. If Doug's a Union prisoner there'll be a way of finding him."

Mrs. Garrett had listened in silence to the soldier's report. Now she put an arm about Mrs. McIntyre's shoulders in a brief, comforting gesture before she went quietly back to the tea party in the parlor. Abbie heard her mother making excuses for Mrs. McIntyre, taking the attention of her guests so that the young soldier might leave the house without being noticed by the ladies. At the door Abbie thanked him warmly for what he had done.

"I'll keep in touch with you, if you don't mind, ma'am,"

he said. "I'd sure like to see that young fellow come through. She's a pretty girl he's going to marry. He talked about you too, Miss Abbie. I guess he felt you were close as a sister to him."

Abbie's eyes misted. "Thank you for telling me."

He went off down the walk, limping slightly, and Abbie returned to the study. Mrs. Garrett had brought Doug's mother a cup of hot tea and she was sipping it and weeping at the same time.

"I've no one to turn to now," she told her friend. "Mr. Mac has changed so—he doesn't care about anything any more. Now I have only Stuart. And Stuart's so young."

Nevertheless, when Stuart came to her side and suggested that they go home and tell his father about this, she rose as obediently as if she had been a child. Obviously she leaned on Stuart more than she realized.

After they had gone there was a moment in the hallway when Abbie was alone with her mother. Rosa Garrett pressed her cheek comfortingly against her daughter's.

"I know it's hard for you," she whispered. "But stay with Lorena for a little while. She needs someone now."

Abbie went back to the study where the French doors stood open upon the flowering garden. Lorena leaned in the opening of a door, staring out at the pattern of sunlight and shadow. She turned at the sound of her cousin's step and Abbie saw how upset she was. The moment of strength she had shown with Doug's mother had dissolved into grief.

"I sent him away," Lorena said miserably. "If he's dead, I'm to blame."

For just an instant Abbie wanted to agree with her, but she managed to check the impulse.

"Douglas had to do what he thought was right," she told the other girl. "Not you or anyone else could really affect that. Besides, he's not dead. I know he's not dead."

Hope came into Lorena's eyes. "Do you feel that, Cousin Abbie? Why do you feel that?"

Why did she feel it? She could not answer. She only knew that if Douglas lay dead somewhere on a battlefield she would know because a little of her heart would have died with him.

Yet later that night in the quiet of her own room, she faced the realization that her feelings about Douglas had truly changed. It had not hurt when the young soldier had told her that she was dear as a sister to Douglas. For he was dear to her as a brother was dear. She could still be impatient and angry with Lorena, but jealousy had gone out of her. She knew now that the hero worship of a little girl did not necessarily turn into the love of a woman. Her belief that it would had been romantic and story-bookish. It had not been real. Now she felt free, released. Her concern for Douglas' safety, his well-being, was as keen as ever, but it was no longer possessive.

In the days that followed, Mr. Curtis and even Mr. Greeley himself made an effort to gain some word of Stuart's brother, but week after week went by without news. The tremendous influx of sick and wounded, the extraordinary number of captured troops had resulted in a chaos in which a man could be lost for months unless he himself made his whereabouts known. The silence surrounding Douglas seemed ominous.

The fortunes of war had turned again, and all that had seemed hopeful to the North in the early summer had now melted into endless defeat. In Washington President Lincoln paced the floor of his study, pondering the document that lay upon his desk—the Proclamation of Emancipation. Many of those about him were against its release, and he himself was not satisfied that it was all he intended it to be. It would proclaim free the slaves in those states that were fighting the Union. It gave no promise of freedom to slaves in loyal states, lest such an act turn those states against the Union and bring it down to defeat. Final freedom for all slaves would have to wait till the war's end.

The President's avowed purpose was to save the Union. All else was secondary at the moment. He believed the Proclamation would help the cause, but he dared not release it in the face of continued defeat. "Give me a victory," he begged his generals. But the Confederate leaders were flinging the Union lines back again and again, and all the great power of the North was helpless in the face of such generalship.

The victory, when it came, was an indecisive one at Antietam Creek, but it was enough to cause Lincoln to announce that he would issue the Proclamation, to go into effect in January of the following year.

It was also during the month of September that first word came of Douglas McIntyre.

Abbie sat alone on the Garrett veranda, enjoying the gentle air of a September evening. Fall was the best season of all on Staten Island, she thought. The sultriness of summer was over, but the days were long and comfortably warm, yet with just a touch of asperity in the sea breeze that stung her into working as she had not worked all summer long.

Stuart opened the gate and came up the walk with a hurried stride that made Abbie start to attention.

"Something's happened?" she said.

"We know where Douglas is," he told her directly.

"I—I'll call Lorena." Abbie got up and went into the house. A moment later she was back on the veranda, her cousin at her side.

"There's no breaking this gently," Stuart told them. "Doug's in a prison hospital in Washington. He's not out of danger yet. He was wounded so badly that it was necessary to amputate his right leg."

Sickness flashed through Abbie like a knife. At her side she heard Lorena's moan and she put out an arm to catch her cousin as she slumped.

Stuart lifted her and laid her in the hammock. He stood for a moment looking down at long lashes against white cheeks.

Then he spoke curtly. "Get your mother to look after her, Abbie. She's just a little girl, really. I'm glad you're not the fainting sort. I need you for something important."

Abbie's father and mother took Lorena upstairs, and put

to bed. Abbie let the flurry about Lorena go on without her and turned questioningly to Stuart.

"You've got to help us," he said and she heard the grim note in his voice. "You know how Papa has been ever since Douglas left. Not even that story of Flynn's brought him back to life. He listened, but he didn't care. I don't think he wants to live any more. He's ill and he's given up what he cared about most—his oldest son. To him Douglas is already dead and there's nothing more to be done. But Doug's alive, Abbie. And we've got to get him home where we can take care of him, pull him through."

"What do you want me to do?" Abbie asked.

"Come over to our house and talk to Papa. We've told him that Doug's alive and he just acts as though he didn't hear us. Mama and I have tried everything we can think of."

"But what can I do that you can't?"

"He thinks of you as a daughter. He's always been fond of you. Perhaps you can make him want to do something. He's the only one who can pull the necessary strings to get Douglas paroled and sent home. We *must* wake him up. Please come, Abbie."

She hesitated a moment longer. Then she stepped to the door and called to her mother that she was going over to the McIntyres' for a little while.

September dusk lay upon the meadow, but an early moon hung in the sky to light their way. And this was a path they both knew well.

"Why do you suppose Doug never got in touch with us?" Abbie asked. "It doesn't seem like him not to let us know where he was."

"I'm not sure," Stuart's voice was grave. "Maybe because of his feeling that his father had disowned him. His leg, perhaps. Lorena. I don't know. The fact that he didn't worries me."

She thought about that as they followed the path. Douglas had always been so vigorous, so ready for action. Not to be able to get around as he had before might be very hard for him to accept. But between two who loved each other, such a thing should not matter. If *both* of them loved. Oh, Lorena had to stand by Douglas now!

"At least they have anesthetics here in the North," Stuart went on. "In the South they have to do without. But the important thing is that he's alive. We can't fail him, Abbie." Then he spoke the very thought that had been in her own mind. "Do you think Lorena will stand by him?"

"She's got to!" Abbie said fiercely. "We'll make her!"

22

Across the Meadow

Lights burned in the dining room of the McIntyre house. That was the room in which Mr. McIntyre spent most of his time these days. He sat bundled in his rocker as usual, a heavy blanket over his knees, his eyes fixed on nothing, waiting only, it seemed, for a release from a life that had become meaningless.

Across the room Mrs. McIntyre knitted in silence. Word that her son was alive had given her new hope, but she was helpless to deal with her husband's indifference.

On the threshold of the room Abbie paused uncertainly. This was a task for which she had no confidence, and she would have turned back if it had not been for Stuart's hand pushing her on.

"A visitor to see you, Papa," Stuart said.

Abbie took a deep breath and went into the room. "Hello, Mr. Mac," she said as she took her old place on the hassock beside him.

He brightened faintly as he always did at the sight of her, but for a moment she could say nothing more because of the hurt in her throat. Hurt that was for Douglas, and for his father, who had grown so shriveled and thin. She turned and managed a wavery smile for Mrs. McIntyre. Stuart stood behind his father's chair where Abbie could look up at him for reassurance and help. He nodded to her gently.

She reached out and took Mr. McIntyre's veined hands in hers, held them tightly. "Stuart has told me the wonderful news, Mr. Mac—that you know where Douglas is."

If the name had meaning for him, Abbie could not tell it. He moved no muscle. His thin hands lay limp in hers.

"I'm talking about your son Douglas, Mr. Mac," Abbie persisted.

His tight lips barely formed the words. "I have only one son. "He is in this room now."

"Listen to me," Abbie said. "Douglas is alive. But he has had a very bad time and he is still not out of danger. Stuart has told you that he is in a prison hospital and if you've heard the stories you know what such places are like, whether in the North or the South."

One hand twitched in hers and she went on quickly.

"You know why he was taken prisoner. He was trying to save the life of a Northern soldier who was wounded. Then Doug was wounded himself. Wounded so terribly, neglected so long, that his right leg had to be amputated. And he may still die if no one helps him."

Mr. McIntyre withdrew his hands from hers and put them on the arms of his chair, his eyes staring at nothing, his face expressionless. For a moment longer Abbie watched him pleadingly. Then indignation began to rise within her. He was Douglas's father, but she could no longer pity him. All the sympathy in her was for the boy who had been her playmate and who now lay far away on some miserable prison bed. Douglas had deserved all things that were good and bright and gay. But he had only Lorena, who perhaps was vain and shallow, and a father who had turned against him.

"You don't deserve a son as fine as Douglas!" Abbie cried hotly. "You're hard and selfish, and if he dies because of you, I—I'll—" she broke off and dropped her head upon her arms to cry as helplessly as a child. Stuart should never have brought her here. She had said all the wrong things, but she didn't care. All the while in her mind's eye there was the picture of Douglas running across the meadow on two good legs, leaping the brook, climbing the path to their Highland cave. A picture that made her heart ache.

Mrs. McIntyre sat in shocked silence. Stuart waited, watchful and quiet. Abbie wept on, her head on her arms. After a time a thin hand touched her tousled hair, smoothed it gently.

"You love him very much, don't you?" Mr. McIntyre said.

At the gentleness of his tone, Abbie raised her head, her face flushed and wet with tears. "I love him better than you do. I'd do anything I could to help get him home. I'd forgive him for anything—no matter what he had done. What right have you to disown him because he is so like you?"

"So like me?" Mr. McIntyre echoed the words.

"You used to be able to give yourself to a cause you believed in. And that's what Douglas has done. I hope he hasn't given up the way you have. I hope he'll come home and make a good life for himself in spite of you."

"What do you think I can do?" Mr. McIntyre asked softly.

Abbie leaned toward him urgently. "Get him paroled to you. Get up out of that chair and do what has to be done. You're his father. It's not as if he were a Southern boy. Oh, Mr. Mac, bring him home!"

"Bring him home for you, Abbie?"

"For me and for Stuart and for his mother. But most of all for you. For his father."

There was a long moment of silence, while Mr. McIntyre stared with unseeing eyes at the plaid blanket covering his knees. Stuart waited tensely, Mrs. McIntyre stilled her knitting needles and Abbie held her breath. Through the window came the distant hoot of an owl and the house creaked uneasily.

Then with a sudden, impatient gesture, Mr. McIntyre flung the blanket from his knees. "Get that hot thing away from me. Stuart, your arm. I can write better at the table. Bring me paper and pen, Miss Abigail Garrett. You know where they're kept."

Abbie flew to the desk in the parlor and was back in a moment, hardly daring to believe in what was happening. Mr. Mac's back had straightened and there was something of the old fire in his eyes.

"That boy of mine has been an utter fool, but I'm going to write and tell him that there's a girl here who needs him home."

In her eagerness Abbie did not grasp the meaning of his words at once. When she did and started to speak, Stuart shook his head at her.

"Better not mention any names, Papa," Stuart suggested. "A young woman likes to speak for herself."

Mr. McIntyre nodded wisely and picked up the pen. "What time is it, boy? I've a lot of letters to write tonight."

Stuart gave him the time and Abbie said good night gently and took her leave. Stuart came with her to see her home across the meadow. The moment they were away from the house she burst into words.

"Stuart, you should have let me stop him. It isn't fair to fool him this way."

"Anything's fair just now," Stuart said. "It's you that Papa wants Douglas to marry. If we threw Lorena at him now we might lose all the gain we've made."

That was true, as she had to admit, and nothing mattered more than getting Douglas home.

"It won't be altogether a lie, Abbie," Stuart said. "There will be a girl waiting for him, won't there? You'd never let him down because of—of what's happened."

She glanced at him uneasily, but the moonlight was pale and his face lay in shadow. Stuart had no knowledge of how her affection for Douglas had changed into something different. If she told him now, he would think—why, he would think her no better than Lorena. He would believe it was because of Doug's leg.

He repeated his question insistently. "Would *you* let him down, Abbie?"

"Of course not! But, Stuart, it's Lorena he wants. I wouldn't do. Why, I wouldn't do at all."

"I wonder," Stuart said. "He may come home believing no woman could love him and if Lorena throws him over . . ."

Abbie was silent and a little frightened. Invisible threads had begun to bind her. She walked more quickly, as if to fling off their cobweb touch. Above them on the hillside someone was singing a melancholy tune of the camps—a man's voice alone.

> . . . Give us a song to cheer
> Our weary hearts, a song of home
> And friends we love so dear.
> *Tenting on the old camp ground.*

"Thanks for coming tonight, Abbie," Stuart said. "I thought you could wake Papa up if anybody could. Abbie, you know something? You're quite a girl."

23

Soldier in Gray

Christmas had come and gone before Douglas McIntyre returned to Staten Island. In January of 1863 government red tape wound itself out and Stuart and his mother set off by train to Washington to bring him home. On the day of his return Hannah Phillips brought the news to the Garretts'.

In the Garrett parlor it was cozy and warm before the fire, though snow blew thick against the windowpanes. Mrs. Garrett sat with a book in her hands, while Abbie and Lorena played checkers at the fireside, the inevitable bowl of popcorn between them. Since the first news of Douglas had reached her, Lorena's moods had alternated between lightheartedness and long spells of being subdued and withdrawn.

After recovering from her first shock, she would not talk about Douglas at all. Abbie had tried to force the issue and find out what her cousin truly felt, but Lorena was like quicksilver these days, slipping away from under Abbie's hands if she sought to catch and hold her. Abbie knew that she had written to Douglas within the first week or two after word had come. What she had said Abbie had no idea, but the fact remained that no answering letter had come from Douglas, though Lorena wrote again. Mostly Lorena tried to evade all dangerous issues, as if she were postponing them until such time as she would be forced to meet them. Abbie had no confidence in her at all.

When Hannah rang the doorbell, Abbie left the checker game to find her friend on the veranda, stamping snow from her boots, patting a crust of flakes from her bonnet. Hannah started talking the moment the door opened.

"Abbie, I just saw the McIntyre sleigh coming from the Factoryville landing. Stuart and Mrs. Mac were in it and Douglas was sitting between them."

So the moment had come. The moment which they had all waited for so anxiously. She let Hannah run on as she led her into the parlor.

"Doug's home," she said softly to her mother and Lorena, without breaking the flow of Hannah's words. Lorena made a sudden movement with her hand that swept a red king from the board.

"You'd never know him," Hannah wailed. "Of course with the snow and his being all bundled up, I couldn't see him very well. But his cheek bones stick out and his eyes look sunken—almost like an old man's. And he only twenty, Abbie!"

Sometimes, Abbie thought impatiently, Hannah could be maddeningly like her aunt.

"Did you speak to him at all?" Abbie asked.

"Well, I called to them from the walk, but the sleigh didn't stop and Douglas didn't even look at me. But Stuart saw me. That's why I'm here. Stuart shouted to me to let you know and to tell you to come over whenever you could. I yelled after them that I'd go tell you right away. And here I am."

"It's nice to see you again, Hannah, after all this time," Mrs. Garrett said, her serenity calming Hannah. "Do come over here by the fire and get warm. How is your Aunt Varina?"

Abbie was grateful for the way her mother had quietly stopped Hannah's outpouring over Douglas. She looked at Lorena and saw something dark and frightened in her eyes. But Hannah could not be kept away from the main topic for long. When she had disposed briefly of her aunt's excellent health, she turned to Abbie again.

"You'll go over to the McIntyres', won't you? I mean you'll go over this afternoon?"

Abbie looked at her mother and Mrs. Garrett nodded gently. "I think you might, Abbie. Not to stay for long, of course. Douglas will be weary from his journey."

"I wish I could go with you," Hannah said wistfully. "But I'd better get home right away. Abbie, do you think Aunt V. will ever get any sense?" She glanced hesitantly at Abbie's mother. "If *you* could talk to her some time . . ."

Mrs. Garrett shook her head. "When Varina Phillips is ready to be friendly, I will welcome her in my house. But I'm afraid I can't seek her out under the circumstances."

"I suppose not." Hannah sighed. "Well, I'll run along now. I just don't dare stay."

When her friend had gone, Abbie returned to the parlor. "Mama, do you really think it will be all right for me to go over to the McIntyres' now?"

Mrs. Garrett did not answer at once. Thoughtfully she put her marker between the pages and closed the book in her lap. "I have a feeling that Douglas will want to see you both as soon as possible. He will need reassurance at this time."

"See us both?" Abbie repeated, while Lorena stared at her aunt.

"Of course he will want to see Lorena."

"Oh, no, Aunt Rosa!" Lorena cried shakily. "I can't go. I'm scared. Scared to death."

Mrs. Garrett held the girl with her steady gaze and would not spare her. "What are you afraid of, Lorena?"

"Oh, don't you see? What if I went over there and took one look at him and then fainted dead away? Think how awful that would be for him. I don't want to hurt him, Aunt Rosa."

"And how will he feel if Abbie goes alone and has to make excuses for you?"

"But how can I know how Douglas feels about me? He never wrote. He never answered my letters."

"You have to make allowances for that," Mrs. Garrett said. "No matter what you wrote him, he may not believe in words on paper the way he'll believe in your presence."

"No—I can't!" Lorena turned away to stare into the fire. Behind her Mrs. Garett's voice went on relentlessly.

"You're a Southern girl, Lorena. Douglas went away to fight for the South. You can't fail him now."

"Do you think I haven't told myself all those things?" Lorena cried. "And it doesn't make any difference in the sickness I feel inside."

"In the South today," Mrs. Garrett said, "women have stopped being helpless. There are women I know, and girls as young as you, working in hospitals under dreadful conditions. They're scrubbing floors and emptying slops and sitting by the bedsides of men who are dying of terrible wounds. It's time for you to grow up, Lorena. You've been a spoiled little girl long enough."

Lorena turned toward her aunt indignantly, but Mrs. Garrett went on without waiting for her to speak.

"If you do faint, it won't matter. Douglas may be moved by your depth of feeling. That is, if you have any depth of feeling. Have you, Lorena?"

Listening, Abbie felt almost sorry for Lorena. Her gentle mother could be as unyielding as granite when the occasion arose. Yet Lorena had just this sort of straight talk coming to her. She couldn't go on running away from the issue of Douglas forever.

For a long moment Lorena did not answer. Then she lifted her chin with an air of resolution. "All right, Aunt Rosa, I'll try."

Snowdrifts piled the meadow so they had to take the long way around by the Shore Road. For the most part they walked on the well-trodden road, stepping to the side only when a sleigh went by. The wind was at their backs so it was possible to talk as they walked along. Lorena would probably have been glad for silence, but Abbie could not help following the line of questioning her mother had begun.

"You never answered Mama's question, Lorena. Are you in love with Douglas? Do you still mean to marry him?"

Lorena moved her head helplessly from side to side: "I *did* mean everything. I had the most wonderful feeling about him when he went away, Abbie. I was so proud to be engaged to him. And I thought about our life together when he would come home. But the things I loved about him were all that he was when he went away. How can I know how I feel about him now? Or how he feels about me?"

Abbie, who knew well enough that feelings could change and that growing up sometimes brought change with it, had no answer for her cousin.

"I just know that we mustn't hurt Douglas now," she told Lorena. "Until he's well and strong again we have to be there for him to count on."

To Abbie's surprise, Lorena slipped a hand through her arm. "I want to do that, Cousin Abbie. Help me to do it."

"I'll try," Abbie said, touched in spite of herself. There were times when Lorena could be so sweetly engaging that Abbie was drawn to her.

By the time they went up the front steps of the McIntyre house each had need for the other. The ordeal of meeting Douglas was hard for Abbie too. It was so important not to fail him. But if he had changed, how could they be sure what he wanted, or what he expected of them?

Stuart met them at the door and took their things. His eyes searched Lorena's face.

"Do you think you can keep from doing that flop-over trick of yours?" he asked.

"I'll try, Stuart. Oh, I'll try!" Lorena said.

Stuart glanced briefly at Abbie. "You'll find him different. Don't expect too much right away."

"Your father—?" Abbie questioned.

"He's being fine," Stuart said. "To listen to Papa, you'd

think Doug had fought for the North and licked the enemy singlehanded.''

"Then everything's going to be all right," said Abbie.

"I don't know," Stuart said. "Come see for yourself."

The others were in the dining room and Douglas sat at the table where he'd played games as a child. A steaming bowl of soup was before him. Mr. McIntyre stood before the window, watching the storm. He turned as Stuart ushered the two girls into the room, and greeted them soberly.

Abbie felt Lorena's hand heavy on her arm and glanced at her cousin. But though Lorena was pale, she moved without wavering as Abbie led her across the room to Douglas. A pair of new crutches rested against a chair, but Douglas was hidden from the waist down by the dining table.

Abbie saw at once why Hannah had been shocked by his appearance. His normally high color had paled to a pasty gray and the flesh was gone from his cheeks, leaving the bone structure marked. His blue eyes seemed to have darkened and they looked out from deepened sockets. Worst of all, there was no smile on his mouth as he looked up at them.

Abbie sought a little desperately to fill the silence that had fallen upon the room. "Douglas, it's good to have you home! We've missed you so. Nothing's the same with you gone. It's no fun climbing the hills and—" she stopped, appalled by her own words.

"You'll excuse me if I don't get up?" Douglas said and the words sounded stilted after Abbie's painful outburst.

Lorena slipped her hand from Abbie's arm and moved toward Douglas of her own accord. Abbie knew she would have gone into his arms at a sign from him, but he held back, watching her almost suspiciously. Then, as if he had no further interest in her, he lifted his spoon and gave his entire attention to the bowl of soup before him.

Mrs. McIntyre touched her son's shoulder gently, tears in her eyes. "He's very tired, girls. A few days of good food and rest and he'll feel better."

Douglas said nothing. Mr. McIntyre's bewilderment was

evident as he looked anxiously at Abbie. This silent, almost surly, boy at the table was someone he did not know how to deal with. His look indicated that he expected something of Abbie.

"We just came over to give you our greetings," Abbie explained feebly. "We—we couldn't wait till tomorrow. But we'll come again as soon as Doug is rested. There's so much to talk about."

She hated herself for her faltering words and sense of restraint. She knew that Doug's father expected some gesture of affection toward his son—some showing of love. And suddenly she knew she must give it. No matter how strange he seemed, this was Douglas; and, if Lorena was going to be held off by his forbidding manner, she must not be. She reached for the spoon in his hand, put it back in the plate and put her arms about him, kissing him warmly on the cheek. Her tears were wet on his face as well as her own and she drew back, laughing a little, reaching for her handkerchief.

"This time I have my own," she said.

Douglas held himself stiffly as she touched him. "Don't cry over me. I'm all right."

But he wasn't all right. She knew that.

"We'll go now," Abbie said steadily. "But we'll come again soon."

Stuart saw them to the door. "Thanks for trying, Abbie. You too, Lorena. At least you didn't go to pieces. But now perhaps you see what I mean."

"We do see," Abbie said gravely.

24

Stray Dog

Spring was late that year, and snow lay on the fields and hilltops of Staten Island clear into March. Not until May did sunshine change dead browns into green life and warm the azalea bushes into flaming bloom.

By that time food and rest had brought Douglas back to at least a semblance of his former physical appearance. He was no longer pale and sunken-eyed. And he was learning to handle his crutches with greater ease. But he was still far from being healthy in spirit. Nowadays he seemed to welcome Abbie's company more than he did Lorena's, and Abbie gave herself unstintingly to his need.

Because he had fought on the Southern side, there was growing feelings against him in the neighborhood. Occasionally small boys gathered in the roadway to shout insults, and there was a marked coolness toward him on the part of their more genteel elders. The rougher adult element was inclined to glower at sight of him and mutter beneath its breath, so Douglas went abroad little. All this increased his despondency, though Abbie tried to cheer him by reading to him, or walking with him in the garden, setting her pace to match his slow, painful movement. The sight of his pinned-up trouserleg no longer stabbed her. She was far more troubled by the inner change.

She talked to Stuart about him one day, and Stuart gave her his own explanation.

"It's easy enough to see what has happened to Doug. He was born to a hero's role. He always reveled in his strength and good health even when he was a boy. He has always been in the thick of action. Now he's a bystander who can't participate. He can't accept that or live with it."

"But why must he be so bitter toward everyone else? He used to be kind and considerate. The change doesn't become him."

"For one thing," Stuart said, "he has an exaggerated fear of pity. He's built up the conviction that a girl like Lorena could never feel anything but pity for him now. Which, unfortunately, is probably true. You're the only one he trusts, Abbie. He knows you haven't changed and that you like him for himself. I don't know what he'd do without you."

Abbie stirred uneasily. Everything—everyone—from Mr. Mac to Stuart, seemed to be pushing her toward Douglas. She was beginning to feel caught by shadowy threads that were strong as steel. If *she* let Douglas down there would be nothing left for him. She knew she mustn't let that happen, no matter what sacrifice she had to make. But sometimes the prospect frightened her.

One afternoon Lorena came home from a visit to the McIntyres', her eyes bright with unshed tears and the diamond solitaire, which she had dutifully worn till now, gone from her finger.

"I gave it back to him!" she told Abbie stormily as she came up the veranda steps and dropped into the hammock. "He's changed, Abbie. He doesn't need me any more. He taunted me and said horrid things—the sort of things Stuart says sometimes. Only I never mind when it's Stuart. In Douglas it's ugly and bitter."

"And you were glad to give him back his ring?" Abbie asked steadily.

Lorena flashed her a defiant look. "Why shouldn't I be? He doesn't want me around—he'd rather be with you. There's no use trying any more."

And thereafter she ceased all visits to the McIntyres'.

Douglas appeared to take Lorena's return of the ring calmly enough. It was as if he were relieved to have something he had expected over and done with. But the bitterness in him did not lessen and his tendency to say sharp, cutting things increased. Listening to him, Abbie could hardly believe that this was her old friend.

Only once did he speak of those terrible days after he was wounded, and then words poured out, as if by talking about what had happened he could free himself a little of the torturing memory.

Abbie closed her eyes, listening, and through his words she could see and feel as vividly as if she had been there herself. He had been carried from the place where he had fallen and taken to an old barn that had been pressed into use to harbor the wounded. He had been just another piece of senseless cordwood to those who handled him, and he had been left like cordwood at the door of the overcrowded barn. Some of the wounded had been lucky enough to be wrapped in blankets, or even scraps of rag carpet. There had been no covering for him. The wounded of North and South had been piled in the barn without distinction that night, and their moans and screams of pain had been terrible to hear.

The night turned stifling hot and the swamp mosquitoes swept down in droves upon the helpless victims. After a while the darkness was split by lightning and it began to rain.

"I was right where water from the barn roof dripped down on my face," Doug said. "There were men on either side of me and I couldn't roll away from that dripping stream of water. No one cared. There was too much suffering all around us. Nothing could be done."

The chilling, monotonous drip that could not be escaped

was harder to endure than all else. Later, in fever and delirium, he had been lifted ungently into a wagon and driven over miles of rough country road, his wound a torment at every jog and jolt. The boy next to him had died that night.

Doug's voice broke for a moment and then he reached out to clasp Abbie's wrist in a grip that hurt.

"Go on hating war, Abbie," he said. "It's not drums and bugles and flags flying. It's dirt and lice and boredom and waste. And it's men crying and screaming and water dripping in the night."

After that he never spoke of his experience again.

Despite her personal problems, a good part of the time Abbie found herself more greatly concerned with the larger problems of the entire country. Everyday affairs went on, of course. Life in its less significant aspects continued, regardless of the war, but always the shadow was there, ready to engulf heart and spirit at any moment. These were dark days for the North.

The bloody battle of Chancellorsville had been fought and lost, though the Confederates had sustained a great loss of their own in the fighting. The Southern hero, Stonewall Jackson, had been shot down in error by men of his own side and had died the next day. Early in June Lee crossed the Potomac, marched his army across Maryland and entered the state of Pennsylvania. For the first time fighting had been brought to Northern soil.

The conscription of soldiers in the North was now impending. All appeals for volunteers had failed to raise a sufficient army. A draft seemed the only solution. In New York the mutterings against such an act were growing apace, and there was the possibility of local trouble if a draft was actually put into effect.

One day in late June Abbie and Douglas sat on a bench in the McIntyre garden. Abbie had been reading aloud an exciting story of love and intrigue and breathless adventure. Yet her voice droned on lazily and her mind did not follow the story. She was thinking of Lorena.

Her cousin's decision to see no more of Douglas McIntyre had not made Lorena happy. She seemed more petulant than ever these days, more bored with her existence.

Doug's voice broke suddenly in upon her reading. "Abbie, you've read that same paragraph over twice. If you're tired, just stop. I'm not listening anyway."

Abbie sighed and let the book fall into her lap. She was beginning to feel hopeless about Doug. There seemed to be no way to show him how little he was doing for himself. He was fast becoming a tyrant of an invalid, and often Abbie found herself wincing at the surly tone of voice in which Douglas addressed his mother. In fact, he was more or less rude to everyone these days. It was as if he had to pay the world back for something it had done to him. Stuart was the only one who would take nothing of this sort from him. The first time Abbie heard Stuart lash out at his brother, she had been shocked and indignant. But now she wondered if perhaps that wasn't what he needed. She could even sympathize a little with Lorena's action. But still she could not bring herself to be unkind to him, to criticize him in any way. Understanding the reasons behind his behavior, she could not censor him. How could she know how she would have behaved in his place?

"Look," he said, breaking in on her thoughts again, "there's some female coming toward the house. Go meet her, Abbie, and steer her away from me. I don't feel like being tea-party polite to a staring old woman."

In the old days he'd never ordered people around the way he did now, and for just an instant Abbie felt like telling him she would stay right where she was and do nothing. Then she realized that she would simply be indulging her own disgruntled temper and went to meet the middle-aged woman who was coming up the walk.

She was someone Abbie had never seen before. She wore a drab brown dress and bonnet, but the pointed little face set in the frame of the bonnet was lively and eager in its expression, the brown eyes earnest.

"Good afternoon," Abbie said politely. "Are you looking for Mrs. McIntyre. Perhaps I can—"

The little woman gave her a bright smile, but her gaze
had sped past Abbie to the man on the bench in the garden,
with his crutches beside him.

"That's young Mr. McIntyre, isn't it?" she asked.
"Douglas McIntyre?"

"Why, yes," Abbie said, "but if you don't mind—"

The little woman brushed past without the slightest
attention to her words and went directly to Douglas.

"I've been meaning to come for so long," she told him.
"But I've been ill and I've only been able to get out again
lately. As soon as I got my walking legs back I had to come
to see you."

Douglas sat where he was. The effort to get up when a
lady approached him was too great these days and he
seldom troubled. Now he looked with frank distaste at the
woman before him. However, if she noted the lack of
welcome in his manner, it seemed not to matter to her in the
slightest. To Abbie's astonishment, she bent and kissed
Douglas on the forehead.

"I had to do that," she said and Abbie saw that tears had
come into her eyes. "I haven't any other way to thank you
for saving my boy's life. I'm Mrs. Flynn."

Abbie caught her breath and watched Douglas anxiously.
Oh, he had to soften now. If anyone could reach him,
certainly it would be this grateful mother.

"Saving his life was somewhat expensive for me, Mrs.
Flynn," Douglas said harshly.

The little woman winced, but she did not shrink from his
words. "I know," she said simply. "I'd give my life gladly
if it would restore your leg."

Douglas had the grace to look ashamed of his own words.
He hesitated a moment and then held out a hand to her.
"Don't mind what I say, Mrs. Flynn. I've developed a
terrible disposition lately. It's good of you to come to see
me. How is your son doing these days?"

Mrs. Flynn blinked the tears from her eyes. "He's back in the fighting again. But he's still alive, thanks to you."

Douglas smiled wryly. "That wasn't much of a turn I did for the South, was it? Saving a Union soldier so he could go back and fight again."

"It was the sort of turn I hope my boy would do if he were in the same position," Mrs. Flynn said quietly.

Douglas looked up into her face for a moment and then he reached for his crutches. "My mother and father will want to meet you. Let me take you to them."

Abbie ran ahead to open doors, to summon the elder McIntyres. She wished Stuart had been home from the office to see that Douglas could still behave like a gentleman when the occasion arose. If he could rouse himself like this even once in a while, there was still hope.

After Mrs. Flynn had left, Abbie told Douglas that she was going home. To her surprise he came with her to the door—an unusual effort for him to make these days. There was still something of shame in him as he looked at her.

"Abbie, have I turned into a monster? The thing I said this afternoon to that poor woman!"

"It was pretty awful," Abbie agreed. "If you hadn't changed your manner I think I'd have done what Lorena did—I'd have gone home and never come to see you again. I felt like it."

A dark flush had come into Doug's face, but he did not avoid her eyes. "I know when I'm being poisonous. Yet I go right ahead at the next chance and try to hurt the other person. I know how many times I've hurt you, Abbie."

Abbie made no denial. She had a feeling that this moment of confession might do more for Douglas than anything that had happened since he had come home.

"What about Lorena?" she asked. "You've hurt Lorena too."

He stiffened. "I'd rather hurt her than have her weeping over me and playing the ministering angel. Do you think I could stand that—feeling the way I do about her?"

So now it was out—the truth. And there was no answer

she could give him. He had to become strong enough to live with the truth, but that was something he would have to do inside himself. No one else could do it for him.

"Let me see you home, Abbie," he said.

She suppressed her first impulse to protest. The trip across the meadow would be a rugged one for him just now. He had never ventured more than a block from home and then only over the smoothest stretches of road. But she knew, somehow, that the physical difficulty of crossing the meadow was nothing if only he decided to make the effort of spirit it required.

"That will be fine," she told him warmly.

So back across the meadow they went, Douglas swinging himself along awkwardly on his crutches, Abbie walking slowly at his side. He was tired long before they reached Bard Avenue, but Abbie made no suggestion that he rest. There had been too much babying of Douglas McIntyre. The time had come for him to do something hard for himself. Her one hope now was that Lorena would not appear to spoil everything.

But Abbie saw her when they reached the street. Her cousin was pushing herself idly back and forth in the hammock on the Garrett porch. Abbie wondered if she could say good-bye to Douglas at the gate, send him away before anything happened. But he had obviously seen Lorena; and, since he was not frightened into retreat by her, Abbie said nothing.

They had crossed the road when Lorena heard them and looked up. She sprang to her feet, ran to the door and pulled it open. In another moment she would have fled inside the house, but in that moment an outcry arose on Bard Avenue.

Up the street from the Shore Road pounded a burly, red-faced fellow, waving a cudgel and shouting angrily as he ran. Ahead of him yapping in terror limped a little brown dog. Abbie took in the significance of what was happening at a glance. The man was the dog tax collector, and she knew it was his duty by law to kill every dog he caught which did not have a license. That was what that knotty club was for. It was a horrible law and had caused much indignation, but the man with the club was well within his rights.

Lorena recognized only the danger to the dog and in the same instant forgot Douglas completely, forgot her own intended flight. She whirled down the steps and into the street, hoops abouncing. She flew toward the terrified little dog and held out her arms. Like every dog that came near her, this one recognized a friend and champion. He leaped into her arms and she held his dirty little body against the white fichu that topped her frock. He whined and licked her cheek and she held him tight.

But the dogcatcher had no intention of accepting such interference as this. He was obviously a bully and this particular cur had aroused his wrath. He advanced upon Lorena threateningly and would have torn the dog from her arms if she had not fled toward Douglas, crying out for help.

"Douglas! Don't let him! Douglas, help me, help me!"

Douglas stepped between Lorena and the dogcatcher. Balancing himself on one crutch and his good leg, he raised the point of the other crutch and thrust it forcibly into the fellow's shoulder. It caught the dogcatcher unaware and it must have hurt, but it only enraged him further and did not stop his assault. He seized the crutch and jammed it back against Douglas' chest. Doug struggled futilely for his balance and then went over backward on the bank at the side of the road.

The dogcatcher stood above him threateningly. "You dirty reb. That'll teach you to interfere with an officer of the law."

He turned back to the girls, but Abbie saw that in the commotion the dog had disappeared.

Lorena stood her ground, though she was trembling. "I let him go. You can chase him through the woods if you like. You—you butcher!"

The man glanced toward the place where the trees and

brush crowded thick along the road and then back at
Lorena. "I ought to have the law on you for this."

Lorena looked him up and down with loathing and his
eyes fell before her unwavering gaze, but he stood his
ground angrily.

Abbie wished she were big enough and strong enough to
go in for a little bloodshed herself at that moment. Once
Douglas could have given the fellow the beating he
deserved, but now Doug was helpless. He could not have
chosen a more humiliating way to show himself at a
disadvantage before Lorena. All the good that had been
done by Mrs. Flynn's visit, by his successful effort in
crossing the meadow had been undone by the thrust of one
brutal hand. Abbie glanced at him unhappily and saw that
he had struggled to a sitting position.

Lorena stayed where she was, but she looked uncertainly
toward Douglas, who had begun to inch his way along the
ground toward the fence beside her. Abbie saw what he
intended and rushed to help him up, but he pushed her
away. Dragging his crutches in one hand, he grasped the
bars of the fence and pulled himself erect so that he stood
beside Lorena. There was sweat on his forehead and his lips
were white, but there was a light in him Abbie had not seen
since the night he went away to war. As even the dogcatcher
watched, startled, Doug let go of the fence, got one crutch
into place beneath an armpit, and caught the other up in his
free hand like a club.

"Now, you!" he challenged. "Let's see you come over
here and take that dog. Lorena, lift your skirts."

Lorena hesitated for only a moment. Then she raised her
hoops to disclose the cringing dog between her feet. The
dogcatcher took one look and lunged forward, but Douglas
swung the crutch so that it whistled within an inch of the
bully's head. The man dodged just in time, but in the
instinctive movement to shield his head, he dropped his
club. Douglas raised the crutch for another blow. Without
his club, and surprised by the unexpected onslaught, the
dogcatcher backed up, tripped over a projecting root and

sprawled on the ground. Using one crutch to propel himself, Douglas swung toward the fellow, the other crutch a dangerous weapon in his hand. The dogcatcher, his bully's courage vanished, watched in alarm. He must have recognized that advancing upon him was a soldier who had been in battle and who meant to stop at nothing. With a yelp of terror, the fellow scrambled to his feet and took off at a run down the hill. Douglas, watching him go, opened his mouth and gave out a wild rebel yell that doubled the dogcatcher's speed.

Not until he reached the safe distance of the Shore Road did the fellow halt his headlong flight and stop to shake his fist at the three who stood looking after him.

"I'll pay you off for this!" he shouted. "Wait and see!" He did not stay to witness the effect of his threat, however, but retreated around the corner, and they saw no more of him.

Her ears still ringing with the sound of Doug's yell, Abbie turned to see that Lorena was watching him anxiously. Doug swung himself toward her and in a moment he had an arm around her, crutch and all, and was searching her face for the answer to some question.

Lorena did not hesitate. Her arms went around his neck and she pressed her cheek to his. "Douglas, I've missed you so! I thought you didn't care about me any more."

"And I thought you were just being sorry for me," Doug said.

"Sorry for you!" Lorena was indignant. "Douglas, I'm so proud of you. What you did for that Flynn boy, and what you did just now to settle that dogcatcher. If only you'd *let* me be proud of you."

Doug grinned in the old way. "You can be as proud as you like, honey." The battle light had gone out of him, but he was exultant as he bent to kiss her.

Abbie felt tears upon her cheeks and knew they were tears of happiness. Everything was going to be all right with Douglas and Lorena after all.

Suddenly a startled look came over Lorena's face. She

pushed Douglas away and lifted her skirts to reveal the little dog licking at her ankle. Doug burst into a shout of laughter and Abbie found herself echoing him shakily. Lorena began to laugh and cry at the same time. The tension had broken and the reaction of relief left them weak.

Astonished at the outburst he seemed to have caused, the dog ran in and out among them, barking and wagging his tail furiously. As far as he, too, was concerned, everything was going to be all right.

25

Manuscript

It was a Saturday afternoon early in July. Mr. Garrett sat at the big teakwood desk in his study, while Stuart perched on a window ledge and Abbie rocked comfortably in her mother's favorite chair. Doug had taken Lorena and Mrs. Garrett for a drive, so the other three were alone.

A number of manuscript pages were heaped on the desk before her father, and Abbie regarded them proudly. He had persisted in the training of his left hand until he could write with reasonable speed and legibility, and had begun serious work on the book he had considered for so long. On this afternoon—Stuart's one day off—her father had invited him to come and listen to the first chapter of the manuscript. So far, only his wife had been permitted to see it, and he said her enthusiasm for it was probably prejudiced.

But the reading had not begun at once. Stuart had troubling news from the *Tribune* about what was going on in Pennsylvania.

"The fighting's pretty bad around Gettysburg," Stuart said. "Union troops are outnumbered and the situation is so serious that the New York militia has been sent into Pennsylvania as reinforcement. New York stands virtually unguarded and the entire city is on edge."

In the quiet of the summer day, with the garden somnolent in the heat and bees hovering about the clover, Abbie found it hard to believe that violence might rise close at hand. She shivered in the warm room.

Stuart turned away from the window. "I'm sorry, sir. I live so much in the excitement of Mr. Greeley's office that I suppose I bring it home with me when I shouldn't. I needn't tell you how eager I am to hear the beginning of your book. I don't even know what it's about."

Mr. Garrett moved his limp right hand on the desk. Abbie knew it often pained him, but now that he was able to write again he seemed to shrug the handicap aside.

"I've been a little fearful of talking my plans over with anyone except my wife," he said. "For one thing, I wasn't sure I could obtain the source material I needed. Or, obtaining it, that it might not be too vast a subject for me to handle. But since I find that I am driven to make the attempt, however futile, I feel I'd like you and Abbie to hear a little of what I've written. I value your opinion, Stuart."

"Thank you, sir," Stuart said.

There was affection in Mr. Garrett's smile. "You think ahead of your years, my boy. I've never discussed the war with you to any extent because I feel that each man must decide for himself what it means to him. But if you are to understand my purpose in this book, I must talk about the subject a little."

Abbie could sense a faint stiffening in Stuart, a readiness to resist any effort of Mr. Garrett's to sway him in favor of the war. From the first Stuart had held to his conviction that to fight was morally wrong and that he must take no part in a controversy which would shed blood. He waited in silence and Mr. Garrett, though sensitive always to those about him, gave no sign that he noticed any resistance in Stuart.

"As you know, I hate bloodshed with all my heart," Mr.

Garrett went on. "I believe that the Sermon on the Mount long ago presented all the precepts men need to live by, if only men would heed them. Few have heeded, even of those who claim strong religious beliefs. Since the beginning of time men have banded together in little groups, each claiming that his way was right, that he and his brothers were superior to all other men."

"I believe I understand all those things," Stuart said. "I will never be convinced that I am so much better than the other fellow that I must fight him to prove my superiority."

Mr. Garrett nodded his agreement. "When I got into uniform it was not to punish the South or to prove that the North was superior. It was to save something that was bigger than either. There has been too much breaking apart on the continent of Europe, too little working together. We must not have that here too. Until every nation is willing to work for the good of all, sacrifice for the good of all, we can never live in peace."

Abbie glanced at Stuart. His face was never expressive like Doug's. There could be no knowing what he thought. But at least he listened.

Mr. Garrett lifted the top sheet of manuscript and began to read aloud. Afternoon faded in the garden as he read— not only the first chapter he had suggested—but all the pages he had written. Abbie moved only once, to light the lamp on her father's desk. Stuart left his window sill and dropped into a chair.

When the last page had been read, a long silence fell upon the room. The message of her father's book was so big, so breathtaking in its importance, that it left them at a loss for words. It was Stuart who spoke first.

"Do you mind, sir, if I don't talk about this now? These are things I want to think about."

Mr. Garrett smiled his understanding. A few moments later Stuart went home, sobered and quiet.

"It's a wonderful book, Papa," Abbie said when he had gone. "It will make people everywhere stop to think."

Her father smiled. "I don't hope for that. Only a few

would read it. My book—if it is ever published—would only be one more link in the chain."

"But the chain is growing bigger and stronger," Abbie said. "You've shown how it is growing. Perhaps some day . . ."

The stray dog Lorena had adopted set up a barking just then and the sound of hoofs and carriage wheels in the road told them the others were home. Mr. Garrett stacked the papers on his desk and put them away in a drawer.

Lorena thrust her head through the beads of the study curtain. "How solemn you two look! Abbie, your mama says she'll take us over to town soon for a real shopping spree. I need so many things and so do you, Abbie. I promised Aunt Rosa I'd check your wardrobe and find out what you need, since you so hate to bother yourself."

Lorena's lighthearted interruption was welcome after the long sober hours Abbie had spent in her father's study. Lorena was a different girl these days and Abbie couldn't help but admire her for the way she was helping Douglas back to real health. She still sulked on occasion, and probably she would always flutter her eyelashes instinctively at every passing man, but Abbie forgave her these tricks. A person does not change altogether, but at least Lorena was growing up.

Oddly enough, Douglas, who, before he went away had been anxious for her smiles, hurt by her frowns, was no longer like that. Indeed, he was the one person who could handle her when she was in a rebellious mood. A look from Douglas, a critical word, and Lorena melted, relented, was tearfully sorry.

Plans for the shopping trip went on, despite the war news that came in from day to day. True, Lee's men were now in full retreat from Gettysburg and for a little while the North went wild with joy. Mobs of cheering men and women thronged the streets of Northern cities. But General Meade did not follow up his opportunity and pursue the retreating Confederates. Slowly, and then in a mounting tide, the terrible toll of dead and wounded became known, and the cheering began to have a hollow ring.

In the midst of the weeping that followed and the concern about a war that did not end, the losses in men occasioned a sudden order that swept down upon New York city. The draft was to go into effect immediately.

26

The Battle of New York

By whose order the draft was commenced no one was ever certain. Strangely enough, it went into effect without any notice being given to General Wood, who was in command of the United States forces, to Governor Seymour of New York state, or to Mayor Opdyke of New York city. Thus the major officials were taken by surprise and unprepared to meet trouble if it arose.

The draft began on Saturday, July 11, in a district where the enrollment lists were excessive and unfair. There was also injustice in a clause of the draft law which put a heavy burden on the poor. If a man chose to pay three hundred dollars, or hire a substitute, he could be exempted. Thus the well-to-do citizen could avoid army service if he wished, while the man who was most needed to support his family would be forced into uniform.

Nevertheless, despite mutterings and even outspoken condemnation of the law, the newspapers and city officials promised that all would go peacefully. Indeed, the first turnings of the lottery wheel on Saturday at the various draft offices, while they brought out crowds of people, resulted in no flaunting of the law. Sunday was a day of quiet and rest, and few guessed the secret work that was going on behind closed doors. That night there was an undue number of fires to keep the fire apparatus busy, but for the most part the good people of New York slept peacefully enough. On Staten Island all was outwardly serene and quiet.

The next day, Monday, was the day Mrs. Garrett had selected for the shopping trip for herself and the two girls. Since the papers were agreeably calm and the action of a handful of rowdies could be dismissed, there seemed no reason to postpone the trip. Mr. Garrett went to work at his usual early hour, and the three women set off some time later.

Jamie, the Garrett coachman, was the only one who protested against the trip. Given, as a rule, to unspoken communion with the mares, and only monosyllabic conversation with humans, he startled the three ladies upon the carriage's arrival at the Factoryville landing by suggesting that they turn right around and go home.

" 'Tain't the good people, the right people, you have to worry about, Miz Garrett," he said, turning in the driver's seat to look back at them. "But there's them in this town what likes trouble. And they don't like things like fighting for their country."

"Have you heard anything, Jamie?" Mrs. Garrett asked. "Have you any reason to think there might be real trouble?"

Jamie nodded darkly. "There's them as say General Lee wouldn't take it amiss if another rebellion started behind the lines. Maybe he'd even be willing to pay good money to get it started."

If Jamie hadn't mentioned the foolish gossip about General Lee, Mrs. Garrett might have listened, or at least have asked more questions. But Abbie knew that her mother, for all that her loyalties had been given to the North, had a secret admiration for Robert E. Lee that almost amounted to worship. To Lorena, of course, he was all the heroes of history rolled into the person of one man.

"That's the most absolute nonsense I've ever heard!" Lorena cried. "It's such a beautiful day. We can't give up our trip. As if General Lee had time on his hands for anything so silly. Don't pay any attention to Jamie, Aunt Rosa."

Jamie, having used up his quota of words for some time to come, subsided into stony silence, and Mrs. Garrett shrugged aside his warning. The ferry had pulled into the dock and they would get aboard at once.

It was a clear day, though decidedly hot. Wind stirred the waters of the harbor now and then in fitful gusts, wind with a furnace breath behind it. The three women found the streets of New York dry and the air choked with dust.

They had a few disquieting moments in the horse car on their way uptown, when a man hopped onto the rear step and rode along for half a block, addressing the passengers in excited tones.

"You folks better all get home fast and lock your doors," he said. "There's bad trouble afoot in this town. I hear they're going to burn down every block of the city that has a draft office in it."

He jumped down from the step, and Abbie saw him turn off down a side street, moving at a trot. The people in the car looked at one another uneasily until an expansive gentleman with a heavy gold watch chain looped across his front nodded at Mrs. Garrett reassuringly.

"Don't distress yourself, madam. The police of New York city are the best in the world. Even if the rabble attempted violence, it would be stopped at once."

Mrs. Garrett thanked him and dabbed at her forehead delicately with a rose-scented handkerchief. "Since we've come this far, we might as well go on with our plans," she told the girls. "Certainly everything seems peaceful as far as we can see."

The usual shoppers thronged the store aisles, and the morning went busily and pleasantly as the three made their purchases. Now and then they overheard talk and gathered that fires were burning here and there about the city. But not until they returned to the street seeking a place to lunch did they find cause for real alarm.

There was a smell of smoke on the hot breeze and what few people were now abroad in the streets hurried as if driven by an uneasy fear.

"Listen!" Mrs. Garrett said as the three stood close together on the curb. Abbie held her breath.

In the distance there was a sound of shouting and then a rattle that was unmistakably gunfire.

Mrs. Garrett moved with decision. "There *is* trouble, girls. We must get back to Staten Island at once. Over there we'll be apart from whatever is happening here."

But now the horse cars that passed were crowded with people endeavoring to get home, and three went by with men standing on the rear step and no inch of space available inside. There were no hackney cabs anywhere. Lorena, whom Abbie still found an unaccountable mixture of little girl fears and mature courage, clung fearfully to her aunt's arm.

"How will we get home, Aunt Rosa?" she wailed.

"If necessary, we'll walk to the Battery," Mrs. Garrett announced resolutely. "It's too bad we have all these parcels to carry, but I think we can manage if we try. Let's march right along and watch what's happening down the side streets so we don't step into something unexpected."

"If we get downtown we can go to Papa's office," Abbie suggested.

Her mother shook her head. "When we get downtown we'll go straight to the ferry. I've no intention of imposing three helpless women on your father's hands. Mind you, girls, I don't think our safety is in the least threatened. The shooting we heard was undoubtedly the police firing to frighten rowdies. Everything is probably quite under control by now."

They heard no more threatening shots as they walked, but the sound of fire alarm bells ringing incessantly was not reassuring; and, when there was a lull in the wind, smoke haze choked the streets. As they hurried along, wasting no breath now on words, Abbie heard the sound of a carriage behind them. She turned, always hopeful that it might be an empty hack, but this was driven by a man who wore a gray beaver and was obviously a gentleman. In the back seat four women huddled together.

To Abbie's surprise, the driver pulled up at the curb and hailed them without ceremony. "Get in, ladies, and I'll take you wherever you're going. Providing I can get there."

There was plainly room for only one more in the carriage, but he gestured at them angrily.

"Get in, get in! Don't stand on ceremony, even if you sit on one another's laps. One of you can climb up here on the seat with me. If you don't get in, I'll leave you right there with your silly mouths open."

Mrs. Garret closed her mouth and pushed Lorena into the carriage. "You climb up in front," she told Abbie. Then she got in after Lorena and somehow the six occupants of the carriage shoved and thrust at their hoops, and wriggled about until they were all more or less settled. Abbie had never worn a hoop on the driver's seat of a carriage, but she managed it now, wishing to goodness for a moment's privacy so she could be rid of the encircling nuisance. Since the war, hoops were smaller than they had been, but they still impeded when you wanted to be anything but a lady of fashion.

The man in the gray beaver hardly waited for her to settle herself before he flicked his whip, and they were off at a good clip.

"Are things really very bad, sir?" Abbie asked as they went careering along.

He gave her a quick, grim look. "With the troops away at Gettysburg and the police outnumbered? What do you think?"

"The—the police outnumbered?" Abbie faltered.

"There are mobs springing up all over town. Hundreds too many for the police to handle. The criminal element is behind the rising, but this sort of thing is contagious. The draft is unpopular and any crowd is tinder when it comes to wildfire excitement.''

''Wh-what are they doing?'' Abbie gasped.

''Burning buildings, homes. Fires everywhere are going unchecked because there are too many to handle. There's been stoning and killing too. I saw a mob over on Third Avenue stone a helpless colored man this morning. They're after the Negroes particularly—as if they were to blame for the war. But they're after the well-dressed too.''

He pulled up the horses suddenly and turned them down a cross street. As they flashed about the corner, Abbie had a frightening glimpse of a horse car with a crowd milling about it. Ruffians on the street were pulling passengers rudely out of the car, but their own carriage managed to circle the danger zone.

The gentleman in the beaver was as good as his word. He let the other ladies in the carriage out at their destinations, then drove Mrs. Garrett and the girls right to the ferry. There was a moment when Abbie wished they could stop and pick up her father, but there was no time for anything but flight. Roundabout circuits were too risky. The moment the ladies were out of the carriage, their rescuer drove off without waiting for thanks.

The three found the boat far more crowded than usual and at every hand they heard tales of violence. The mob, it appeared, was learning its own power in the unprotected city and that was a dangerous knowledge.

Everyone on board the ferry seemed glad to be returning to safe and peaceful Staten Island. There would be no rioting there, they assured one another. But while the boat was still offshore, Abbie saw the black smoke of a fire in Tompkinsville and began to wonder if Staten Island was to escape after all.

27

Rescue

Abbie knew her mother felt that she should stay quietly in her seat on the ferry and behave in a ladylike manner, but she was stirred by an uncontrollable restlessness. She kept worrying about her father over in town, and about Stuart in Horace Greeley's office. The name of Greeley stood for all things a mob would most abhor. If it wanted a scapegoat to blame for the war, the *Tribune* might well serve. And if Stuart were there . . .

Abbie went out on deck to stand for a while in the bow of the boat watching the approaching shore line. When she turned back to rejoin her mother and Lorena, the first person she saw was the colored woman who ran the confectionary shop in their own neighborhood, and who had come to Abbie's help the day Lorena had fainted over a hurt dog.

Mrs. Hill sat quietly in the midst of the excitement about her. Her hands were folded in the lap of her black dress and her dark eyes stared straight ahead at nothing. Her brown skin was ashen and Abbie knew at a glance that here was someone in trouble. She went to her quickly and sat down at her side.

"Is there something wrong, Mrs. Hill?" she asked gently.

The colored woman gave her a startled glance of recognition. "Thank you, Miss Abbie. The trouble is I don't dare get off this boat. I started home a couple of hours ago, but the ferry men said there was trouble at the landings. In New Brighton a white lady was being driven to the boat by her colored coachman and some men stopped the carriage and tore him down from the seat and beat him. Miss Abbie, I've got to get home to my boy and my little store. But the ferry men say I'd better wait till dark. So I've just stayed on the boat."

Abbie listened in concern. Everyone liked and admired Mrs. Hill. It seemed impossible that she might be harmed. But there must be real reason for her fears if the ferry men had been concerned about letting her go ashore.

"You wait right here," Abbie told her. "I'm going to talk to Mama and see if we can think of any way to get you ashore."

She hurried back to her mother and Lorena and told them her story. Lorena was immediately indignant.

"Why in the world would anyone blame a woman like Mrs. Hill for the war, or try to hurt her?" she demanded. "It's not the Negroes who started all this."

"Hush," Mrs. Garrett said. "It isn't a matter of reasoning. Hush a moment and let me think."

Abbie watched her hopefully. She felt the way she had as a child when her mother could always be counted on to solve difficult problems. Now her mother was looking thoughtfully about at her fellow passengers. Two benches away sat a woman in widow's weeds, with her back toward them.

Mrs. Garrett nodded in her direction and spoke to Abbie. "Honey, when you were walking around, did you happen to notice whether that is Mrs. Lawrence from Port Richmond?"

Abbie shook her head. "I didn't notice." Mrs. Lawrence had once been a teacher at the New Brighton Academy for Young Ladies, which Abbie had attended.

"Stay here, Lorena," Mrs. Garrett said. "Abbie, come with me. We'll walk to the door and then start back so we can see. If it is Mrs. Lawrence, I have an idea."

Abbie tried to move with the same casual air her mother adopted, but it was difficult because of her inner excitement. They walked slowly to the door, looked out at the shore line and saw that the boat would be reaching the Factoryville dock in another ten minutes. There was little time in which to act.

They started back toward Lorena and in the instant of turning Abbie glanced hopefully at the woman in black. The heavy veil had been thrown back over her bonnet so that her face was visible. It was not Mrs. Lawrence.

"Never mind," said Mrs. Garrett. "This is an emergency. Come with me, Abbie."

She went straight to the woman who sat at the end of the bench, with Abbie following somewhat breathlessly. Mrs. Garrett bent toward the unknown lady, urgency in her voice as she spoke.

"Madam," she said, "I know this is an imposition, but will you permit me to introduce myself?" At the woman's assent she went on at once. "I am Mrs. Roger Garrett of Elliottville and this is my daughter Abigail. I wonder if you would be willing to do a service that might save the life of an innocent person?"

The woman was elderly and her cheeks were a meshwork of lines left by the years. She had lived a long time and what people did no longer surprised her.

"What is it you wish be to do?" she asked simply.

Abbie listened as her mother hurriedly explained her plan. The woman accepted the suggestion as calmly as if such a request had been an everyday matter.

"I will be glad to aid you," she said.

A nod of her mother's head motioned Abbie back to her seat beside Lorena. While Abbie was explaining to her cousin, Mrs. Garrett, the strange woman, and Mrs. Hill all disappeared in the direction of the ladies' cabin.

The boat was docking at the Factoryville landing when the three reappeared. The woman in widow's weeds no longer wore her veil. The veil had been transferred to Mrs. Hill's black bonnet and now hung in heavy folds over her face. Mrs. Garrett had given the colored woman her own dark gloves. But the disguise was not completely effective. Anyone looking too closely might question the brownish tint of the face behind the veil.

As they moved toward the gangplank, Mrs. Garrett walked confidently ahead and the two girls followed, each with a hand on the elbow of the woman between them. Lorena was the best actress of them all. She chattered away as they went down to the dock and Abbie wished she could give an impression equally carefree.

Abbie noted at once that there were more men than usual standing about on the dock. Surly looking fellows, they were, poorly dressed and lacking the upright manner of the honest laborer. They watched the handful of passengers with shifty-eyed interest, molesting no one, but giving the impression that they waited only for a spark to inflame them as the crowds in the city had been inflamed earlier that day.

Abbie could feel her tongue turn to flannel, while her forced words died in her throat. But Lorena chattered on guilelessly.

"My, it's good to be home again, Aunt Sarah." She squeezed Mrs. Hill's elbow. "My feet sure do hurt after all that walking over in town. Now I can't wait to get home and try on my new tassled boots."

Lorena was pretty enough to take any masculine eye away from every other woman in her vicinity and for once Abbie was grateful for her cousin's special gift. The men lounging about the dock were no exception to the rule. Abbie could see the way their gaze followed her cousin, ignoring the woman in the black veil. One fellow, younger than the others, insolently sang a few lines of a popular tune and the words followed them along the walk.

> With tassels on their boots,
> A style that surely suits
> These Yankee girls with hair in curls
> And tassels on their boots.

Lorena tossed her head and hurried on, her hand firmly upon Mrs. Hill's elbow. At the end of the dock a man stepped suddenly toward them and Abbie saw with sinking heart that here was one who had no interest in Lorena's pretty ways. It was the erstwhile dogcatcher with whom they had clashed that day Doug had first crossed the meadow. His attention was upon the black veil and the face behind it. Abbie felt sure he meant to reach out and throw the veil back from Mrs. Hill's face. But before he could take another step, Rosa Garrett brushed by him with a little cry of pleasure.

"Look, girls! Someone's come to meet us. Isn't that fine?"

The burly fellow paused and looked around, while Mrs. Garrett walked purposefully toward a carriage of strange gentlemen, the girls and Mrs. Hill hurrying after her. In another moment, Abbie was sure, her mother would have managed to get them right into the carriage of strangers, but a welcome voice hailed her just in time.

"Over this way, Miz Garrett! I been thinking you might get home earlier'n you told me."

Bless Jamie! Abbie thought as relief swept through her. He had been loyal enough and anxious enough to wait goodness knows how long at the dock. She dared not look back as they went toward their own carriage, but no footsteps sounded on the dock behind them, no shouted command ordered them to stop. She did not glance toward the dock again until they were driving off. Then she saw that the dogcatcher was staring after them suspiciously. But it didn't matter now. They were on their way home. Nevertheless, his look made her recall the threat he had made to pay them off. She could only hope that he would not be too curious.

Jamie clucked to the horses and volunteered no further remarks until Mrs. Garrett directed him to stop first at Mrs. Hill's candy store.

"I wouldn't do that, Miz Garrett," he said. "There's been some trouble hereabouts. They ain't burned the store, but they broke into it and it wouldn't be safe to go back there right now."

Mrs. Hill moaned softly. "I left Bobby there by himself. He always takes care of everything for me real good and I never thought . . ." her voice trembled to a stop.

Jamie showed no surprise at the identity of the veiled lady in the carriage. "I wouldn't worry none about that Bobby, ma'am. He's a right smart lad and he'd use his head if there was trouble."

"You'll come home with us," Mrs. Garrett said gently, patting the colored woman's arm. "Then Jamie can go back to your neighborhood and see if he can find out what's happened. Will you, Jamie?"

"I'll go, Miz Garrett," Jamie said. "I'll be all right. It's the nobs they're after. And the Black Republicans and the colored people and anybody who helps 'em."

"You shouldn't help me, Mrs. Garrett," Mrs. Hill said quickly.

"Do you think we'd fail a friend when she really needed us?" Mrs. Garrett demanded. "Now you just settle back and catch your breath. Everything's going to be all right."

But later, as they got out of the carriage and hurried into the house, Abbie found herself wondering if her mother's words were true prophecy.

28

Hide-out

Abbie's father did not come home at his usual time that evening. Though Mrs. Garrett made a show of outward confidence, Abbie was aware of her mother's concern. She would be worried, not only about her husband's safety, but about the safety of this household, harboring as it did a Negro woman.

The fearful Mrs. Coombs went home to stay for the time being, leaving her duties to Abbie's mother and the two girls. Mrs. Garrett put herself and the girls to various tasks at once and Abbie was glad enough to be kept busy. Fortunately, Jamie stood by.

In the late afternoon he went out on a scouting expedition and returned with news both reassuring and disturbing. He reported that Mrs. Johnson had several colored people hidden in her barn, Bobby Hill among them. Jamie had managed to get word to Bobby that his mother was safe. So far, acts of violence on the island had not reached the proportions they had in New York. There had been isolated instances of rowdyism, but no concerted action, no real gathering of the mob.

One could not tell, however, at what moment a rising might occur. There were frightening threats abroad, threats of death to all who had sympathized with the cause of the colored man, threats to clear the island of every Negro and every Abolitionist found upon it. Since the abolitionist stronghold had always been their own neighborhood, trouble, if it came, might be expected here.

After Jamie returned the Garrett doorbell rang and Abbie, opening the door cautiously, found Mrs. Phillips and Hannah on the veranda.

"Well, let us in, child, let us in! I must talk to your mother at once," Aunt Varina said testily, as if it had been only yesterday she had set foot in this house.

Mrs. Garrett, hearing voices, came into the hall and gave her hand graciously to Mrs. Phillips. Aunt Varina brushed the hand aside and took Rosa straight to her black bombazine bosom.

"I've behaved dreadfully, dreadfully!" she cried. "And to my sweetest friend! Rosa, can you ever forgive me?"

Hannah wriggled past her aunt, smiling impishly at Abbie. "I did it!" she whispered. "I scared her to death about what might happen to the Garretts with all this terrible rioting going on."

Mrs. Garrett showed her guest into the parlor, murmuring that there was nothing to forgive, and Aunt Varina rushed on.

"No, no, Rosa dear, I can't sit down. I can't stop a moment. I want you all to pack your things and come right over to my house for the night. Everyone knows I've never sided with the Abolitionists and you'll be quite safe there. Hurry now, Rosa. You can bring your Southern niece along, of course. It simply isn't safe to stay overnight in this house with only an undersized coachman and your husband with his one poor hand to guard you."

Mrs. Garrett waited calmly until the rush of words subsided. With difficulty Abbie held back a rush of indignation at Mrs. Phillip's reference to her father. This was for Mama to deal with.

Mrs. Garrett made her answer quietly. "It is most thoughtful of you, Varina, to think of us in this way. But I intend to stay right here in my own house. I have every confidence in my husband's ability to protect those he loves." She said nothing of the fact that Mr. Garrett had not come home.

Varina Phillips sighed. "Sometimes I think you are a very foolish woman, Rosa. Nevertheless, I admire you. We are friends again?"

"Of course," Mrs. Garrett agreed, smiling.

Hannah made joyful gestures behind her aunt's back and whispered, "Come over soon," as she followed Aunt Varina out the door.

But when they had gone, Mrs. Garrett turned uncertainly to Abbie. "Honey, do you think I've behaved foolishly? Should I have sent you and Lorena over to Varina's for the night?"

"And leave you here?" Abbie demanded.

"You know Varina would never allow Mrs. Hill to take shelter in her house," Mrs. Garrett said. "And Mrs. Hill is my responsibility until she is safe."

"Do you think Lorena and I would go off and leave you two here?" Abbie said staunchly. "After what Aunt V. said about Papa, I wouldn't accept her offer anyway. I think you did exactly right."

But after supper, with dusk growing outside and the twilight breathless and still, Abbie found her gaze moving uneasily toward the windows, as if she feared to see threatening faces peering in at them. The three women gathered in Mr. Garrett's study, not wanting to light up the parlor at the front of the house. The French doors were closed and locked and the heat was oppressive. Mrs. Garrett and Lorena stilled their nervous hands by sewing, while Abbie attempted to read a story that made very little sense because her thoughts darted restlessly from one thing to another.

Was Stuart spending the night at the *Tribune* over in Printing House Square? Would the mob attack the *Tribune* as it had attacked other buildings in town, burning it to the ground, stoning those who tried to escape? And what of Staten Island? At best they had only a handful of constables here. With all the troops away, the island was at the mercy of the mob if it chose to take over. But most often her thoughts returned to Stuart.

Two or three times Abbie or Lorena tiptoed upstairs to look in at Mrs. Hill, who lay asleep in the spare room, exhausted from the strain of the afternoon. She had not stirred and the girls left her undisturbed.

At seven-thirty the sound of someone coming up the side steps to the study doors startled them all. But they quickly recognized the step and Lorena rose to go to the door.

"Yes, it's Douglas," she told the others. She unlocked the French doors and flung them open. Doug put his crutches over the sill and swung himself into the room. Crossing the meadow was no longer the ordeal for him that it had been the first time and he made the trip often now.

" 'Evening, Mrs. Garrett. Hello, girls. I thought I'd come over and see how you were doing. Papa's got our house barricaded like a fort and he's standing guard."

"What about Stuart?" Abbie asked.

Doug shook his head gravely. "We hoped he'd come home this afternoon when he saw there was going to be trouble. But it would be like him to stay on the job over there if they need him. Where is Mr. Garrett?"

"We've heard nothing from him," Mrs. Garrett said.

"Then I'll stay here tonight, if you're willing." Douglas reached beneath his jacket and took out an army pistol. "Papa had two of these, so if you'll fix me up with a chair on the front veranda I'll take up my post right now. I don't think we need to worry. A mob is a pretty cowardly unit unless it's sure it has the upper hand. A man coming up the walk in the moonlight makes a good target. Just don't put a light behind me."

"Thank you, Douglas," Mrs. Garrett told him gratefully.

"I know we'll breathe more easily for having you here. Between you and Jamie, I'm sure we'll be well protected. But Douglas, it's only fair to tell you that we have Mrs. Hill hidden upstairs. We believe we got her into the house without discovery. But her presence, if it is suspected, might lead a mob to attack."

"All the better that I'm here," Doug said.

Lorena got him a chair and pushed it out to the veranda. Then she sat for a while at his side, her hand in his there in the breathless darkness.

There was a sort of glow about her cousin tonight, Abbie thought wistfully. The evening had worn on and she and Lorena were out in the kitchen fixing lemonade and sandwiches for a late snack.

"We're going to be married as soon as the war is over," Lorena told her gayly. "Though I had to do the proposing. Doug has more silly ideas about not being worthy of me. Oh, Abbie"—her hand reached out toward her cousin's for a moment—"it is I who have to work to be worthy of him."

Abbie patted her hand affectionately. As her mother had pointed out, and Stuart before her, it sometimes took real trouble to make a person grow up. In the last few weeks Lorena had begun for the first time to accept mature responsibilities, and the acceptance was making a different person of her.

"When the war is over," Lorena went on, "Douglas and I want to go South to live. Abbie, we love the South and there will be so much to do down there. We want to be there to do what we can."

When the war was over, Abbie thought. How often that phrase was on all their lips these days.

The neighborhood remained quiet; and, though once in a while they heard distant shouting, no one turned up Bard Avenue, no mob materialized. Over in the sky above New York low clouds glowed with a flickering yellow light—the reflection of fires burning in the city.

And that was the first night.

Roger Garrett came home by an early morning boat, his

eyes shadowed from lack of sleep and concern for his family. There had been trouble in the neighborhood of his office, and it had not been safe to set foot on the streets. But by daybreak the crowds had wearied and broken up, and the office force had been able to escape.

Relieved of his post, Douglas went home to sleep. Jamie, back from another scouting trip, assured them that the trouble was not over.

Shops were closed everywhere. Most transportation, except for the ferries, had ceased. A crowd had broken into the Tompkins Lyceum and taken all the muskets from the drill room—so now a good portion of the mob was armed. Again the island waited fearfully for night to fall.

Toward sundown Abbie sat on the side veranda peeling green apples while her mother made the crust for her father's favorite dish, hot apple pie. The thought of Stuart had scarcely been out of Abbie's mind for all these long hours. He *had* to be safe. Nothing must happen to him. The worry that tugged at her now was far stronger than any she had felt when Douglas had gone away to war.

Her fingers moved automatically, peeling apples, slicing them, but her thoughts were distant from her work. She could remember the way Stuart had looked that day when he had stood beside her easel up on the hilltop and had titled the daub she'd been painting. That was the day he had suggested that she go after Douglas herself. But in the end it had not been Douglas she had wanted. She had not seen the truth then, but she was beginning to see it now. She could talk to Stuart as she had never been able to talk to Douglas. She turned to him always when something troubled her. It was Stuart's opinion she cared about, his praise she sought, even though she had not always been conscious of the fact.

Now Stuart was over in New York in quite probable danger. Her busy hands stilled and she forgot the apples because of the mingling emotions that swept through her.

"This is the way it feels to love someone," she thought. "This is the way it feels to worry about someone you love."

She knew he had never given any personal thought to her.

She had merely been someone to help him with Douglas. He would have been happy to see her married to his brother. There were even times when she had been sure that he disliked her. But those things didn't matter now. All she asked was that he come home safely. The future would take care of itself once she knew he was safe.

Her apples were browning in their bowl and her mother would not like that. She picked up the knife again and reached for another apple. As she peeled, a whimsical thought seized her. She would try the old wishing trick she used to play as a child. She would remove a curl of apple peel carefully so that it would all come off in one long strip. And she would wish while she peeled. Wish for Stuart's safety. If she could remove the peeling in one piece her wish would come true.

The green strip of peel lengthened beneath her fingers as she turned the apple, holding the knife with the utmost care, while the tangy, acid smell of green apples spiced the air. A step at the side gate startled her and she looked up. The knife slashed through the strip of peel and it dropped in a springy coil to the floor of the veranda. But now it did not matter that the charm had been broken, for Stuart McIntyre was coming up the walk.

She had to hold onto herself to keep from running to him in her relief and joy. He was bareheaded, his face dirty and unshaven. A purpling bruise welted one cheekbone and his coat was torn. But he was home. He was safe.

"You've been hurt," Abbie said and her voice shook.

He brushed her concern aside. "It's nothing. I haven't gone home yet. I stopped here first on the way. Do you know how the folks are?"

"Everything's fine at your house," she told him quickly. "Doug stood guard for us here last night. Stuart, I've worried about you so!"

As always, his reaction was mocking. "I am touched by your concern, Miss Abigail."

She would not let him prick her. She reached for the strip of apple peel and dangled the green coil before him. "I was making a charm to bring you safely home, but I spoiled it when you walked through the gate."

"That's fast-working magic," Stuart said. He came up the steps and sat wearily down at her feet. "Where's your father, Abbie? I've just heard a rumor down at the dock and I thought I'd better let him know right away."

Mr. Garrett had heard their voices and he came through the study doors before Stuart had finished speaking. "It's good to see you safe, my boy."

"Thank you, sir. There's a rumor going around that you're hiding a colored woman in your house."

So the dogcatcher *had* been suspicious yesterday, Abbie thought.

"Mrs. Hill has taken refuge with us," Mr. Garrett told him. "We are proud to protect and shelter her."

Stuart made an aimless gesture with the back of his hand across his sweating face, streaking the grime still more. "My head feels foggy. It's hard to think things through. Isn't there some way you can get her out of the house? All that crowd needs is a leader. Somebody to yell, 'Burn out the Garretts!' It won't help to keep Mrs. Hill here and have her torn to pieces. They did that today to the old apple woman over at the dock in the city."

Abbie shivered. She remembered the friendly colored woman who had sold apples at the docks for so long.

"There's the cave," Stuart said. "She'd be safe there. And you'll be safer with her out of the house."

Abbie made an effort to rid herself of the frightful picture Stuart's words had brought to mind. It was more important now to think of the living.

"The cave would do," she said. "I could take her up there after dark. Don't you think that would be best, Papa?"

"I want to do everything possible to protect her," Mr. Garrett said. "This may be the most sensible way."

Stuart stood up wearily. "Then it's settled. Abbie, I'm going home and get a couple of hours' sleep."

"Wait," Abbie said. "Stuart, tell us what happened to you."

"Mr. Greeley and the others are standing guard over at the *Tribune*. They've practically made a fortress of the office, with enough weapons for an arsenal. There'll be a fight if the mob attacks. I wanted to stay and lend whatever help I could, but Mr. Greeley himself sent me home. He said the Union needed me and I couldn't go throwing my life away in a riot." Stuart grinned wryly.

"It looks as if you'd had a bit of a scrap getting away," Mr. Garrett said.

"It wasn't much. I went out the back way and somebody yelled that there was another *Tribune* rat. One ruffian jumped me with a club, but I could twist and duck and run faster than he could."

Jamie came around the side of the house just then, hurrying a young colored boy before him. It was Bobby Hill and he looked thoroughly frightened.

"Look who I found in the back yard," Jamie said. "I thought he was a smart boy, but he had to go and sneak away from Mrs. Johnson's and come over here."

"Please, Miss Abbie, I want to find my mother," Bobby pleaded, his eyes shining with tears he was trying not to shed.

Abbie went down the steps and took Bobby's hand gently. "I know how you feel. Your mama's inside and she'll be all right. Do you think anyone saw you on the way over?"

"I didn't see nobody," Bobby told her. "I came sneaking through the fields where the grass is high."

"Well, scoot inside." Abbie gave him a little push and then turned to face Stuart. "There will be two in the cave tonight."

Stuart tried to smile through his weariness. "All the better. I'll be back after dark to help you get them up there. Don't worry—we'll manage."

29

Drums on the Shore Road

After supper, when it was dark, Stuart returned, refreshed and clean, but with the welt on his cheek looking angrier than ever.

Mrs. Hill had agreed readily to the plan to take her son and herself up to the cave in the woods. Indeed, she said, she would be relieved to go. Her big worry now was that she might bring trouble down on the heads of those who had helped her. Mrs. Garrett packed a hearty lunch for the two, and Abbie gathered up a blanket and a couple of pillows so they would be as comfortable as possible. Then the four started up the hill, Abbie leading the way, fumbling through the darkness for the path she knew so well by daylight. Mrs. Hill and Bobby came next, while Stuart made up the rear guard. The night was cloudy and the moon lighted the way only intermittently. A lantern, however, could not be risked.

The cave seemed farther up the hill than ever before. Abbie and Mrs. Hill had both left their hoops behind, but bushes caught at their full skirts in the darkness, tearing rents in them as the two women pushed heedlessly on. As they stumbled upward, Abbie found herself remembering the times she and Doug and Stuart had climbed this path in play, with an imaginary enemy hot in pursuit. Tonight the game had come alive and the danger was real.

The blanket and pillows made the cave reasonably comfortable and at least it was cooler here on the hillside than lower down toward the water. The bush before the cave's entrance made a perfect screen and it would lend shelter in the event that rain blew up during the night.

"We'll bring you more food and water tomorrow," Abbie promised. "And we'll keep you posted on how everything is going."

As they felt their way back along the path, Abbie had a sense of time rushing away too swiftly. Now that Mrs. Hill and Bobby were safe in the cave she was no longer concerned, and she wanted to reach out to Stuart and pull him back, slow his pace. After all, she had just come to a surprising realization and she wanted to enjoy these moments of being alone with him.

"Must you hurry so?" she gasped. "There's nothing to rush for now."

"I'll feel better when you're safely home," Stuart said, but he came to a halt on the path ahead. "Want to stop a minute and get your breath?"

"Yes, please," Abbie said and stood near him there in the warm darkness, her fingertips touching his sleeve. She was aware of the denser blackness of the trees about them and the damp, earthy smell of the woods.

"This gives me a chance to tell you something, Abbie," he said.

She waited, her lips parted with her quick breathing.

"As soon as this trouble is over, I'm going to enlist," he went on. "I've had a taste of a little civil war these last days and I know there's a time when you have to fight. Not to fight is to give up to the forces that oppose freedom."

"Oh, no!" Abbie whispered. "Not you, Stuart."

He seemed not to hear her. "Your father's book gave me a glimpse of a bigger pattern than the one I've been looking at. If there's a chance of working together, then that is worth fighting for. What's the good of refusing to fight if the other fellow means to anyway?''

She was proud of him, even though she felt a little like crying. But how could she let him go now, when he had become so dear to her? As she stood there an unfamiliar sound reached her ears—a strange, distant wave of sound that was almost a roaring.

"Listen!" Stuart cried softly.

Abbie moved closer to him and for a moment they stood there hardly breathing, listening with all their might. The sound was almost like the steady booming of a drum—yet it could not be a drum.

"If we were in Africa," Stuart said, "I'd think the jungle tom-toms were sounding."

"Could it be army drums?" Abbie whispered. "The troops coming home?"

"No army drum ever sounded like that," Stuart said. "There's no roll to it, no beat. It's just a steady roar."

"Fire?" Abbie breathed.

Stuart took her hand and pulled her along the path. "Not fire. I've had plenty of chance in the last two days to learn what fire sounds like. Let's get back in the open where we can find out what's going on."

They slipped and scrambled through whatever way offered. They had lost the real path now, fighting their way through the underbrush, paying little heed to scratching thorns or tearing branches, seeking only some opening that would lead them back to the road. And all the while the steady roaring went on, the tone of it threatening, promising disaster. Whatever it portended, that sound was not one of peace.

They stumbled at length upon the road and stood close together, listening, striving to pierce the darkness. The roar was plainer than ever now and it came from the direction of the Shore Road. Abbie felt the muscles in Stuart's arm tighten beneath her hand.

"I know what it is, Abbie. Don't you recognize it?"

In the same instant she knew. The plank walk that ran from New Brighton to beyond Factoryville was raised above the ground and it always gave out a hollow sound when you walked upon it. Now the plank walk roared with the tramp of many feet, giving out its warning in its own way.

"We'll have to get back to your house quickly, Abbie," Stuart said softly.

As they stepped into the open street they could see the flickering lights at the end of the road. Those were torches held aloft and lanterns being swung as the men marched along the echoing boards.

The two on the road hurried now, fearing there might be a break in the roar at any minute as the mob poured up the side streets. But before they could reach the gate of the Garrett yard, the shadow of a nearby tree suddenly widened as a man stepped from behind it. Abbie's heart nearly stopped. There was menace in the shadowy figure that moved toward them.

"What're you two up to anyway?" came the rasping challenge.

Though she could not see his face, Abbie knew she had heard that grating voice before and the knowledge chilled her. It was the dogcatcher who had watched them so suspiciously on the dock the day before.

"Hurry," Abbie whispered to Stuart. "Let's go by without answering him."

Stuart nodded and they started down the road. But the fellow stepped into their path, blocking the way. The sour odor of liquor was sickening on the air.

"It's that dogcatcher who knocked Douglas down," Abbie whispered to Stuart and then spoke to the fellow directly. "There are no dogs around here tonight. You'd better go back to your friends."

The fellow lurched a step nearer. "That's right, lady. I'm out for bigger game tonight. I been watching your house for a while."

Did that mean he had been there earlier? Had he seen them hurry Mrs. Hill and Bobby up into the woods?

He reached out suddenly and caught Abbie by the arm. "I gotta grudge to fix with you. Though at least you got a bantam with two legs to fight for you tonight."

Stuart struck out so swiftly that Abbie hardly saw his fist swing. She heard the crunch of the impact and saw the man stagger under the blow. But he did not go down. As he lunged back at Stuart, Abbie cast desperately about for a weapon, a stick, a tree branch, anything. Stuart's weight and size were nothing beside his assailant's and she didn't mean to stand there and see Stuart take a beating.

In the grass near the roadside her fingers found a stick and she whirled back to the struggling men. The dogcatcher was drunk and, thanks to the training of Fergus McIntyre, Stuart, though he lacked weight, knew how to use his fists. The second time the fellow went down like a tree falling and lay inert, while Stuart stood above him waiting.

Clouds inched away from the moon to illumine Bard Avenue. The man on the ground did not move.

"He'll keep for a while," Stuart said.

He turned to look at Abbie and at the sight of her he laughed out loud. "Abbie! What do you think you're going to do with that?"

Abbie found that she was holding a toothpick of a stick menacingly aloft and lowered it sheepishly. "I—I didn't want you to get hurt," she faltered.

"Thanks, Abbie," he said and the amusement was gone from his voice. The man on the ground moaned faintly and Stuart leaned over him. "We'll have to carry this fellow into the stable where he can sleep it off locked in. It won't do to have him get back to his friends tonight. Tomorrow we can tell him we found him on the road and let him go. I doubt that he'll have a clear recollection of what happened. Go get Jamie, Abbie."

She flew to do his bidding. Jamie and Stuart lugged the dogcatcher's limp weight into the stable, where, after a bit of incoherent grumbling, he fell fast asleep.

Afterward they went back to Mr. Garrett's study and Abbie found herself watching Stuart whenever he wasn't looking her way. What was she to do about him? Probably he would only be surprised if he knew how she felt. Probably he would just think it was funny and laugh at her. No lady should ever speak out her feelings for a gentleman, she knew. But in a few days he'd be going off to war and she'd be left to eat out her heart, without his ever knowing how she felt about him.

What was it Stuart himself had said about the "polite fol-de-rol" to be found in novels? He'd said a lady had her own subtle ways of going after the man she wanted. But how was she to be subtle about this, when all she wanted was to be simple and direct?

Late in the evening, when Stuart picked up the pistol Doug had left with them and went for a patrol around the house, Abbie slipped out to go with him. Down on the plank walk the roar had died away a little, and the swinging lanterns, the torches, were farther apart. Abbie and Stuart circled the house silently and found that all was well. But now that she was alone with him, she had nothing to say. When he turned back toward the house she slipped her hand into his.

He paused to look at her in the light that fell across the lawn from the study doors. Then he said, "Things are quiet enough for the moment. Let's have a talk."

He led the way to the little summerhouse and helped her over the dark threshold. It was cooler here than in the stifling house, but she could feel the beads of perspiration on her nose. Yet Stuart's hand seemed cool as he held hers and drew her down on the bench beside him.

"Before I go away, Abbie," he said, "I want you to know how much I admire you. I'm not blind. I've known for a long time how you felt about Douglas. And I think you've been fine about the way you've hidden your own hurt and kept a generous attitude toward both Lorena and Douglas. Not every girl could have managed that."

She listened in mingled astonishment and exasperation. "You're giving me credit I don't deserve," she said stiffly.

He reached out for her two hands and held them gently in

his. "Abbie, I couldn't give you more credit than you deserve. There just isn't anyone like you, Abbie."

She felt unreasonably angry. Admiration! Credit! What did a girl in love want with such things? She snatched her hands away and jumped up.

"If that's all you wanted to tell me, let's go back! But first I'll tell you a couple of things, Stuart McIntyre. Once, about a thousand years ago, Doug was my hero. My head was full of a lot of romantic notions about him. But I wasn't ever really in love with him. So it didn't hurt anything but my pride when he chose Lorena. And after he'd been gone a little while, my pride healed up too. When he came home and everyone started pushing me at him, I didn't know how to make you understand that I didn't want him for me. Not at all. So now will you stop all this silly talk about how fine I am. I don't want to be fine. Stuart McIntyre, you make me so mad!"

She whirled toward the faint patch in the darkness that was the summerhouse door, but Stuart caught her before she went through and pulled her back. Then she was in his arms, held close to him. For a moment she remained stiff and unyielding. Then he kissed her and as he did the resistance melted out of her.

"I think I've always loved you, Abbie," he whispered. "Do you suppose you could stop fighting me for a while?"

"I don't want to fight you," Abbie said. "I won't ever fight you again."

"That's fine," he said. "Now we'd better return to the house."

He let her go and she stepped back in surprise. Surely there was more to be said. But Stuart was behaving as if a kiss and a single embrace were all. She went quickly out of the summerhouse ahead of him and started across the yard. He was laughing as he fell into step beside her.

"So you aren't going to fight me any more?"

She sniffed without replying and hurried toward the house. At the veranda steps he stopped her.

"I'm going away, Abbie. There's a chance that I won't come back. We mustn't count on anything until the war is over. I hope you'll wait for me. But I don't want you to promise that you will. Years and circumstances change people. Abbie, let's wait and see. And don't be angry with me now."

It wasn't what she wanted, but she couldn't be angry with him. She slipped her hand into his and they went up the steps together.

When they were with the others, Abbie tried to pretend that everything was just as it had been before. But she knew that for Abbie Garrett the whole pattern of life had changed.

In the early morning hours the island quieted and everyone went wearily to bed. Abbie was sure she would never fall asleep, but her heavy eyelids closed the moment her head touched the pillow.

And that was the second night.

The next day the mob went wild and carried out its threats against distant McKeon Street, where so many colored people lived. But by that time the Negroes of the island had hidden themselves in the deep woods or escaped to New Jersey where they were safe. Houses were burned, but those who lived in them had fled.

In the city the *Tribune* office remained in a state of siege, but no attack came. The crowds had no leaders, no plan behind them—which disproved the claim that the South had attempted to organize a rebellion.

On the third night a rain storm broke over the island and most of the crowds, wet and bedraggled, weary of their own game, gave up and went home. On Thursday the militia and some of the regulars from Gettysburg marched into New York and thereafter there was only spasmodic trouble. When the tragic toll was taken it was found that more than fifteen hundred had died, most of them rioters, but also many of their victims. The number of wounded and injured could never be calculated.

On the following Monday Stuart McIntyre enlisted in the Union Army, though he was still too young for the draft to touch him. All this was in July of the year 1863.

The war was to go on for nearly two more years.

30

Sound of Music

Chickamauga, the siege of Chattanooga, Lookout Mountain and the Battle above the Clouds. Grant at last in high command. Fighting in the Wilderness. Spotsylvania. The taking of the Shenandoah Valley. The fall of Atlanta and Sherman marching through Georgia.

So the drums of history rolled, and the names went down on the record in letters of blood. And behind every name there were tears and valor, heartbreak and tragic waste. Then the guns held their fire and a hush fell upon the broken nation. At Appomattox Court House on an April day in 1865 a man in a gray uniform took the proffered hand of a man in blue as Lee surrendered his armies to Grant. A few days after the Stars and Strips flew again above Fort Sumter, Abraham Lincoln, President of a nation whose wounds must now be healed, attended a play called *Our American Cousin* at Ford's Theater in Washington. Into that theater came an actor named John Wilkes Booth.

* * *

May was bright again in Staten Island.

Douglas and Lorena had been married just two weeks before in the Garrett parlor. The ceremony had so much happiness in it that no one seemed to notice that the bridegroom was on crutches. If anyone thought about it at all, it was only to admire the confident way in which he moved about as vigorously as anyone present.

Afterward, in the warm, sunny afternoon, a reception had been held in the parlor and on the lawn. That night Doug and Lorena had started their journey south to Charleston, where Douglas was to enter his duties in the Charleston office of a shipping concern that was to carry goods by sea between New York and Charleston. For the past year he had been learning all about the work in the New York office in anticipation of the end of hostilities.

"The best part," Lorena told Abbie happily, "is that we will get free passage once a year to New York as part of Douglas' work. So this won't be good-bye to the North, Cousin Abbie."

Now, as Abbie Garrett climbed the hill path above Bard Avenue, she thought back over all that had happened. Her step was light and she felt like singing. The war was over, over, over! And Stuart McIntyre had come back to Staten Island. She had not seen him yet, but she was to meet him this very morning in the woods near the cave. A letter had come from him a week ago and she had read it so many times that she knew it by heart. Its words were running through her mind as she followed a path that was dappled with May sunshine:

Dear Abbie:

So I am coming home after all and now I can say the things I did not say before I left the island.

I have thought of you many more times than you know. You have sat beside me at campfires and we have had long talks together. You have marched with me when I have been wet and cold and discouraged. But you were never gloomy. You smiled that special smile of yours that has your heart in it for whomever you smile upon. Your hand was strong in mine and there was always hope in the words you spoke to me.

Anxious as I am to see everyone, I want to meet you alone the first time, Abbie, and not with your family or mine at hand. I will be home late Thursday night. So will you climb the woods path Friday morning sometime after ten? If you do not come I will know that the past two years have changed you. If that is the case, I will understand, Abbie, and never blame you.

If you come—but I will leave that for Friday morning.

                                        Stuart

Not for anything would she have failed him—or herself. She took the final bend in the path eagerly and saw him standing there. He was taller and heavier than when she had last seen him. His face was dark from the Southern sun, his hair bleached pale where the forage cap did not cover it. His uniform was stained and faded, the cuffs frayed, but probably his civilian clothes would no longer fit him. At least his smile was the same.

She went toward him and he opened his arms. His kiss was not like the gentle one he had given her that night in the summerhouse so long ago.

"You're crying, Abbie," he said.

"Because I love you," she told him. "Because you're home, and because of your letter, and because the war is over."

He held her close for a few moments and there was no need for any words. Then he held her away to look at her.

"There's so much to talk about," he said. "So many plans to make. That rock over there isn't as soft as a sofa, but it's a good place to sit in the sun and swing our legs."

He took her hand and led her to the big slab where she and Lorena had once sat in those long ago days when the war had just begun.

They talked of themselves first and of the future for which it was now possible to plan. Stuart had sent back despatches to the *Tribune* all these months, acting as a sort of fighting correspondent. Mr. Greeley approved of using talented young men and there was a regular post waiting for Stuart now on his paper. That meant they could be married without delay.

When that was settled, Abbie sat for a while basking in the sun that warmed their rock, her head comfortable on Stuart's shoulder. But they could not forget the war completely. It had been so long a part of their everyday lives that it was hard to believe that it was over. For a long time to come they would remember and their children's children would remember.

Abbie sighed and stirred in Stuart's arms. "If only President Lincoln had lived. We need him so much now."

"Lincoln!" Stuart spoke the name softly. "It seems strange now to think how slow we were to believe in him. Do you remember how he was laughed at and discounted, and then how, one by one, the great men of the country came to trust and respect him, and count on him?"

"The little men too," Abbie said.

Stuart went on, half musing to himself. "I remember something he wrote in a letter a couple of years ago. He hoped then that peace would come more quickly than it did. I memorized his words, Abbie, because they gave meaning to what I was doing. This is what he said:

" 'Peace does not appear so distant as it did. I hope it will come soon, and come to stay; and so come as to be worth the keeping in all future time. It will then have been proved that, among free men, there can be no successful appeal from the ballot to the bullet; and that they who take such an appeal are sure to lose their case and pay the cost.' "

Abbie listened in silence and after a moment Stuart continued.

"Perhaps what we have done in this war will be useful to those who still belong to the future. Maybe they'll take up this United States we've held together and make it something important, not just to Americans, but to the world."

They were quiet for a little while and the spring about them hummed in the warm air.

"Listen," Stuart said, "do you hear the music?"

She held her breath, listening intently. There was no sound of music anywhere, except for the coming-to-life singing all about them.

"It's the music of peace," Stuart said. "It's around us now. Maybe some day we'll learn the tune a little better." He got to his feet and pulled her up from the rock. "Come along, Abbie. We've done enough philosophizing for one morning. Let's go tell your mother and father our news."

Hand in hand they went down through the woods together. And now there was a special rhythm to their walk, as if they kept step with faraway music.

About the Author

Phyllis A. Whitney was born of American parents in Yokohama, Japan, and lived the first fifteen years of her life in Japan, China and the Philippines. Her adult years have been spent in the world of books—first and foremost as a novelist who is read around the world, and also as bookseller, librarian, reviewer, and teacher of writing.

Although she is perhaps best known for her romances, DREAM OF ORCHIDS, RAINSONG and EMERALD among them, Ms. Whitney has also written numerous books for young people including THE FIRE AND THE GOLD.